praise for psychics of oracle bay

Not in the Cards

An Exciting Introduction: Amy's books immediately go to the top of my queue when they are released and they never disappoint. This was an exciting introduction to Oracle Bay and I'm looking forward to getting to know the rest of the inhabitants in future books.

Found Another Great Author!: I didn't know what to expect when I went into this book. The premise of the book sounded like something I would enjoy. At first, as I started reading the book, I wasn't sure I was going to like it. However, after a few pages, I was drawn into the book and it never let me go. In fact, by the end of the book, I was so ready to find out what was going to happen next from all the hints that were given, I wanted the next book right then. This book was well-written, had a great plot (both romance and intrigue), and I loved the characters, even the villain who I loved to hate. Can't wait to read more and I highly recommend!

Fantastic: A well written story with great characters and the location of Oracle Bay was inspired. The heroine in this story is a tribute to enduring heartache and finding a new life and love.

· · · ★ ★ ★ ★ ★ ★ · · ·

First Hand Knowledge

The author does a bang up job of making this mythical place not only enchanting, but a place I'd want to go. To live, even if I were the only mundane in the lot. She also expands characters from her previous book 'Not in the Cards' and keeps the story arc alive and moving forward. There's something to be said for a series that continues with the lives of all the characters, even when the focus is on only two at a time.

· · · ★ ★ ★ ★ ★ ★ · ·

Wing and a Prayer

I have this terrible problem with Amy Cissell's books. I get hooked within the first few sentences, and want to read the whole thing in one sitting. They're addictive, fun, clever stories about people you wish you knew.

· · · ★ ★ ★ ★ ★ ★ · ·

Belle of the Ball

This is the third book in the series, and I think this series is getting better each book. I love how silly, fun, and interesting this book is. Drew and Bill's romance was great, touching, and romantic. And, the mystery was great, too. Add to that, there were some revelations that were hilarious. There was a also point at the very end of the book that made me laugh out loud because when Drew couldn't see Bill, I thought he'd been turned into a toad. What really happened and why? You'll have to read this and find out. If you love a fun, cozy, romantic mystery, give this book and series a try; you'll love it! Highly recommend! I was provided a copy which I voluntarily reviewed.

Hell and High Water

I throughly enjoyed this book. It touches on so many possibilities of paranormal people. It has a good lead in, full rich characters with quirks and an unexpected ending.

Tempest in a Teapot

The ending got me! I have really enjoyed this series, and I was so darn excited to see another one in the series.I was extremely happy with this book as I couldn't figure out who the villain was. I had ideas, but the author was skillful at red herrings. Then the end hit...I was so darn angry! LOL! Highly recommend.

There are curses and bonds, mystery and mild romance, friends and family-both related and found. I do love Oracle Bay. I'm excited for the next story for Morgana

Psychics of Oracle Bay

Not in the Cards
First Hand Knowledge
Wing and a Prayer
Belle of the Ball
Hell and High Water
Tempest in a Teapot
Elements of Surprise
Dead Giveaway*
Bad to the Bones*
Shoot for the Stars*
Fun and Prophet*

Box Sets (ebook only)
Seeing is Believing in Oracle Bay (Books 1-4)

* forthcoming

hell and high water

PSYCHICS OF ORACLE BAY
BOOK 5

AMY CISSELL

HELL AND HIGH WATER
Amy Cissell

A Broken World Publication
13820 NE Airport Way, Suite K395495
Portland, OR 97251-1158

Hell and High Water: A Paranormal Fallen Angel/Psychic Romance
Copyright © 2022 by Amy Cissell
ISBN 978-1-949410-55-6 (ebook)
ISBN 978-1-949410-56-3 (paperback)

Cover Design: Cissell Ink
Edited by Suzanne Lahna, The Quick Fox
Edited & Proofread by Christopher Barnes, Cissell Ink

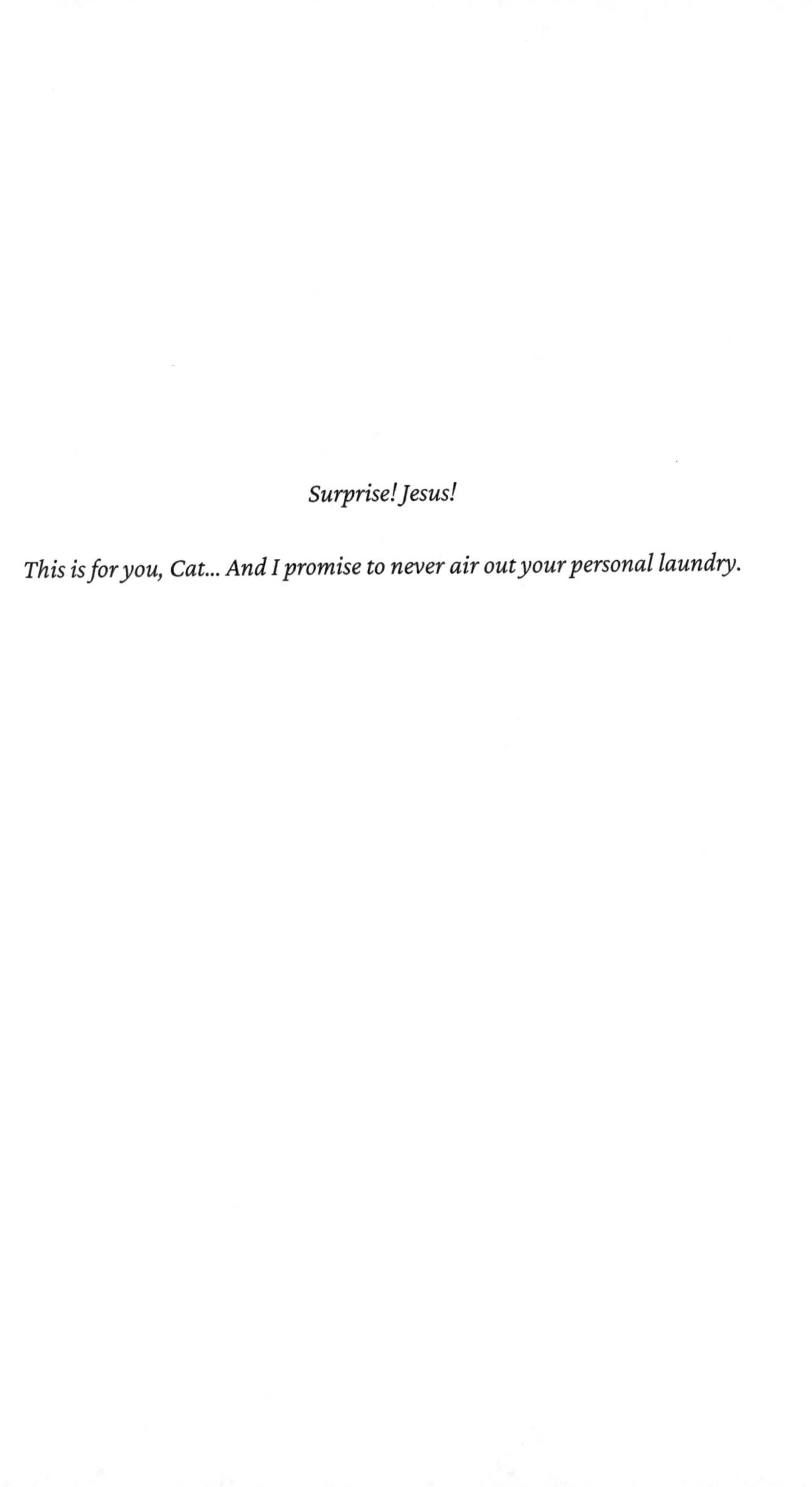

Surprise! Jesus!

This is for you, Cat... And I promise to never air out your personal laundry.

one

Ceridwen Kenny stood outside The Pour House, Oracle Bay's local brewpub, and pursed her lips, trying to slow her breathing. The season was turning; winter storms were giving way to spring squalls, and the cold wind whipped her long red hair across her face until only her blue eyes, a few patches of pale white skin, and the tips of her pointy ears shone through.

She didn't want to be here. It'd be different if she was meeting the rest of the psychics to discuss their local businesses, or the latest mystery, or which supernatural creature had shown up this week. Having someone else there as a buffer made a world of difference. She couldn't count on Brandy, the brewpub's business manager, or Zeke, the pub's head bartender, newly appointed assistant manager, and part-time prophet of the Lord.

She shook her head. She was a grown-ass woman, fast approaching her fourth century of life, and she wasn't afraid of anyone or anything. Not even the arrogant, ridiculous fallen angel who owned the place and whatever he'd done to her that was making her fall apart.

Ceri took a deep breath, let it out, and allowed her gaze to drift from the front of the bar to the Pacific Ocean. The grey waves were curling into the shore but breaking too quickly for the few surfers, braving the cold water and colder air. She glanced at her phone. She'd left home an hour and a half ago, and even considering that it'd taken an hour to walk from her place to the bar, she'd still burned almost thirty minutes doing...nothing.

It was out of character, but she couldn't deny what was going on. She was procrastinating, and she was avoiding. Just because they'd spent the better part of two months in each other's beds didn't mean they couldn't have a friendly, cordial relationship, and the fact that she'd ended things when he wanted more and she didn't was no reason to expect him to turn down the request she was dreading making.

She pushed the door open and strode in. Her temper was already flaring, even though he hadn't done anything. Yet. He'd invaded her mind, her dreams, and her habits—she seldom slept, she'd removed the mirrors from her house, and was now the kind of person who avoided confrontation instead of facing it head on—and that was enough.

Felicity, Oracle Bay newcomer—there'd been a lot of those after the near-apocalypse—and one of the Pour House's newest servers looked up from where she was putting away clean glassware behind the bar and waved. She was always cheerful, almost to the point of annoyance. She was a white woman with long, dark brown hair that was caught back in a clip decorated with miniature violets that sparkled when she moved.

Zeke was on the floor talking to a white woman dressed completely in black and shrouding her face with her black hoodie. She was sitting alone—one of the few people who'd shown up for the early afternoon opening time on a Tuesday in March—and probably intimidating the crap out of the other customers. Ceri had heard him complain more than once about having to be anywhere besides behind the bar on the rare occasions he graced the rest of the psychics with his prophetic presence.

Ceri pulled her attention away from the woman—focusing on a stranger was just one more way to delay—and paused, not sure what to do now that she was here. Asking for Andy seemed weird. Presumptuous? Ridiculous at best.

"He's in his office," Brandy said from her place at the end of the bar where she was poring over her laptop. She looked at Ceri and grinned, amusement dancing in her hazel eyes.

"Who?" Ceri asked, then rolled her eyes at herself. Only two people had offices, and one of them was talking to her right now.

Brandy didn't even try to hide her smirk. "Oh, honey. I don't know what is going on between the two of you, but whatever it is, you need to get it straightened out. It's making you stupid. I say that with friendship and love."

"Sure thing, Brandy. You're definitely not calling me out because you want your boss to pull it together and brew some new award-winning beers. It's friendship."

Brandy winked at Ceri. "I really love running this bar, so I was telling the truth. Mostly."

"Is he busy?"

"Never too busy for you. It's a standing order. The boss's only order, actually. You're allowed unfettered access to anywhere and anything at the Pour House. You want to examine the books? I'll log you into the accounting software and glare at you from the other side of the bar."

"Just Andy's office for now. I'll let you know if I need to check your math later."

"Have fun, but don't scare the clientele."

"Pinky promise," Ceri said, letting the grin that had been threatening to sneak out during her conversation creep across her face.

Ceri strode over to the stairs, then stomped up to the second floor. His office door was closed, as usual, so she raised her hand to knock.

The door opened before her hand dropped. Andy stood in the

doorway, mere inches from her. She was conscious of his closeness, his body heat, and his scent—wood smoke, leather, and peat.

"What do you want?" he snapped. Silver wings popped open behind him, sending sparks into the air that flitted down to singe his shirt. The scent of sulfur intertwined with the other smoky smells that made up Andras Sterling, fallen angel, former Grand Marquis of Hell, and current owner of the best brewpub on Washington State's Long Beach peninsula.

Ceri cringed inwardly. He was already angry with her, and all she'd done was show up. Her eyes drifted from the sparks flying off his wings to his body, then up to his face. Andy was white with lightly tanned skin, tall and broad-shouldered, had grey eyes like the sea after a storm, and silver hair that contrasted sharply with his unlined, ageless face. He was, in a word, beautiful.

Ceri's breath hitched, and she blushed when Andy's lips curled in a sardonic smile. Dammit. He affected her, and she wished he didn't know how much.

"Well?" he prompted. "Did you come all the way over here just to admire me, or did you have something to say?" Andy tapped his foot, and the sulfur smell intensified. Sparks flew with each tap of his toe, and she watched, mesmerized and afraid to say what she'd come there to say.

"I am tired of games, Ceridwen," he said. The silver-grey wings that had torn through his shirt drooped, the tips brushing against the floor. "You said it was over between us, that it was an apocalyptic fling you never meant to last longer than the final battle. And yet, you keep seeking me out, raising my hopes, and my well..." His voice trailed off, and he arched an eyebrow at her with a smirk. "Say what you want and leave."

Shame heated her skin and pushed a lump into her throat. She'd treated him poorly, and that was no lie. She hadn't said anything that wasn't true, but she hadn't approached it with kindness, trusting that the several millennia of experience and life he had behind him meant he didn't need kindness.

"I'm sorry."

"Save it," Andy ground out. "Get to the point and get out."

Ceri bit her lip. She knew she had to tell him, to ask for his help, but admitting she needed him after walking away was almost too much. A small wave of dizziness pushed through her hesitation. "Our connection didn't sever," she said, the words coming so fast they tumbled over each other in their effort to be free. "When I scried you and was pulled into you, into all of you, the visions and the memories stayed longer than with anyone else I've ever read."

Andy took a step back, and the sparks died in the air; no more appeared to take their places. He motioned towards one of the two chairs facing each other near the window, and she sat.

"I told everyone the aftereffects would fade eventually because that's what always happens. But they didn't. Not only is it still incredibly taxing to use my skills for anyone else, half the time I see you instead of them. I'll be scrying Joe's future as a senior accountant before he goes for the big promotion he's too scared to apply for, and then he's burning in hell while demons torture him. While *you* torture him." She didn't add that every time she glanced in a mirror without purpose, flames leapt to the surface and consumed her mind with nightmares of being the one Andy was torturing.

Andy reached forward as if to grab the hands that were shaking in Ceri's lap but stopped himself. She didn't like to be touched without invitation, and she'd revoked his invitation.

"And the dreams," she continued. Her voice broke, and she curled in on herself. Looking at her hands twisting in her lap, she could no longer maintain the confident façade she'd been wearing for months. "I can't tell if I'm dreaming your memories, or if it's my brain taking bits of everything I've learned and mixing it into something new."

"What makes you think we're still connected, and it's not just your brain having trouble handling everything it downloaded?"

"I can still see your present and your future, and it changes based on what—" she'd almost said, "what I do," which was not what she wanted to convey. "Based on what you do," she finished clumsily. "I know where you are and what you're doing. I know how your decision to brew a salted caramel porter will affect sales and what awards it will win.

"And if that wasn't bad enough, I can never turn it off. It's draining me. Every day, things are a little more difficult, and the parts of me that are *me* are a little more faded. The parts that are you are stronger. I'm tired. I haven't worked in six weeks because I can't risk getting pulled into a hell I can't control and can't escape. It took me an hour to make the twenty-minute walk here, and I'm drenched with sweat from the effort."

Andy's wings flared out and curved around him. The rotten egg odor of his anger diminished. "What can I do? What should I do? I never meant..."

Ceri smiled sadly. "I know. Neither of us did. I didn't realize at first. It wasn't until..." She trailed off. The symptoms hadn't intensified until she stopped spending nights, and a few afternoons, and some unforgettable mornings, with Andy. "Can we try something? Hold my hand?" She reached out to him. He took her hand and pulled her closer to him.

"Does it help? The contact?" Concern reverberated through his voice, and he placed his other hand on her upper arm. Wood smoke and leather once again were his dominant scents.

"A bit," she admitted. "But not enough. Andy, it's killing me. I don't know how much longer..."

"I will stay here and hold you until we figure out how to fix this. You're going to be fine. I did this, and I will find a way to make it right."

"You're gonna hold me and figure out how to fix me at the same time?" Ceri laughed. "That's some multitasking. Besides, I'm still fine. Just tired. We have time to figure this out. At the rate things have been deteriorating, I'd estimate I have at least four to five months before it gets really bad. I wouldn't have waited until the end to come to you, no matter how stubborn I am."

"We'll figure this out together, and whenever you need relief, my body is yours." He winced. "That isn't what I meant. I mean that, too, but..."

"I know. Thank you. It doesn't change things, and I don't want it to get weird."

"Ceri, in the last year, we've seen magical goats turn into goddesses, had an apocalypse, and gotten drunk with a wine god, and that barely scratches the surface. It's already weird."

"You know what I meant."

He sighed regretfully and retracted his wings. "I know. Have you told your friends?"

She shook her head. "Not yet. Everyone's so busy, and Drew was preparing for his and Bill's first long vacation. I'm waiting for them to get back, so I don't have to tell the story more than once."

"And then find another excuse? Misty is getting ready for the grand opening of two new businesses, or Sandy is headed out of town to visit Dionysus for some father daughter time, or the Autumn Bazaar is only five months away..."

Ceri wrinkled her nose at him. Maybe procrastination wasn't as foreign a trait as she wanted to believe. "Rude. But true. I'll tell them as soon as Drew returns. He should be back in three days."

"In the meantime, you should get plenty of rest. I'll drive you home."

"Fine. I'll let you do that, but only because I'm really tired." Ceri's eyelids drooped a bit, but she mustered a smile. "Let's go. I haven't been sleeping well at night, but maybe I can manage a nap. If it's not asking too much, perhaps you can lie down with me?" She held her breath; asking that question was harder than it should've been knowing how much it would help, and if he said no...

"Anything. Always. There's nothing I wouldn't do."

"Thank you." Ceri stood up and smiled at Andy and stepped back, breaking their physical contact. The smile slid off her face. Flames leapt into her mind, pulling her into hell. The blood drained from her face, and she gasped for the air that wouldn't quite fill her lungs. The world turned grey, and her knees buckled.

Andy's arms were around her before she hit the ground. The hellfire shrank back, but it didn't bring the relief she'd felt from his touch moments before. Shivers wracked her body, and only the heat from his kept her teeth from chattering. Her heart raced, and the pressure she hoped was panic and not a heart attack landed on her chest, making it even harder to breathe. The grey in her vision was quickly darkening, and she closed her eyes. The sound of his wings snapping out kept her on this side of consciousness, and his roar of anger forced her eyes open. He launched himself upwards, one fist raised to break the ceiling before it could break them, and flew through the roof of his pub into the late morning sky.

"Brandy is gonna be mad you broke the roof," Ceri coughed out. Her strength drained from her body, leaving her limp in his arms. The sun blazed down at her, filling her field of vision with bright white light—too bright to look at—then the darkness pulled her down.

The jumble of noise separated into voices she couldn't identify. Except for his. Always freaking his. No matter how much Ceri'd tried to distance herself from Andy, to put her fling with a half-fallen angel behind her, something always drew her back. The memory of his wings wrapped around her, shutting out the world and making her heart skip a beat, was overtaken by the one of him breaking through the ceiling of his office with her in his arms. She didn't remember what came next, but from the smell and the steady beep, beep, beep in the background, she was in a hospital. The panic she'd felt before passing out in Andy's arms threatened to return, and the beeps kept pace with her pulse.

Now wasn't the time for journeys to the past. Now was the time to figure out what the hell—if that was even the right place to look— was happening, why she was so thirsty, and whose voices were joining his in a quiet murmur of conversation?

She concentrated on filtering out Andy's voice so she could focus on the others. It took a while to sort through them, even though they all sounded familiar. Morgana's was the easiest to pick out—the oldest in their coven, although Misty preferred it if they called it a "loosely organized unofficial union." She had a powerful voice that could pull you out of your chair and into a curtsey if she was angry. And right now, she was angry.

Morgana did not like being dragged to places she hadn't planned to go, and whatever was going on, it was definitely unplanned. If Ceri didn't tell them she was awake soon and that she'd been eavesdropping, she might end up being caught in Morgana's crosshairs.

Her heart stuttered again, but no one seemed to notice the interrupted rhythm of the machinery.

Paska was there, and that was a real shocker. He liked spontaneous get togethers even less than Morgana. Maybe it was an age thing. He was almost as old as Morgana—sometimes he felt even older—and cranky, especially when what was happening did not match his plans.

Once she'd identified and filed Morgana and Paska, the others were easier to sort out. Sandy, the newest member of their group, her fiancé Vincent, Misty—the only psychic in Oracle Bay who was actually from Oracle Bay—and her boyfriend Joseph, and Jezebel, the resident astrologer and the funnest person in town, other than Ceri and Drew of course.

Speaking of Drew, his voice was noticeably absent. But he was still in Mexico, wasn't he? On a long-overdue romantic getaway that Ceri knew was leading to his engagement.

The psychics of Oracle Bay were so wonderful, kind, caring, empathetic—you have to be when you can see things no one else can—and supportive. But they were also the nosiest bunch of people Ceri had ever encountered. When they didn't know something, it grated against the edges of their precognition and drove them to question until they found answers that satisfied them. That they were here, all of them except Drew and Russell, who was out-of-town spending time with his aunt, couldn't mean anything good. They wouldn't be here if she was going to be okay, would they?

She sighed internally. She'd have to be honest about her deterioration if Andy hadn't already told them everything. There was no way around it.

Or... She was stiff from lying on whatever uncomfortable surface they'd put her on and wanted to stretch. Maybe she could duck into the restroom and flee out the window? It was an option.

Ceri opened her eyes. Or tried to.

It didn't feel like something was preventing her from opening them—not exactly anyway. It was more like being in a deep sleep. One where she knew she was sleeping but couldn't quite claw her way out of.

"I brought coffee for everyone," Drew said. "Unfortunately, not Bill's, but there are some decent places in town."

This was not good. Not good at all. Either Drew was home early or she'd been asleep long enough for him to return. Either option was bad.

Ceri tried to center her breathing and concentrate on pulling herself up and out. Finally, she pried her eyes open with a gasp.

Light flooded her eyes, and she closed them again involuntarily. The voices were louder, clearer, as if Drew's coffee comment had turned up the volume in the room.

"Why are we even here?" Morgana said, her voice sharp with... was that fear? No. It couldn't be. Morgana wasn't afraid of anything.

"Where else would we be?" Misty's voice was sharp. "You don't have to stay, of course. We'll call you if anything changes."

"That's not what I meant. Of course we are by her side to keep the vigil. I meant why is Ceridwen here, in this place? The hospital can do nothing for her." A deep weariness accompanied Morgana's voice.

Vigil? Was she dying?

Fear quickened her pulse, but no one in the room but the beeping machine noticed she was awake. Mostly awake.

"She's here because the hospital can monitor her vital signs and keep her stable and hydrated," Drew said. His voice was smooth and calm, but Ceri heard the frustration underneath. It likely wasn't the first time someone had explained to Morgana why hospitals weren't all bad.

"She's awake." Andy's voice, deep and growly, sent a shiver through her body even now.

She let herself grow more aware of her surroundings. She had an IV in her left hand and an odd pressure on her right. She moved that hand experimentally, and the pressure increased. Someone was holding her hand.

The pressure disappeared as her eyes fluttered open, and everything rushed back. Eons of torment and suffering. Torture she'd experienced from both sides of the knife.

Her eyes flew the rest of the way open, wide with shock and the pain of remembering.

The room was too bright, and for a moment, her vision swam and unconsciousness threatened to drag her back down. She took a deep breath, and her vision cleared. There were too many faces leaning over her, staring at her. She recognized all except one. A hooded figure with no aura stood at the foot of her hospital bed, wedged between Misty and Jezebel, although neither of them seemed uncomfortable with the stranger's proximity.

As if sensing her attention, the figure reached up and pushed back the hood, unveiling a too-wide smile before dissolving into nothingness, revealing another figure. The face was hauntingly familiar, but she couldn't place it.

Then she realized why there was no aura. It was because there was no life, no soul to project an essence of being.

It raised a hand to the side of its head, slowly enough to be almost melodramatic, and waved slightly before walking towards the length of the bed and passing through her. Ice trailed in its wake, and her heart stuttered when the chill passed through it. She opened her mouth, but her scream froze in her throat.

Then the hand that'd been holding hers returned. The visions of hell and the reality of the malevolent shade disappeared. She slumped back into the bed, willing herself into unconsciousness again.

Unfortunately, she stayed painfully aware of her surroundings and the eight faces staring down at her. Nine, if you counted Andy, who was still by her side and not in her direct line of sight.

"I just saw a ghost," she croaked.

· · · ★ ★ ★ ★ ★ ★ ★ · ·

"Why can't I go home?" Ceri asked for at least the fifteenth time since she'd woken up the day before. She shifted on the semi-elevated bed, bumped her IV, and winced in pain. "I'm awake. I'm fine. I just passed out from..."—she racked her brain trying to come up with a reason she'd lost consciousness for three freaking days that wouldn't end up with an even longer stay in the hospital or a visit with the psychiatry department—"...lack of sleep and dehydration." There was no need to talk about the dizziness that persisted if she moved too quickly, bringing with it a pounding headache that blurred her vision further. A little rest in a comfortable bed and a lot of hydration would take care of that.

"As soon as we know you're stable, we'll discharge you," the nurse said from the foot of her bed where she was charting. "A coma is a pretty serious thing, you know. Don't you and your husband want to make sure you're not going to have a repeat episode before you get home?"

"My...husband?" Maybe she wasn't stable yet, because last time she'd checked, she was pretty sure she didn't have one of those.

Andy, who'd barely left her side since she'd woken up the day before, squeezed her hand tightly. She glanced over at him, and he shook his head.

Ceri glared. There had better be an excellent reason he'd introduced them as a married couple, and she'd be looking for an explanation on how he'd gotten through the red tape and privacy laws to convince the hospital.

"He's been so attentive, never leaving your side." The nurse sighed and looked at Ceri's brand-new surprise spouse. "We should all be so lucky to have such a devoted partner."

"He brings all the luck to my life," Ceri said. She hoped Andy knew she didn't mean good luck. By the twinkle in his eye, it was pretty clear he was catching her subtle and cutting insults. It was also clear he didn't care about the insults at all.

Ceri turned her attention back to the nurse. "My wonderful *husband* will take excellent care of me at home. And now that I'm awake and unhooked from most of your machinery, there's no reason to stay here when I will be more comfortable somewhere else."

The nurse looked up as she put the chart back at the end of the bed. "I agree completely, and that's why you will be discharged."

A smile started spreading across Ceri's face.

"As soon as we have the results of the CT scan and the new bloodwork." The nurse graced Ceri with a sunny smile that softened when she looked at Andy. "Get some rest while you can. The doctor will be in to see you in a couple hours."

Ceri's smile had stopped in its tracks, leaving her face stuck in an awkward grimace. She turned to her *husband*. "Since we're married now, *sweetie*, what say you break me out of here and take me home?"

"I thought husband sounded a lot more plausible, and it wasn't hard to find a moment while you were in triage to alter a couple things. As your spouse, I get unlimited visiting hours so I could hold your hand and keep the nightmares at bay, more so than an 'ex-friends-with-benefits,' a 'local brewer who gives you a discount,' or a 'kind-of friend who doesn't even know anything about your insurance situation or next of kin.' I'm glad you had your wallet with you so I could at least provide that."

She couldn't find anything intrinsically wrong with his argument, but still... "Why not fiancé or boyfriend? Or brother?"

He reared back, a look of absolute disgust on his face. "Brother?

Woman, if I was your brother, the thoughts I have about you would get me arrested."

Ceri felt the flush start low on her chest, and she willed it to stay there. Unfortunately, her pale, lightly freckled skin was not obedient when it came to exhortations to suppress visible signs of humiliation. The heat spread up her neck and over her face until even the tips of her slightly pointy ears were on fire.

Andy turned over the hand he was still holding and examined her palm—the way Misty did when she was pretending her psychic powers came from reading lines on a hand and not reading their futures through touch.

She wouldn't ask what he was doing. She didn't care. She'd snatch her hand out of his in a second if she thought she could avoid another flash of whatever it was. The thought was enough to push another wave of dizziness through her, along with the accompanying eyeball stabbing. She took a deep breath, and the pain receded.

"What are you looking at? And don't call me woman. I have a name, and I know you haven't forgotten it."

Andy met her light blue eyes. His impossibly long eyelashes framing his sea-grey eyes were as incandescently silver white as his hair. Heat filled his gaze, the kind that reminded her how quickly he could stoke her fire. Her breath hitched in her chest, and she gasped involuntarily.

"Are you okay? Sounds like you're having a little trouble breathing. Should I get a nurse?" Andy smirked at her, but his voice was laced with barely perceptible concern.

"You didn't answer the question," Ceri replied, ignoring his. "Why are you looking at my hand?"

He raised it up, cupping it in his palm, and held it less than an inch away from his mouth. He exhaled slowly, and the feel of his breath on her skin sent goosebumps cascading up her arm. She held her breath, certain he was going to kiss her palm. He licked his lips, and she followed the movement of his tongue.

He dropped his hand back to the bed, taking hers with it. "Just seeing if I'd learned how to read palms yet. Misty's been giving me lessons, you know."

Ceri hadn't known and wasn't sure if he was being serious now. But she still had to ask, even if she resented how breathy she sounded. "And? Did you see anything?"

He traced the lines of her palm with the index finger of his other hand. "Your lifeline is uncommonly long, but your love line is even longer. I'm no expert, but it sounds to me like you're destined for the kind of love that'll last beyond the grave."

Ceri screwed up her face. "I've heard every faux fortune telling method you could imagine, and that, my friend, was pure amateur hour. Right up there with 'a tall, dark stranger is in your future,' and 'you've had loss in your past.' Telling people what they want to hear, or in your case, what you want to hear isn't prescience. It's..." She wracked her brain, trying to come up with the word that was hiding on the tip of her tongue. "...it's chicanery."

"Chicanery?" He laughed so deeply, she couldn't stop an answering grin from stealing across her face.

"It was the best I could come up with."

"Is it really deceit if we both know it's pretend?" The humor had fled from his face, and the look he leveled at her was too serious for a faux fortune telling conversation.

"No. As long as both parties are on the same page, then it's not chicanery." She heard the hint of an Irish lilt color her voice, something that only happened when she was tired, turned on, or tipsy.

This time, his smile was sad. "And what if expectations change halfway through the reading? Is it still above board?"

Ceri shook her head. "The oracle and their supplicant would be bound by the rules they started with unless the change in scope was immediately disclosed, negotiated, and agreed upon."

Andy ran his finger across her palm again, and her fingers curled inward towards the sensation. He sighed, and Ceri winced at the exhaustion evident in the sound. "There will be time enough to discuss any changes in scope. For now, let's get you home, figure out how to manage what's going on with you until we can fix things, and talk about your ghost."

"My...ghost?" The subject had been assiduously avoided by the rest of the oracles before they'd filed out when visiting hours ended. "If I remember correctly, it was widely agreed I was hallucinating as I came out of my coma."

Andy nodded. "You're right. Your friends believe you were not quite back to yourself when you saw something as you woke. Maybe it was a ghost—this is a hospital, after all, there are bound to be spirits leaving their bodies—but the overall opinion is it was nothing important, if it was even something at all."

She didn't know why his opinion mattered so much—he was just a friend. A friend she'd spent a good deal of naked time with over five apocalyptic and a couple post-apocalyptic weeks, but not someone she knew as well as the others, nor someone whose opinion she was interested in for anything beyond idle curiosity. She didn't do long-term relationships, and she never had trouble moving on after ending things. Still, she held her breath when she asked, "What do you think?"

His grey eyes bored into hers, and she blinked against the intensity. "I didn't see anything. I didn't feel anything. I'm usually sensitive to shades and spirits of the dead and damned."

Tear prickled in the corners of her eyes. She fixed her gaze on the clock above his head and pulled back towards the center of the bed. Not enough to break their skin-to-skin contact, but enough to remove the cloak of intimacy that had spread over them.

He held on, circling her wrist with his long, strong fingers. "Wait." He tugged her a little closer, and she allowed him to do so, returning her gaze to his face and the expression she didn't want to examine too closely. She'd ended things with him because he'd looked at her with that expression too many times for a casual relationship. She didn't expect to feel guilty about it, to wish things could've been different, to worry if she'd hurt him when she walked out of his bedroom for the last time.

He squeezed her hand gently. "It doesn't matter what's usual or typical for me. You saw something, you know it was a spirit. And you felt its deliberate and unfriendly disposition. Who am I to argue with your experience if it doesn't match my expectations?"

The tears that had threatened fell. "Thank you," she whispered.

He shrugged; when his shoulders fell, they pulled down the mask he usually wore in an attempt to look unremarkable and unmemorable. The mask he'd stopped wearing around her when they were together.

Ceri tried not to be hurt that his public persona had fallen into place while they were in private. After all, she was the one who'd built the boundaries between them, hand holding or not. She had his belief, and that was enough. It had to be enough. She couldn't give him more, and it was selfish to expect to receive more than she could offer.

"Thank you," she repeated, steadily this time. She was going to need him more than she liked in the next few weeks, and it wasn't fair to either of them to pretend it was anything more than a need born of necessity, or that anything would change once they figured out what was wrong with her and how to fix it.

And it would be more than unkind to let her guard down, to give him hope her heart was more open than she'd let him believe. Especially if, as she was beginning to suspect, her sojourn on this planet was nearly at its end.

You can't mourn what you don't have.

<h1 style="text-align:center">three</h1>

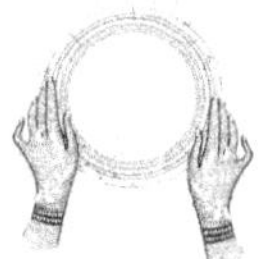

The large table in the tucked-away alcove at the back of the Pour House was nearly full by the time Ceri arrived with her arm through Andy's. She couldn't stop the blush from rising in her pale cheeks at Drew's raised eyebrow. She pasted a smile on her face and flipped him off with her free hand.

Felicity appeared at her elbow almost before she got to the table. She grinned, her expression so friendly and open that Ceri couldn't help but smile back. "What can I get you, Ms. Kenny? We have a new tap—a Kolsch-style ale to push you into summer. Of course, I probably don't have to tell you what's on tap!" She wiggled her eyebrows up and down in an expression so over-the-top that it cut through Ceri's embarrassment at having to show up on Andy's arm.

"That sounds wonderful. Thank you, Felicity. And please call me Ceri." Ceri flashed the server a quick smile. Her gaze slid down the server's arm where a hint of a tattoo peeked out from under a shirt-sleeve. "Nice ink! Is that a...?"

Felicity pulled up her sleeve so the entire tattoo was on display. It was a black and white skull nestled in a bouquet of scarlet flowers. Buds and leaves poked out through the eyeholes, and the overall effect was beautifully macabre. "It's a memorial tattoo. Gotta have something to remind me of the good things in the past, right?" Felicity smiled again, pushed the sleeve down, and headed back to the bar to put in Ceri's drink order.

Ceridwen shivered. Somewhere, somctime, someone would've said a goose had just walked over her grave. She shook her head and slid into the booth next to Drew. Her arm lost contact with Andy's for a moment, and it was all she could do to hold back the gasp as the images that'd been swirling around in her head for the last six months pushed their way to the front of her cerebral cortex. She took a moment to thank all the gods that she was pale enough that no one would notice any more pallor.

Andy sat next to her and pressed his leg into hers. The contact was too intimate, and this time the heat that rose wasn't on her face.

She cleared her throat and looked around the table. No one had said a word since she'd walked through the door, and that was so unusual that she struggled to find the right words as well. "Um. Hey?" she offered with a slight wave. "How are things?"

The six assembled psychics—all real, true, genuine seers who offered honest oracular skills and not the usual rip-off fortune telling one usually found in a touristy coastal town—looked at anything but her.

Okay. This was weird, and a sinking feeling she almost didn't recognize as insecurity and fear started churning in her stomach. "Y'all are freaking me right out. Someone say something. Is there something wrong?"

As one, five of the oracles turned their eyes to Drew. Drew had been her best friend for almost a century, one of the few people who knew her darkest secrets and hidden sins, and the most attractive man she'd ever met. The pressure of Andy's thigh against hers made her revise her internal statement. The second most attractive man.

She waited and watched Drew squirm.

"I don't know what's going on, but if one of you doesn't tell me in the next thirty seconds, I'll..." She racked her brains for an appropriate threat. "I'll give Dio your personal cell numbers and ask him to share with everyone he's ever met."

Paska laughed, breaking the silence that had hovered around the table. "Fair enough, lass. Although that's not the kind of threat you can use more than once or twice... If that asshole wine god hears his name invoked too much, he'll show up, fill our wine glasses, and demand our numbers, and we'll be too drunk to say no."

Ceri smiled appreciatively at Paska. She didn't know him well—she didn't think anyone did, except Morgana maybe—but she'd always appreciated his dry wit, gallows humor, and the fact that he was significantly older than she was. "I'll keep that in mind. But since you didn't tell me what's going on, only warned me about my information extraction method, I think every one of you is still under threat."

When no one spoke, not even Drew, who'd apparently been appointed spokesperson, Paska let out a noisy sigh with more than a hint of exasperation coloring the sound.

"Fine. I'll speak since the rest are too cowardly to say what's on their minds." Paska reached out his hand, and she placed her free hand in his without reservation. "Ceridwen, this is an oracular intervention. We are concerned about you."

"Okay?" She didn't know how to react. "I get that you're worried because I just got out of the hospital two days ago after a coma-situation. And I didn't talk about what was going on. That's on me. I should've trusted all of you with the burden I was carrying."

"That's not it," Drew said. He stopped abruptly as Felicity showed up with Ceri's beer and pitchers for the rest of the table.

Andy took the tumbler of whiskey and pint of pale ale that were left on the tray. "Thank you. Brandy made a good choice when she hired you."

The server flushed and bobbed in what almost looked like a half-curtsey before turning around and stopping at the next table.

Andy drained his glass of whiskey in one gulp and took a long drink of beer, then looked around the table. His stare landed on

Drew. "You were saying?" His voice had an edge to it Ceri had seldom heard.

"You don't belong here, Andras," Morgana said. "You aren't one of us, and it was you who brought the battle between Heaven and Hell to Oracle Bay. We tolerated you in the hospital, but your usefulness has faded. Why don't you go tend your bar and send Ezekiel over?"

Ceri didn't bother to stop the gasp from leaving her lips. Morgana was never one to sugar-coat anything, but that was sharp, even for her.

"Ceri, do you want me to leave?" His voice lost the hard edge he'd had a moment before and dipped into smooth, rich and honeyed like the whiskey he'd just downed.

She shook herself. Now was not the time to dwell on how his voice made her feel. She bit her lip and considered. "I'll be okay for a bit, I think."

"Fine," he bit out, all the warm honey leaving his voice. "I'll stay out of conversational earshot, but yell if you need me, and I'll be back before you know it." He squeezed her hand, then pulled away.

This time, she couldn't contain the small cry of pain that escaped her lips at his absence. Sweat broke out on her brow. She hunched over the table and tried to get her breathing under control. When she could breathe again, she straightened up and looked at Andy. "I'm okay. Pinky promise."

A ghost of a smile flitted across his lips, then his eyes shuttered into that unreadable expression he used to reserve for everyone but her. He turned and walked to the bar. She watched him order another whiskey and throw it back.

"Ceri," Drew said, bringing her back to the table. "Stop looking at your man candy. This is serious."

Ceri looked at him, picked up her beer and took a long sip, then exhaled slowly. "He's not my... You know what? Why don't we get this intervention going? If it's not about me losing all the bits of myself, what is it?"

Misty put her cellphone on the table, open to her messaging app, and slid it into the middle of the table.

Ceri looked down at it. "This is our group chat." She glanced up at Misty and tilted her head, trying to ignore the pain that reverberated through her skull at the subtle movement.

"Read it," Misty commanded.

Ceri picked up the phone and scrolled through. Most of the recent messages were from her and were about the ghost she'd experienced when she was waking up from her coma. She'd thrown out theories and asked for help to figure it out.

"I've seen all this before. Obviously. I sent these messages. Why are you showing them to me now?" She heard the note of panic threading through her voice and hoped no one else did. She covered it with an attempt at humor. "Are you kicking me out of the group? Is this my last glimpse of our group chat? Stop beating around the bush and tell me."

Jezebel, a Black woman with an impeccable sense of style and a sense of humor that snuck up on a person and left them wheezing in laughter, leaned forward and dozens of tight black braids brushed the top of the table. "You were hallucinating. And you can't seem to tell the difference between fantasy and reality. We are worried, and we want you to get some help."

Ceri looked around the table. "Is this why we're here? Because the lot of you don't believe in ghosts? After everything else we've seen in the last few months, this is what pings the unreality button?"

"We believe in ghosts," Sandy said quietly. The young white woman with olive-skin was the newest member of the "fortune-telling and wine-drinking" club, and the hesitance in her voice betrayed her lingering uncertainty. "We'd have to, right? Even if I didn't before—and I didn't, to be clear—there was no escaping it after Russell pulled Martha back to finger Adriana for the murders earlier this year."

Paska snorted, and a dusky stain rose on Sandy's cheeks.

"You know what I mean," she huffed. "You're so juvenile, Paska."

"We are here, not because we doubt ghosts exist, but because none of us saw anything, felt anything, or have seen anything. You were coming out of a coma, so you may have seen an unquiet spirit, but insisting that a random spirit—in a hospital, no less—is anything to do with you is worrying. If there was something to know, someone here would know it. That is what we do, girl." Morgana pushed her long black hair behind her bare milky white shoulders, took a sip of her beer, and grimaced. "When will that insufferable demon get a good wine list?"

Ceri tried to keep her expression even. So maybe she'd sent a few text messages about her encounter, throwing out theories, concerns, and requests for help with research and warding. She'd noticed her messages had largely gone unanswered since she'd been released from the hospital with nothing to do but rest and recuperate but figured everyone was busy. She pushed Misty's phone back to her, then looked at Drew. His blue-grey eyes met hers, and for the first time in over a century, she saw guilt in them. "You, too?" she whispered.

He shrugged but didn't meet her gaze. "None of us have seen anything, and you were in a coma. Not only that, but there is something clearly going on with you if you're gluing yourself to Andy's side like that. Between the ghost, the secrecy, and the collapse, you've got us all worried." He finally looked right at her. "I'm worried. You've never had delusions before, but you've also never been in a coma. I don't know what to believe."

Ceri closed her eyes. She didn't know why their disbelief hurt so much. She'd spent the first few decades of her life alternately being called crazy or being accused of witchcraft. Acceptance wasn't something she'd expected. But she'd let herself become accustomed to it since she'd moved to Oracle Bay twenty years ago at Drew's insistence.

"Does anyone here need another round? Another pitcher?" Felicity's voice broke through the beginning swirl of Ceri's oncoming panic attack.

"I think we're good—" Drew said, before being interrupted.

"I want two fingers of your oldest whiskey," Paska said. "And a bottle of whatever wine Andy has stashed behind the bar for psychic emergencies." He looked around. "Make that two bottles of wine."

"Of course," Felicity chirped. "Let me just refill your waters, and I'll be right back with your drinks." She leaned over the table with a large pitcher of water and started to fill Jezebel's glass.

Ceri didn't see what happened, but seconds later, Jezebel was cursing under her breath and grabbing bar napkins to wipe off her jeans as an expanding pool of water spread across the table.

"I'm so sorry!" Felicity said with a hand across her mouth. She took a step backwards, wobbled when her heel skidded on something, and dropped the pitcher on the table. "I'll be right back!" She turned and fled, leaving the pitcher and water-logged table.

Ceri looked down at the table. It was a glossy wood, and with the sheen of water covering it, it was almost reflective.

Pain ricocheted through her brain, and she grabbed her head, trying to keep it from flying apart. Images flew at her so quickly she couldn't do more than absorb the horror. Interspersed with Andy's memories of hell, of battles, torturing the damned, cavorting with beautiful demons, and suffering for daring to fall in love were snippets from her past. She saw the first time she'd been accused of being a witch, the last time she was chased out of town for seeing too much, her short stint as a private detective in Los Angeles, every face she'd failed, Misty's worry that Joseph's interest in her was already waning, Paska in the dark wearing dramatic robes and chanting by candlelight, the life kindling in Sandy, and Bill proposing to Drew. There was a dark shape in her peripheral vision, but when she tried to focus, it slipped away.

Someone was screaming, and she wanted to tell them to stop, but the words wouldn't come.

And then it drifted away like a sandcastle at high tide. Washed out to sea. Still there, but no longer in the solid form it'd been moments before. Light and clarity returned.

"Someone get the water off this table immediately," Andy barked. He'd pulled her into his arms and was cradling her, pulling her face to his shoulder, hiding her eyes from the mirror-like surface of the table.

"I'm so sorry, I'm so sorry, I'm so sorry," Felicity chanted from behind Ceri. "It felt like someone pushed me. I'll clean this up and get my things!"

"Why would you do that?" Andy sounded genuinely confused.

"So I'm ready when you fire me," she replied softly.

"Don't be ridiculous," Andy said. "Everyone makes mistakes, and accidents happen. Clean it up and take a break to regain your composure. Once you've calmed down, I want you back on the floor. Two new tables filled up in the last couple minutes. Shawn can cover for you until you get back. Send them over on your way out."

"Thank you!" she squeaked.

Ceri stopped listening and buried her face deeper into Andy's shoulders. He smelled like he'd taken a dip in a sulphur hot spring, but it wasn't unpleasant. Maybe she'd gotten used to the smell of his anger. Her friends were once again uncharacteristically silent as Felicity finished cleaning up, and Ceri knew what they were going to say. She hadn't made up any ground in the "I'm totally sane and not hallucinating" campaign she'd debated launching. If anything, she'd made it even more unlikely they'd listen to her at all.

CERI RAISED HER HEAD FROM ANDY'S SHOULDER. SHE'D KEPT HER FACE hidden until the shuffling noises of her friends—former friends?— disappeared. Her eyes caught on Andy's face. The look of tenderness he gave her made her heart skip a beat.

"I'm sorry," she whispered.

"Never apologize," he said fiercely.

A grin cracked the tight muscles in her face. "Love means never having to say you're sorry?" The look on his face when she dropped the "L" word had her squirming in discomfort. It wasn't what she'd meant, and now... "I didn't mean..."

"I know you didn't." He looked at her, and she couldn't read his expression.

"AHEM!"

Ceri whipped her head around, then had to hold on to the table when her head swam from the motion.

Paska smiled at her.

"I thought everyone was gone," she said.

"I know. But before I leave, I have something to say to you—something you should hear." His face was placid. Paska looked at Andy. "What are the chances I can get the whiskey I ordered before your new employee dumped water over everything in front of the resident scryer?"

Andy stared at Paska long enough for Ceri to feel second-hand discomfort. "I'll get it."

"Don't!" Ceri wrapped her arms around his neck, willing him to stay. "Please. I can't."

Andy reached a hand up and stroked her cheek. "I'm not walking away from you. As long as you need me, I'll be here."

He raised a hand and waved. A minute later, Zeke was at their table.

Ceri stared at him. Zeke intrigued her. She'd never been able to read him. He was medium build, with the dark skin of a native of the Middle East, and deep brown eyes that looked like they'd seen almost as much as Andy had.

Zeke cocked his head at Ceri and raised his left eyebrow. "Did you need something, seer?"

She flushed but didn't answer.

"Don't get mouthy, Ezekiel," Andy said. He sounded amiable enough, but Ceri heard the threat in his voice.

"Apologies, boss. What can I do for you?" Zeke's smile was insincere.

"Knock it off, prophet," Andy growled.

"As you wish, demon." Zeke shot back.

Ceri rolled her eyes, sending another shard of pain through her head.

"Three fingers of your best whiskey." Paska looked at Andy, who was smoking from his ears. "And a second for the boss. Bring two of your lagers with those. And for the lady…"

"I'll have the same." She didn't drink much—numbing her gift was uncomfortable and unwise—but sometimes, a lady just needed a bit too much alcohol to dull the pain.

After Zeke headed back to the bar, Paska caught her eyes. "Lass, you are in trouble, but I need you to know I believe you. The rest of those assholes are too young to understand their gifts aren't the infallible compasses they believe. Except Morgana—her disbelief surprised me. I know enough to know truth when I see it, even when I haven't *seen* it."

Paska took the glasses Zeke handed over, took the whiskey in one drink, then drained the beer. He stood and inclined his head toward Ceri. "Whatever happens, whatever you need, I'll be here for you. And I'll remind the rest of those assholes that the second sight doesn't mean they see everything. Take care of yourself, lass. There aren't too many of us old ones left, and I'd like it if you stuck around."

Ceri stared at his back as he walked away. They'd always been friendly, but they'd never been friends. That he was the one who believed her, that it wasn't Drew, was both gratifying and deeply distressing.

Andy sighed and handed her one of the whiskeys. "Shall we toast?"

"To what?" She didn't even try to keep the bitter hurt out of her voice.

"To better times. To clarity. To belief?" He held up his tumbler.

She clinked her glass against his. "Better times," she agreed, then downed her whiskey, hoping it would drown the visions that lay in wait just below the surface.

four

A faint glow was the only light when Ceri's eyes sprung open. Her breathing was too quick and too shallow, but she didn't know why. She closed her eyes and ran through a breathing exercise she'd learned from the internet when she was searching for something—anything—that would help quell her too-frequent panic attacks.

Breathe in two, three, four. Hold, two, three, four. Exhale, two, three, four, five, six, seven, eight.

Once she felt she was unlikely to have a heart attack, she sat up and looked around. She was in Andy's room, in his bed, and he was asleep next to her. One of his arms brushed against her left leg. His face, always beautiful, was resplendent in repose. Without the subtle expressions he employed to avoid notice, the lines smoothed out, and his cheekbones were prominent. He looked like a sculpture. She'd once seen the sexy Satan sculpture—she couldn't remember its proper name—in Liege, Belgium, but Andy could give him a run for his money.

He stirred and reached out. She took his hand and placed it on her abdomen. He quieted immediately.

Things weren't right. She couldn't rely on him always, and soon she wouldn't be able to be apart from his touch at all. Even if they were partners in all senses, life bonded and handfasted, constant togetherness would wear on them. As it was, when one person desired a relationship and the other was content with only the sexy-times, constant togetherness would ruin them more quickly.

Either they needed to find a solution, or she needed to go.

"Stay," he murmured before wrapping his arm around her middle and holding on firmly.

"For a little while, at least," she whispered, running a hand through his soft, silver hair. "I don't deserve you, you know? And you sure as hell don't deserve this mess. No matter what happens, how this turns out, I hope you know you were the rock I needed, that you're the reason I could hold on as long as I did. You were wonderful. No, you were perfect."

Ceri extricated herself from under his arm, took a deep breath, and got out of bed. She kept her eyes on the ground on her way to the bathroom, peed, flushed, and washed her hands. As she dried them, she glanced up and her gaze caught in the mirror.

A dark shade stood behind her. Its features were barely distinguishable, but still human. It opened its mouth in a silent scream and walked forward. Ceri tried to shrink out of the way, but there was no room to avoid it. It walked into her, briefly obscured the mirror, and disappeared.

Without the shade to grab her attention, Ceri's gaze was transfixed by the mirror. She knew she should stop, look away, save herself, but she couldn't. It held her gaze, held her soul. The mirror, any reflective surface, had been the only thing she'd looked forward to when she was young and had to hide her second sight from anyone but her nan. It had been the bane of her existence and something she'd tried to ignore for the first couple decades of the twentieth century. And now, it'd been the one thing that connected her to this group of completely disparate people. The psychics were an odd mix, but they worked because they believed in each other.

And now, she'd walked outside of even *their* suspension of disbelief.

She stared into the mirror, willing herself to see something besides the visions of hellfire and loss that had plagued her recently. All she wanted was one thing not rooted in pain. She'd seen nothing but the worst of everything in the past few months—the worst pain, the greatest losses, the biggest failures. Promotions denied, marriages ended, death, dismay... Nothing good. Not since she'd accidentally taken Andy's memories—past, present, and future—into herself.

But...hadn't she seen Drew's engagement and Sandy's new pregnancy? Those weren't negative. Maybe the tide was turning.

Ceri pulled her eyes away from the mirror, away from the flames that licked the edge of her vision, and stumbled back to bed. She grabbed her cell and shot off two quick texts.

Sandy - congrats! Let me know if you need any baby garments knitted. I can outsource to Etsy like a pro.

Drew. You're engaged. I can't believe I haven't heard the whole story. Spill or else.

Drew's answer was almost immediate. *I didn't want to detract. But yeah.*

Ceri pursed her lips at her phone. *Your good news never detracts. Can we have coffee tomorrow? I promise not to talk about ghosts if you promise to tell me the engagement story.*

The three dots that indicated he was responding appeared and disappeared several times before his message finally popped up on her screen. *Coffee at the mermaid shack, ten?*

Ceri frowned. If he was suggesting coffee at the inferior chain instead of his fiancé's local amazing coffee shop, something was up. *Sounds perfect. See you then. xoxo.*

He replied with an emoji heart.

Ceri grimaced at her phone. Something was clearly off. She looked back at her messages to see if Sandy had replied. Seeing nothing, Ceri cringed. Maybe she'd messed up. A lot of people didn't like to talk about their pregnancies until they got past the first trimester. As she stared at her message, wondering if she could retract, a response arrived.

Good to have early detection. No congrats please. Don't tell anyone else. I'll find you tomorrow.

Ceri replied with a thumbs up. What else was there?

She set down her phone and slid back under the covers. Being away from Andy wasn't as hard here—in his home, in his room—as it was elsewhere, but she was reaching her limit. Ceri wrapped an arm around Andy's waist and pulled herself close. Her eyes fluttered closed as she told herself not to get used to this.

Nothing good ever lasted.

· · · ★ ★ ★ ★ ★ · · ·

Ceri woke with a gasp, clawing her way from drowning to air.

"Shhh." Andy's voice washed over her. "It's just a bad dream. You're safe. You're protected."

Ceri rolled over, falling further into his arms. "Sorry. Thanks. Both. I don't know." It would be so easy to lose herself in his embrace. She was safe. Protected. Things she'd not felt for longer than...forever. She'd spent three centuries taking care of herself, and she didn't like depending on anyone. She wasn't one of those people who desired to lose themselves in their partner. She was her own person, could take care of herself, and didn't need another half to complete her.

She started to pull back, to keep the contact she needed to keep the *literal* demons at bay but put distance between her and the fallen angel whose bed she shared. Andy's arms tightened around her, and she surrendered. She didn't have the strength to insist.

"You don't have to be strong with me," Andy murmured into her hair. "I can help you bear this burden that I gave you."

She laughed, then flinched at how bitter she sounded. "I wish I could give it back. I don't want this. I never wanted this."

"I know. I didn't want it, either." His hand slid down her body to rest on her hip, and his breath teased the wisps of hair near her ear.

Ceri tensed. She knew how much he liked her delicately pointed ears, how much he liked teasing the points with his tongue, and she was sure he was going to give into the temptation.

Instead, he rolled onto his back with a groan, his hand leaving her hip and the warmth of his body disappearing from her back. Only the arm trapped under her body remained in contact. "I need to take a shower," he said. "Will you be okay for a while?"

She bit her lip and tried to be grateful he was maintaining the boundaries she'd set up, because she clearly wasn't capable of it right now. *Probably the exhaustion and nightmares,* she told herself. *Definitely not anything else. Not desire.* "Of course! I'll be fine. I wish there was another way..." She rolled forward so he could free his arm.

"I do, too. For a lot of reasons, but mostly because it'd be easier for you if you didn't have to rely on touching someone you've no desire to touch to keep your sanity." Andy slipped out of the bed, grabbed a couple things out of a drawer, and went into the bathroom.

Ceri kept her eyes fixed anywhere but on the way his soft pajama pants rested low on his hips, showing off the tattoo high on his right thigh that he said was the symbol of his servitude in hell. The original fallen had been marked by their god when they left her service. Each had a tattoo somewhere on their bodies that advertised who and what they were to anyone with the magic decoding ring.

Nope. She definitely wasn't seeing the way his muscles bunched and flexed with each movement. And she was too busy looking out the window on the other side of the room to see the definition in his shoulders and back before he disappeared from view.

Ceri exhaled in relief. This whole thing would be a lot easier if he hadn't caught feelings. If he'd stayed as disinterested in more as she was, they could've continued on with their arrangement that was mutually beneficial and a lot of fun. Someone always had to ruin things. Someone who was never her. She pushed back the internal conflict that had been growing the last few days as well as the lingering suspicion that she was the one who'd messed up things this time and concentrated on her centuries of certainty that romantic entanglements were not for her.

It was easier having someone she trusted nearby. Traveling to fulfill her needs was annoying and time-consuming, but in a town full of psychics, there hadn't been a lot of choices other than an occasional fling with a tourist passing through. Most of the people who came to their tiny town were families, but every once in a while, a single person showed up for a solo getaway.

Heat pooled low in her belly, and she grimaced. It didn't matter now. She couldn't take Andy back into her bed, not now—not when it would be borne of necessity and proximity. And she couldn't be away from him long enough to find another lover, even if she could find someone she trusted well enough to not freak out if the nightmares showed up or she walked past a mirror.

If she kept deteriorating at the rate she had been lately, she might die before another opportunity came her way. She laughed. Wouldn't that be something? To die in a rare period of celibacy?

Ceri fluffed up some pillows and arranged them behind her so she could half-recline while she waited for her turn in the shower. There was an amazing view from the bed, and it was an excellent place to watch the seagulls swooping on the updrafts between here and the ocean. It was mere coincidence that it was also an ideal place to watch Andy emerge from the bathroom.

She suppressed her disappointment when he came out in low-slung jeans. At least she could see his hip bones, the hint of the tattoo, and his chest.

"My eyes are up here," he said with amusement.

She flushed. "I don't know what you're talking about. I'm watching the birds."

He dropped the towel he'd been using to towel off his short, silver hair and stalked towards her. "Sure you were. You always lick your lips like that for seagulls." His wings flared out behind him, and he smirked. "I think we both know what kind of feathered friend you're ogling."

At his teasing accusation, Ceri's senses returned. There was no harm in admiring his angelic form, but admiration was the limit—and her admiration had to be secret.

"My apologies," she said rather stiffly in an attempt to keep a polite distance between them. "It won't happen again. You are an attractive man, but I shouldn't objectify you like that. I will do better."

He sighed, and Ceri swore she saw his shoulders slump slightly. "Of course. I appreciate the compliment and your future efforts." Andy pulled on a black t-shirt with the Pour House logo emblazoned on it, the material stretching tight across his chest. After grabbing a pair of socks and a long-sleeved button-up shirt, he looked back at her. "How are you doing? You good to shower and dress now? Or do you need a few moments to drive the demons away?"

The only demon I need to drive away is the only one I want to hold on to.

"I'm good for a little while yet." Ceri pushed the covers back and got out of bed, only wobbly slightly this time. Andy stepped forward and steadied her. "I'm okay now."

He let go but didn't step back.

Ceri grabbed her overnight bag and walked into the steamy bathroom.

"I'll be in earshot," he promised.

CERI WALKED OUT OF THE BATHROOM FOLLOWED BY A BILLOW OF FOG. SHE'D gotten most of her clothes on, but the moisture in the air had stymied her efforts to hike up her blue jeans. She hadn't heard anyone on the other side of the door and figured she had a few minutes to fully dry off and finish dressing before Andy reappeared.

She dropped her bag by the door and moved out of the pervasive steam cloud so she could towel off her legs. When she judged she was dry enough for another attempt at blue jeans, she sat on the chair near the low vanity she loved, even if Andy had covered the mirror while she was showering.

Ceri finished dressing, shoved her dirty clothes into the bag, and straightened up to untangle her long red hair. The horror was encroaching on the edges of her vision, and she knew she didn't have long before she'd need Andy's touch again. She closed her eyes, as if that would keep the monsters at bay, and ran the wide-toothed comb through her hair. When it was smooth and tangle-free, she reached behind her head and started braiding.

Her arms and shoulders were shaking by the time she finished the French braid, and she shook her right shoulder out, holding the end of the braid with her left hand. She opened her eyes to look for a hair elastic.

The mirror, uncovered and steam-free, caught her before she could even try to look away.

She felt the scream tear through her but couldn't hear it. Her eyelids refused to close. A parade of the damned marched towards her—so many different people, different sins, different expressions. There was the downtrodden, the guilty, the smirking, the triumphant.

The mirror disappeared with a crash, but she still couldn't close her eyes.

A silver wing appeared in her field of vision, and she grabbed onto it, memorizing the feathers, counting each rachis, marking each barb. She blinked and became aware of Andy's body pressed against her, his wings wrapped around her.

She took a deep breath. And another.

"What happened?" she asked.

"You tell me," he bit out. "Why'd you uncover the mirror? That was a stupid move."

"I didn't!" she protested. "It was covered when I came out of the shower. I was sitting here braiding my hair with my eyes closed, and when I opened them, it was uncovered, not a hint of steam on it. I don't understand."

Andy picked her up, walked across the room, and kicked open the French doors that led to a balcony, then launched into the air.

"Where are we going?" she asked against his chest, knowing he'd be able to hear her.

"Your place. You don't have mirrors on your walls. It'll be safer there while I try to figure out what to do, how to keep you shielded until we can figure this out." He put on a burst of speed and took them higher, high enough that anyone looking up in Oracle Bay wouldn't immediately recognize an angel flying over the town.

· · · ★ ★ ★ ★ ★ ★ ★ · ·

ANDY PACED BACK AND FORTH IN HER LIVING ROOM, SOMETHING MADE awkward by the fact that he refused to let go of her hand.

"What happened to the mirror?" Ceri asked.

He stopped at looked at her. "I threw it out."

She bit her lip, hesitated, then asked, "Did you throw it out the window?"

"Yes." He resumed his pacing.

"I really liked that mirror. That vanity is my favorite piece of furniture, like ever." She tried not to think about the state of the mirror or the window it'd likely gone through.

"It's yours then. I'll have it brought over here, fully repaired, as soon as you can stand to have mirrors again."

"I like your optimism." When he directed a single raised eyebrow at her, she clarified. "That you think I'll ever be at a place I can have mirrors. It's much more likely that this—" she raised the hand firmly held in his "—is merely delaying the inevitable. Don't get me wrong, I'm grateful at the moment. I have things to do yet, but when it's time, when I'm ready, you'll have to let me go."

"I don't like what you're implying." He knelt in front of her and pulled her forward until he could wrap his arms around her.

"I'm not implying. I'm telling you there will come a time when this will be too much, too difficult, and too painful. When that time comes, it will be a kindness to let me go."

"I will never let you go. Do you hear me?" He reached up and cupped her face in his hands. "I am not letting go, and you are not giving up. We will find a way."

Ceri smiled at him. She wasn't going to argue anymore—she wouldn't change his mind anyway.

She rested her forehead against his, exhaustion threatening to render her unconscious. She'd lived a long, long time. She'd had so many adventures, met so many wonderful people, and had finally found a home in Oracle Bay. It was hard to imagine this being over, but he knew where the path she was on would lead. She'd gone too far into hell, into madness, and there wasn't a way to turn back. Not anymore.

It was too late to save her.

eri glanced down at her watch and cursed under her breath. "It's five minutes to ten," she told Andy.

"And?"

"And I told Drew I'd meet him for coffee at ten. I need to see him. There's something going on, and I don't know what it is, but he needs me." Ceri stood and headed to the kitchen, stopping short when Andy didn't come with her. "Come on—or let go. I have to grab my wallet."

"You can't go out. You're too fragile." Andy's eyes widened almost before he'd finished speaking. "That's not what I meant. You're not fragile, but you need to stay home. Call Drew and tell him to come here instead."

"I'm going. I'd love it if you'd come with me, but I know you're busy. Maybe I can just..." Her eyes darted around as she tried to figure out something that would help keep the madness away. "Borrow your shirt?"

"You want to borrow my shirt? Do you think that'll help?" He already had the long sleeve shirt off.

Ceri wrinkled her nose and gritted her teeth. "Um. Can I have the t-shirt instead? It's more...you? It's old, it's been touching your skin, and it's not generic like the other."

"Okay. Whatever you need." He stood close enough to press his legs against hers, then dropped the long-sleeved shirt and slowly pulled the t-shirt up his body and over his head. He handed her the shirt, and she looked down. She promised not to objectify him less than an hour ago, and here she was fighting her hands' desire to reach out and trace the line of hair that led from his belly button down to disappear into his...

"Why do you have a bellybutton?" She stood and took off the sweater she'd donned against the chill from their flight over.

"What do you mean?" Andy picked up his other shirt and put it on, buttoning it almost all the way up.

"You're an angel. You were created by your god, not kindled in another. You had no umbilical cord, no need to draw what you need from the life of another. So why a belly button?"

Andy looked down at the flat pane of his abdomen. "Huh. I never thought about it before. I'll ask Barachiel next time he visits. Even if he doesn't know, it'll be fun to see how his mind tries to work it out."

Ceri took a deep breath, then took off her light-yellow tank top, replacing it as quickly as possible with Andy's black shirt and tried not to think about the fact that she was wearing the pale pink lacy bra that Andy'd given to her for Yule.

Surprise flitted through his eyes and disappeared.

"Do you know why the mirror was uncovered?" he asked. "If you didn't do it, and I believe you when you say you didn't, how did it happen? It was securely covered—I would never take a chance—so how did it happen?"

Ceri blinked at the abrupt change in subject, tucked in her borrowed shirt, and put her cardigan back on. "I don't know," she finally answered. "It just was."

"I wonder if it was your ghost. Can ghosts have that much effect on the material world? Isn't that a lot of work?" He scooped her into his arms, snagged her purse from where it was tipped over on the kitchen table, and flew into the air.

"I wish Russell was here," Ceri muttered. "He'd be the perfect person to talk through this stuff with. I mean, I guess it's good that he's taking some time with his Aunt Sybil to figure out who he is and what he can do, but it's inconvenient timing for me." She felt Andy's suppressed laughter, and a slow smile spread across her face. She loved making him laugh.

He landed lightly in the alley behind Caffiend Dreams—Bill's amazing coffee shop.

"Ugh," Ceri muttered. "I forgot to tell you we were meeting at the Mermaid Shack."

Andy looked at her, and for the first time since all of this had started, she thought he might believe she was actually going crazy. "Drew wants you to have burnt chain coffee instead of the amazing, caffeinated concoctions created by his boyfriend? Are you sure?"

Ceri showed him the text and shrugged. "Your guess is as good as mine. But I'm late, and Drew is not a patient person."

"Whatever you say. Something weird is going on with him. It's good you're meeting with him to get to the bottom of it. I'll walk you there, then hang out across the street until you need me." He held out his arm, and she tucked her hand through his elbow.

"Thank you. For everything." She leaned her head against his arm as they walked down the street to meet her best friend.

Drew was looking at his phone and muttering to himself when she walked in.

"You're late," he snapped.

"I'm sorry. It's been a rough morning. Do you need another coffee?" She stepped towards the counter. There was usually a short line—some tourists preferred the familiar over the good—but there wasn't today. Only one person was in front of her, and her black leggings and hoodie tugged at her memory. She shook herself out of it—probably a long-term tourist—and turned her attention back to Drew.

"Yeah. Quad shot Americano with plenty of room."

Ceri widened her eyes but just nodded. She put in his order and got an iced vanilla latte for herself. She needed as much sugar as possible to get through today.

When she set his coffee on the table in front of him, topped up with cream, and dropped into the chair across from him, he finally looked at her.

"You look like crap, Ceri." He took a drink of his coffee, grimaced, and took another long drink.

"You're not looking so hot yourself," she retorted.

Drew sighed and dropped his face into his hands.

Ceri scooted her chair around to sit beside him and pulled him into a side hug. "Drew, you have to tell me what's going on. I thought you'd be so happy when I saw..." Oh. Oh no. She'd only been seeing pain and misery and had held onto Drew's engagement and Sandy's pregnancy as the bright spots, but neither seemed happy. Dammit. Had she twisted this for them? Was this her fault?

He was shaking his head. "I am happy. I love Bill. He's my everything."

"I'm not an expert in happy, but you're not selling it. What happened?" Ceri nudged him with her shoulder until he looked up at her.

"Nothing. I don't know. I mean, I said yes. How could I not? He was so excited, and even though his whole proposal plan had been ruined by the sudden appearance of an angry fallen angel, he made it so perfect, so romantic. It was wonderful." He sighed again and took another drink of his coffee.

"But..." Ceri prompted when he didn't say anything further. "Something must be wrong if you're making me drink this instead of getting a caramel latte from your honey."

"You'll think I'm stupid. Or shallow." Drew pushed away from her a little, and she let go and scooted back to her side of the table.

Ceri shrugged. "I'll tell you the truth, but you have to tell me what I'm judging first. I can't say you're being an idiot unless I know why."

"He's going to die," Drew blurted.

Ceri felt the blood drain from her face. "Oh my god. What's wrong? Is he sick?"

Drew was shaking his head before she finished speaking. "No. He's not sick. He's in fantastic shape that doesn't ruin his sexy dad bod, and his stamina is incredible."

"TMI, Drew. But if he's not sick, what do you... Oh." She bowed her head and looked down at her hands. They were shaking a little, and she didn't know if it was from the jolt of caffeine or something else. "You mean he hasn't been blessed with the ridiculously long life we have? You don't want to tie yourself to him in case you don't love him anymore when he's old, and you're still walking around in the body of a thirty-year-old?"

"No!" Drew roared at her.

Ceri flinched and nearly tipped over her chair.

"No," he repeated, more quietly this time. "There is nothing that will ever destroy my love for him. I will stay by his side as long as he'll let me. But..." Drew took a deep breath. "What if his feelings change? What if he doesn't want me when I don't age with him? What if he decides he wants to spend his life with someone who will age with him?"

Ceri blew out a long breath. It wasn't an angle she'd ever considered. She didn't form attachments—partially to avoid questions like this, and partly because relationships involved too much energy to maintain. "Too bad there aren't vampires," she said. "We could get one on retainer and have them turn our favorite mortals into blood sucking creatures of the night to keep them young and by our sides forever."

"That would be a solution." Drew drained his Americano. "Want another?"

"What? No. Don't do this to yourself." She stood and held out her hand. "Walk with me to Antonia's. We'll get a cup of tea, a couple pastries, and then you will go home and tell yourself not to be an idiot."

He glared, but stood up anyway, grabbing her purse.

She opened her purse to drop her wallet back in, and gasped.

"What is it? Are you okay?" Drew asked.

Ceri reached into her too-large purse and pulled out a vintage gold tiara. It was decorated with rubies in settings shaped like roses and surrounded by emerald "leaves." Diamonds circled the bottom of the tiara, and even with age evident, it sparkled like it'd just been polished.

"It's pretty, but it's not really you, babe," Drew said.

"It's not mine, and it wasn't there when I grabbed my wallet to pay for our drinks." She looked around the coffee shop but didn't see anyone lingering suspiciously.

"Okay, but you look way more upset than 'surprise antique jewelry discovery' warrants. Does it mean something?" Drew pulled her out of the coffee shop.

"Yeah. Yeah, it does. I can't quite place it, but this makes me think of LA." She tried to piece together the fragments of memories flitting around in her mind. They were playing tag in the middle of the minefield that was the worst of Andy's eternity.

"You haven't lived in LA since the early twentieth century, have you?" Drew asked. "You didn't stay too long after I showed up and ruined your case with my condescending misogyny and Chicago brashness."

"I stayed for one more case." The pieces snapped together in her mind. "I stayed for one more case but couldn't ever close it. It was the only one I ever walked away from without finding the murderer."

"I thought you never walked away," Drew said.

"I didn't. But my client died when I didn't take her fear that she'd be the next victim seriously enough. She was the seventh—and last —victim of a serial killer. Without a client and without a killer, I had nothing. The only link I ever found between any of the victims was that in each case, there was exactly one piece of jewelry missing from their collection—and it was always a bejeweled flower. My client, Helen Williams, was found just like the rest—no immediately visible signs of violence and fully dressed in a long, white gown that was a cross between a lacy wedding dress and a funeral shroud. Perfectly made up and peaceful until you removed the gown and saw a body that'd been drained of blood, dismembered, and reassembled. Her brooch was missing—it had a bouquet of flowers in platinum and diamonds on cobalt blue enamel and encircled by pearls." Ceri took a breath. The images from the case—the crime scene photos—were coming in too quickly, and she cursed her brain for being so willing to call these images up. "But the first victim was missing the ruby tiara her husband had given her for her fortieth birthday three days before he died of a heart attack."

"A tiara just like the one you found in your purse?" Drew's brows were pulled into low V in the middle of his forehead.

"Not just like this one. This *is* the tiara that was taken by the serial killer I never found. And somehow it appeared in the space of fifteen minutes when my purse was at our table the whole time." She started shaking, and Drew wrapped an arm around her shoulders.

"Where's your guard dog?" Drew asked looking around.

"I am not a dog," Andy said as he walked up. "What's wrong with her?"

"I will let her explain, but keep a close eye on our girl, okay? Don't let her out of your sight." Drew glared at Andy until the latter dipped his head in acknowledgment.

Ceri reached out her hand and grabbed Drew's wrist. "Drew, talk to him. Tell him your fears. Tell him everything. Don't decide for him. If you do, then you will be a shallow idiot."

"I'll take it under advisement," he said.

"Dumbass," she muttered.

"Drama queen," he shot back.

"Love you. Do the right thing. I just gotten used to drinking the good coffee again." She tried to fix as much command into her voice as possible, and when he gave the barest hint of a nod, she let go of his wrist.

"Love you too, Ceri." He walked away and, by the direction he took, was headed towards Caffiend Dreams.

Ceri reached out her hand and sagged in relief when Andy took it.

"What's wrong?" His voice was low and urgent. He pulled her closer, and she let him.

"I can't... Not here. Do you have to go to work?" Ceri looked around, but the streets were strangely empty. "Where is everyone?"

"What do you mean?" Andy glanced around briefly before turning his attention back to her.

"The streets are empty. There wasn't a line in the coffee shop. Things have been bananas busy for months, but today feels... empty. Like we're the only ones here." She shivered, and Andy's arm tightened around her.

"If the texts I'm getting from Brandy are any indication, they're all at the Pour House for the brand-new weekday brunch she started this week. It's not the best day for Felicity to be late." He growled a bit in frustration.

Ceri squeezed his hand in sympathy. "Are you thinking of firing her? This is kinda the second big strike in two days, although the spill was an accident."

"And I'm sure today was, too. And she did finally show up a couple minutes ago, so at least I'm not having to go wait tables. I hate waiting tables more than anything else I've ever done on this mortal plane." Andy glanced at his phone again and shoved it back into his pocket. "To answer your question, I do need to go to work. There's nothing pressing I need to do today in the brewery—the new brewer Brandy hired can manage most everything without me at this point. But I need to stop in and show my face to remind myself—and

Brandy—that it's my bar and not hers." He grinned down at Ceri, and she returned his smile.

"You love it. You love not having to be responsible for anything but creating new beers and occasionally charming your customers." She briefly rested her head on his shoulder while they walked down the street that would take them to the brewery. Ceri tried to hide the fact that she was out of breath. It was only a mile to the Pour House, and she'd made the walk dozens, if not hundreds, of times.

He stopped abruptly. "You're out of breath."

"I'm fine."

"You're not fine. Lie to the others if you have to. Lie to yourself. But don't lie to me, Ceridwen." He dropped her hand, but before she could even register his absence, he had her in his arms. "Hold on, woman. As soon as we turn down the next street, I'm ducking into an alley, and we're taking off. I've got these wings, and I might as well use them."

"You're going to start rumors if you keep flying around every-where," Ceri said.

"Not as many rumors as the ones we just created by strolling down Main Street hand-in-hand," he smirked. He crouched, tightened his hold, and shot straight up into the air.

Ceri gasped as her stomach failed to rise as fast as the rest of her. They burst through a flock of seagulls before he adjusted his direction and headed to the bar.

Seconds later, he landed gently on the roof. He kicked open a trap door she hadn't seen before and jumped through, landing lightly on his feet in what looked like...

"Is this a storage room?" Ceri asked. Then she blushed. She recognized it now. It was the supply room at the far end of the brewery. The only room besides his office no one else had a key to. It also had several pallets and a pile of shipping blankets. They were a little scratchy, and her knees hadn't been the same since, but they made a nice enough nest for an afternoon quickie.

Andy set her on her feet, flew up to pull the trapdoor closed, then landed in front of her again, taking her hands in his. "Are you okay?"

"As much as I can be right now. But I would really like to sit down and learn a little more about Brandy's week-day brunch. I'm so hungry." She pulled him towards the door.

He unlocked it and followed her through—or tried to.

Ceri stopped when her grip on his hand didn't keep moving. She turned around in time to catch him tucking away the wings that had impeded his passage through the door. She laughed at the look of embarrassed consternation on his face.

"It's not funny," he grumbled.

"You got stuck in a door," she gasped. "How is that not funny?"

A grin threatened to crack his stony visage.

"How many times has that happened to you?" Ceri was still giggling.

He laughed. "This was not the first time, but it was the first time in a very long while. You turn me upside down, Ceridwen. I lose all sense of space and time when I'm with you." His expression changed from wry embarrassment to soulful longing.

Ceri's chest tightened, and she had to work to keep her expression passive. For a moment, she let her mind play through the possibilities of giving in to him, giving him what he wanted. It'd be so easy, but it wasn't what she wanted, was it? She was having trouble believing herself anymore—perhaps another symptom of the hell she was going through and the deep connection that had formed between them. But it didn't change anything. She wasn't long-term material, and there would come a day when she'd walk away and break his heart.

"Don't look at me like that," he said. "Don't look at me like you're saying goodbye."

"I'm not saying goodbye. I can't walk away from you now. Not until…"

He closed his eyes, but not before she saw the profound sadness in his gaze. "I know. You don't have to say it again. Let's go get you some food. A short stack with extra bacon would do you a world of good."

Ceri let him lead her out through the maze of the brew house and into the back of the bar where two people she didn't recognize were flipping pancakes and frying eggs.

"Tom, Luis—lookin' good," Andy said.

The men, one white and one with light brown skin that pointed at Latin American heritage, looked up. "Hey boss," the Latino man said. "Here for breakfast?"

"I'm not, but the lady here is gonna need a stack of your best pancakes and four strips of bacon when you have time, Luis." Andy started towards the door, then stopped. "You know what? I want breakfast, too. Can you make me a veggie omelet, extra mushrooms, and those breakfast potatoes I've heard Brandy raving about?"

"You're the boss, boss," the white man said. "We've got a couple orders ahead of yours, but you'll be eating the best breakfast on the peninsula soon."

"I like your confidence, Tom," Andy said. "I hope your food is as good."

"You won't be disappointed," Luis said. "But..."

"I can take a hint. We'll get out of your kitchen and snag a table in the back. I'll let Felicity know we already put in our orders." Andy pushed open the swinging door that separated the kitchen from the bar. He waved at Brandy, who was on her laptop at the end of the bar, frowning at the screen.

After sliding behind the table in the back alcove that was permanently reserved for the town psychics—too big for two people, but not one that would take a regular table out of circulation—Ceri closed her eyes. "Thanks for the food and the flight."

"You deserve to be taken care of a little from time to time. You're worth it."

Ceri was saved from having to respond by Felicity's appearance. Andy ordered two cups of coffee, a pitcher of cream, and waters while Ceri stared at the table, blinking away the tears that prickled her eyelids. She was trying not to let Andy's words get to her, but she'd never been told she was worth it before. Worth the trouble. The regard. The consideration.

She shook her head. This was getting dangerous—maybe ever more dangerous than living with the encroaching madness.

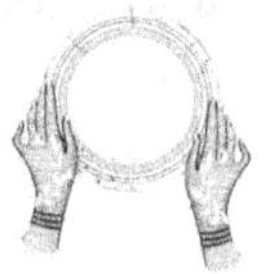

six

"Angel. Demon. Whatever you are. I have an idea."

Ceri looked up with a start, pulling herself out of her brunch coma. She was leaning against Andy, who was on his laptop, looking at spreadsheets and frowning.

"Paska? What are you doing here?" Ceri sat up straight and tried to create the appearance of distance between her and Andy without losing contact.

"You don't have to play that game with me, lass," Paska said with a roll of his eyes. "I know why you've become so attached to your lover when you've spent your life avoiding any attachment. And that's why I'm here. Even if you were madly in love, this level of physical contact would be tiresome after a time. I think I have a temporary solution while we look for the cure for your madness."

Andy closed his laptop and looked at the ancient human who looked no older than forty, and a well-kept forty at that. "Talk, magician."

Paska rolled his eyes again. "You may be a true immortal being whose beginning was written in the stars before you were spoken into existence, but you don't know shit about living in this world. You've been here what, half a century at most? Show a little respect for your elders."

"I don't know why you're butting heads, but stop," Ceri interrupted. "We're all old and wise and blah blah blah. Why not humor the very young woman in the room and tell me why you're here, Paska? What will help?"

Paska winked at her and put his hands on the table. They were the only part of him that didn't look young. His hands were scarred and blackened by fire and ash. "Close your eyes, girl. I know you don't read the bones, but let's not take any chances. You don't need any more future climbing into your brain." Ceri closed her eyes and heard him scatter the contents of his hands across the table.

"Did you come here to help or tell my fortune?" Andy's voice was sardonic, but Ceri heard the thread of hope under the surface.

"Shut up and look," Paska said. "This is the same reading I've gotten six times in a row when concentrating on Ceri's dilemma. I don't understand the answer, not completely, and I hate not understanding. But what I do know is that feathers are the answer."

"Feathers?" Ceri asked. She opened her eyes and stared at Paska, carefully keeping her eyes off the surface of the table, no matter how much she wanted to see the story the bone runes were telling.

Paska held her gaze and swept the bones towards the edge of the table where they clattered into the black leather pouch he carried everywhere. A black leather pouch she was a little afraid to ask the origin of.

"Feathers. So, I was thinking—who do I know that might have access to magic feathers? Because clearly plucking a chicken isn't likely to work. Unless…" Paska trailed off with a thoughtful expression on his face. "Would it be something that simple? It seems unlikely, but sometimes the simplest is the thing we overlook."

"Paska, feathers." Ceri tamped down the impatience she felt at being so close to something that could help.

"Right. We'll look into chickens later." Paska looked at Andy. "Can you pluck a feather?"

"Can I what?" Andy looked as if Paska had just suggested he pull an eyeball out and set it on the table.

Which... Ceri didn't know if angel feathers were pluckable like a bird's, or if they were part of them—like skin or eyeballs. He'd certainly reacted enthusiastically and positively when she'd touched his feathers.

"You heard me. Can you give the girl a feather?" Paska tapped a finger on the table. "This won't work if you can't, and I'll have to go back to the drawing board. Or see if Joseph has any more magic farm animals willing to give me a feather. I don't think it'll work as well if it isn't you, though."

Andy opened his mouth, closed it, then said, "I could give Ceri a feather, but I'm not doing it right here."

"Fine, of course. No one's asking you to pop your wings out in the middle of the bar. The residents of Oracle Bay might be used to pretending not to see what's in front of their faces, but the tourists aren't, and they have cameras. I love having the internet in my pocket, but I hate that I can't do anything without being watched." Paska grimaced. "But we do need a feather, and I have some questions and a small experiment. Run along and grab a feather for your girl."

"I'm not his girl," Ceri huffed.

"Maybe not yet," Paska said. "Sometimes the timelines twist in my mind. Ignore my previous comment, Andy. Go get a feather for Ms. Kenny. Then we will talk."

Andy slid out of the booth, and Ceri gasped at his sudden absence. Her peripheral visions dimmed as the monsters approached.

She saw Andy pause at the top of the step that led out of the alcove and into the main bar.

"Go, boy," Paska barked. "The sooner you leave, the sooner you'll be back. Hesitating makes it all so much worse."

Andy walked towards the stairs leading to his office at a pace quick enough to almost be called a jog.

"Look at me, lass," Paska said. "Take my hands. I'm not him, and I can't dampen what you're seeing, but I can distract you and help keep the nightmares from overtaking you. And, if I'm reading the bones right, we might have a temporary stopgap that won't leave you gasping in pain and fear every time he walks away. It should make going to the bathroom easier, too."

Ceri put her hands in his and tried to breathe through it. "It's worse during the day. In the mornings, it's not so bad. But the visions, the memories, the nightmares—whatever they are—grow in strength during the day, and each night, they die back a little less."

Paska squeezed her hands. "I know, lass. And we're going to figure this out. I wish you'd said something sooner. You hid it well until you collapsed and went into a coma. Imagine how much closer we'd be to a solution if you'd not tried to be strong and independent!"

"Fine. You're right, and I was stupid. I should've asked for help." Ceri stared at the place where their hands connected.

"You should've, but I wouldn't call you stupid. I don't know your story, but whatever happened when you were young isn't the story you have to tell forever. You have friends here—friends who are family. There's no need to walk alone anymore."

For the second time that morning, tears pricked at Ceri's eyes. What was it with these men trying to make her feel things she didn't know she could feel? "Thank you. I'm trying."

"No you're not," he said. "You're avoiding. But you'll have to try soon if you want to live."

Andy slid back into the booth and up against her side before Ceri had a chance to reply. He placed a feather in the center of the table. It was almost two feet long and shimmered silver in the light. Ceri reached out and ran a finger along the rachis. "It's so beautiful."

"How far apart do you have to be to stop getting the numbing effect of his presence?" Paska asked.

Ceri considered. "If I'm ready for it, I am usually okay for a while if we're in the same room, or if I'm in his room."

Paska nodded in satisfaction. "That's what I was hoping for. Now, before I tell you my theory and we do some tests, I need a little information. Part of this is to satisfy my curiosity, but mostly, I need to know what's going on in your mind so I can try to figure out what the bones are telling me. We will fix this. I promise."

"Do you also want to know what her ghost has been up to? It's becoming actively malicious, and I worry that will impact any short-term fixes you come up with." Andy reached out and grabbed her hand.

"Yes. I want to know everything. And I have a theory about your ghost as well. It's something I'm holding close for the moment, but tomorrow I'll share at the regular meeting." Paska pulled out a small notebook and a stubby pencil. "Okay, I have questions; you have answers. Let's go."

"I won't be at the meeting tomorrow," Ceri said before he could get going. "Even if I could stand it, I'm pretty sure everyone there thinks I'm going crazy."

"What do you think?" he asked, piercing her with his dark brown eyes.

"I know I'm going crazy, but I also know the ghost is real." Ceri crossed her arms over her chest and jutted out her chin.

"Both true. And we'll get to that, but first... First a drink."

Ceri tilted her head. Long conversations with Paska were a rarity, and following him from start to beginning involved a lot of wrong turns, roundabouts, and arguments with a navigation app.

"Hey everyone!" Felicity chirped from just out of view. "I would love to get you a drink, Mr.... I'm sorry, I don't know your last name, sir."

"It's Cooper. Mr. Cooper. And I'll take a pint of your finest whiskey." Ceri saw Paska wink at Felicity, and she widened her eyes.

"A...pint? Um." Felicity's eyes flicked to Andy, clearly unsure how to handle Paska's weird order.

"Or just the bottle if it's over half full. And you can bring me a rocks glass if it makes you feel better," he said.

Andy shook his head. "Bring him the bottle, two glasses, and for Ceri?"

"Mimosa?" Ceri asked hopefully.

"You got it!" Felicity said.

"Tell me what happened," Paska commanded. "Start at the beginning."

"Do you mean with the ghost? Or with?" Ceri twirled her index finger around her ear.

"Which of those is the beginning? I asked for the beginning." Paska huffed, then leaned back.

Ceri shook her head and tried to pull her thoughts together. "You know when it started. You were there."

"Humor me, girl. Besides, I don't know if from your perspective. I was a mere observer. You lived it."

Ceri paused for Felicity to set down the drinks.

"Thanks Felicity," Andy said. "No need to check on us again. I'll let you know if we need anything."

Felicity glanced around the table, her gaze lingering on Ceri a moment too long, then landed back on Andy. "Of course. I'll be here!"

Ceri took a sip of her mimosa. "I might become a regular at week-day brunch. Brandy is a genius."

Paska poured two glasses of whiskey to the brim of the glass, downed his in one gulp, and refilled it. "Alcohol can dull the knowl-edge, but it's a fine line between self-medication and self-abuse. It's a line I've learned to dance on both sides of in the last thousand years."

"And before that?" Ceri asked, suddenly certain he was older than that.

"Before that, I stayed far away from the line—switching sides every decade or so. But we're not here to talk about my unusual life choices. We are here to figure out what's going on with you. Keep talking."

Ceri took another fortifying drink of her mimosa, wished she had a whiskey glass, and dove back into her narrative. "The angels showed up, an apocalypse happened, and then the murders. And all while this was going on, I started having dreams. At first, it was just a dream a couple times a week. I was dreaming about Andy's life. His past. I was seeing what he'd lived through in hell. What he'd done, and what'd been done to him."

"How did you know it was Andy's mind yours was pulling from?" Paska propped his elbows on the table, leaned forward, and propped his chin on his clasped hands.

Ceri mulled over the question. "I don't know. I saw so much—too much—when I scried him. It was overwhelming. I saw who and what he was—from his creation to his fall to his unexpected rise. I saw the apocalypse coming, even though he did not. And I knew I was reliving events he'd lived through. I felt him inside of me."

Paska snickered.

"Inappropriate timing for juvenile humor, old man," Andy murmured.

"Apologies, Ceridwen. Please continue." Paska tipped his head forward to hide the grin that lingered on his face.

Ceri took another unsatisfactory and unfortifying sip of her mimosa and eyed Andy's whiskey. He slid it over to her, and she smiled gratefully at him before taking a drink and sighing in gratification. "I love that you have the good stuff—none of that bog whiskey from the wrong side of the sea." After another long sip, she nudged the glass back towards Andy. "The dreams increased in frequency, and soon it wasn't just nightmares. If I let my mind drift while awake, I was overtaken by visions of hellfire, torture, pain. The end of the earth. The first major battle. The last." She held out her hand, and Andy pushed the glass back into it. She gulped. "And now, it's not even when I'm drifting. The visions encroach on me all the time. I'm barely sleeping. I have trouble eating. I see armies of the dead marching towards me."

Andy slid closer to her and wrapped an arm around her. "If it's too hard, you don't have to talk about this."

"Don't listen to him, child. You have to talk about this. We can't find the answers if you don't give us the questions. Keep talking. I have enough whiskey to get you through this." Paska tipped the bottle and refilled the glass she was sharing with Andy.

"It's harder now to do anything. I can't see the answers anymore. I try to scry for clients, but all I see is the worst possible outcome, and always flames lick the edges of my sight. When I stopped... When we stopped..." Ceri paused, looking for the right words to describe what happened between her and Andy.

"When she ended things between us," Andy inserted.

"Right. Then. When we weren't spending so much time together, it got worse. I was walking to see him, to see if it would be better if we were together, to test that hypothesis. It took me an hour to walk from my place to the brewery, but it worked. When I touched him, the horrors receded. But then I stepped back and was pulled into hell." Ceri shuddered at the last memory she had before waking up in the hospital.

"You know what happened next," Andy said, taking up the thread of the narrative. "I picked her up, shot through the ceiling, and took her to the hospital. I called Misty, and as soon as you lot descended on her, I hopped a plane to get Drew when Morgana told me he was the only one who could save her."

"Wait, what?" Ceri asked. "I didn't know that."

"Nor did I," Paska said. "Interesting. Continue."

CERI LEANED BACK AGAINST THE BOOTH. SHE WAS DRAINED, NOT AS DRUNK AS she wanted to be, and no less confused than she'd been when she'd

started. She'd told Paska and Andy everything. Now she was waiting for Paska to process and tell her his brilliant idea.

Paska cleared his throat, and Ceri sat at attention. "Okay. There's a lot more to this than even I was anticipating. I was ready for your apocalypse nightmares and the ghost—although I didn't know it was malevolent—but I wasn't ready for the serial killer angle. I'll need to think about that a little more, but I still think my original idea is worth a try." He pushed the feather towards her. "Pick this up, close your eyes, and hold it against your chest."

Ceri looked at Andy, who shrugged slightly. She picked up the feather, held it close to her, and closed her eyes.

"Take a deep breath."

Ceri did as instructed. Then took another.

"Okay, open your eyes." Paska's voice was quiet and calm.

She opened her eyes and looked at Paska. He tipped his head to his right, her left. She looked to her left, to Andy. He wasn't there. "Where?"

"I'm right here." Andy walked back into the alcove.

"But how?" She looked down at the feather still clutched tightly in her hands. "This?"

"Put it down now," Paska commanded.

She pulled it away from her chest and reluctantly put it on the table. Pain wracked her body as the visions redoubled in her mind. It was over in an instant—although it felt like an eternity—and Andy had his arms around her again. "Shhh, you're okay." He caressed her hair and ran his thumbs along her cheeks.

"It worked reasonably well," Paska said, leaning back and looking all too pleased with himself. "That should give you both a little freedom and peace—and Ceridwen, it will give you relief during the day, although I recommend you still spend as much time as possible in each other's company. There will be no substitute for that."

"Thank you," Ceri whispered. "But how?"

"It is more a part of me than a chicken feather is to a chicken," Andy said, shooting an indecipherable look at Paska. "It *is* me."

"And it will protect you almost as well as he can. And I suspect it will even keep the ghost at bay, at least a little. Bring the feather tomorrow night—you need to be at the meeting when I tell the rest of those idiots how profoundly stupid they're being." He stood, bowed, doffing an imaginary hat, then turned and walked away.

seven

Ceri turned the feather over and over in her lap and avoided looking at the man who was driving her home. She was going to grab more clothes, the rest of her toiletries, and a few books so she could move in—temporarily—with Andy until Paska figured out how to fix her brain.

Her phone buzzed, and she grabbed it out of her handbag without looking. She wasn't sure she could deal with anymore vintage murder jewelry right now.

Ceri tapped open her messaging app.

Sandy: *Hey. Vincent is gone this afternoon. Can you come by? I hate to drop stuff on you now, but you're the only one who knows, the only one I can talk to about this.*

Ceri looked over at Andy. "Can you drop me off at Sandy's after I grab my stuff?"

Andy glanced at her out of the corner of his eye. "Are you sure you're up for a social visit? You've already had to spend time with Drew and Paska today. You should rest."

She typed out a response to Sandy. *I'll be by in about 30 minutes. I have to stop at home, then Andy'll drop me off.*

Sandy: *Perfect. I have snacks and bubbles.*

Ceri pursed her lips at Sandy's message—bubbles and pregnancy didn't go together—but merely gave a thumbs up reaction. There'd be time enough to figure it out in person.

"Don't try to manage me, Andy. And yes, I'm up for a social visit. With my friend who needs me right now." Ceri glared at him. She hated being told what to do, no matter how well-intentioned it was.

"Someone has to make you take care of yourself. You're certainly not doing it," Andy muttered under his breath but just loud enough for her to hear.

"You know what? I'd almost rather see visions of the horrors you inflicted on the souls of the damned on repeat in my head for the next hundred years than have you make snide remarks about me when I'm sitting right here. I am in charge of myself, of my life, and of my self care. Not you. And it doesn't matter if you think I'm doing the right or wrong thing, if I'm not resting enough, eating enough, *fucking* enough, because at the end of the day, this body and this mind are still mine." Ceri felt her temper rising; the tips of her ears were burning with rage. This is why she didn't get involved. It didn't matter where or when a man was from, the minute you give them an inch, they take a mile of control in the name of "taking care of their woman."

"I'm just trying to help."

Ceri closed her eyes and counted to ten. Then did it again. She shook her head. It was no use. "It's hard to believe an ancient immortal being can sound as petulant as a child denied a lolly, but you managed it. It doesn't matter that you're trying to help. What matters is I didn't ask for this help, nor do I want it. You'll know if I want help because I will say, 'Hey Andy! I need some help with this.' Alternatively, you are allowed to say, 'Ceri, I was wondering if you want me to remind you when to eat and rest.' But you are not allowed to tell me what to do in the name of helping, then sulk when I don't want your aid."

"You seem to have a lot of strong feelings about this," Andy observed, most of the petulance gone from his voice.

"You try being a woman—a white woman, anyway; I can't speak for anyone else's experiences—and you'll soon develop a very strong hatred for being managed by men who think they know better." Ceri deliberately kept the edge in her voice. If he couldn't see what was wrong with his protective instincts, there'd be no hope for anything between them ever. Not that she was really considering it.

"Okay," he said as he pulled into Ceri's driveway. "I will try. Tell me when I screw up—and I will. Probably a lot. But I will try."

"Do or do not," Ceri muttered.

"Don't go all Yoda on me now," Andy groaned. "There has to be room for trying sometimes, right?"

Ceri grinned. "We'll see. Will you come in with me? I'm fine, but it'd be nice to have you there in case of ghosts."

"Of course. I'd love to aid you since you have explicitly asked for my help." Andy got out of the car and opened her door, helping her out of the car.

"Was that so hard?" she teased, tucking her arm through his.

"I guess not, but ask me later when I think you're too exhausted for what you've planned next." He unlocked her front door with the key she'd given him last week when she'd moved in with him in self-defense.

Ten minutes later, Ceri was ready. She had a bag packed with enough clothing and other supplies—the worst part about being a long-lived woman stuck in the prime of her life was the unending fertile time between menarche and menopause—for the next week.

"To Sandy's, then?" he asked.

"Please. I'll text you when I'm ready to go home unless I can con Sandy or Vincent into driving me." Ceri climbed into the front seat of the car and fastened her seatbelt.

Andy got in next to her, and she saw a smug smile settle on his face.

"What's got you looking so pleased with yourself?" Ceri asked.

"You said 'home.'" He started the car with a wide grin on his face.

"What?" Ceri was completely lost.

"You said you'd text me when you were ready to go home. Home. My home." He pulled out of the driveway, then glanced over at her again. "Sounds like mi casa es su casa."

Ceri rolled her eyes. "It's just a figure of speech."

"A figure of speech that has you considering my house your home."

Ceri scoffed. "Don't read too much into this, Dr. Freud. I'll see you later. At your place."

He stopped in front of Sandy and Vincent's home and waited for her to open the door. She clasped the feather in her hands and got out. "Later, Andy."

"Later, Ceri. And don't forget, home is where the heart is."

She slammed the door against his laughter and watched him drive away.

· · · · · ★ ★ ★ ★ ★ · · · ·

Sandy opened the door before Ceri could ring the bell.

"Come in. Have booze." Sandy yanked Ceri inside.

Ceri followed her to the back porch, sat in the chair Sandy pointed at, and took a glass of... "Is this Champagne?"

"Seemed a good idea. Don't argue. I'm freaking out and don't know what to do." Sandy sat in the chair next to her, drained her glass of bubbles, burped, and refilled her glass.

"I'm not an expert, nor a doctor, but I think if you're looking for what you're supposed to do, it doesn't involve shooting Champagne." Ceri set down her glass and looked at Sandy. "I take it this isn't happy news?"

"Oh, you must be psychic! How else could you tell?" Sandy put down her glass and burst into tears.

Ceri tucked the feather inside her shirt and stood to shove in next to Sandy and enclose her in a hug. "Hey, friend. Whatever you need,

I'm here for you. Tell me what's going on in your head, and we'll fix this. Nothing's happened that can't be undone."

A few minutes later, Sandy sniffed and raised her face from Ceri's shoulder. "I snotted all over you."

Ceri waved it off. "It's fine. That's what friends are for. Snot on me whenever you want. Do you want to talk about it?"

"Give me a minute." Sandy got up and headed into the house.

Ceri sat back in her chair and picked up her glass of Champagne. It really was rather fantastic.

When Sandy returned, she was a lot less splotchy and was carrying two glasses of water. "Sorry about all that."

"Don't say 'sorry.' Women apologize way too much, and you have no reason to be sorry. I hit you with a big piece of news I thought you already knew, and you're having emotions about it. Nothing about that requires an apology." Ceri held up her glass and waited for Sandy to raise hers.

"I don't want to be pregnant," Sandy said. "I mean, Vincent and I have talked about it, and we agreed that the future was an excellent time for that. Like seven to ten years in the future. Not now. In fact, I got an IUD when we moved in together. This shouldn't be possible." She took another long drink of Champagne.

Ceri looked at Sandy and weighed the words she wanted to say. "I think you've already decided what you want to do. Today's Champagne is my big clue, not being psychic, by the way."

Sandy sighed and refilled her glass again. "I have, but... I don't know."

"You haven't talked to Vincent?"

"No. Not yet. I needed to be sure first, and then I wanted to talk to anyone but him. What if he's mad? What if he wants this? What if he's anti-choice?" Her voice was thick with tears again.

"Okay, calm down, Sandy. You talked about timelines, you agreed on you getting an IUD, right?" When Sandy nodded, Ceri continued, "And you know him well. Did you ever talk about pro-choice versus anti-choice before you shacked up?"

"We did, but that was before I... Before I..." Sandy sniffled loudly, then took a deep breath and continued in a steadier voice. "Before I had a surprise pregnancy test."

"Okay, I get what you're saying. It's always different when it's your reality and not a philosophy that affects other people. But Sandy, you have to tell him. And while it matters what he thinks and how it feels, it matters more about what you want. This is your body, your life, your future. Don't assume he'll be on a different page than you, but you are the final decision maker. There's no debate, no popular vote. You decide. And know I have your back with whatever you decide."

The front door closing jolted Sandy's eyes from Ceri to the house, a look of panic rising on her face.

"Hey, it'll be fine. Why don't you scoot into the bathroom real quick and wash your face—you blotch a bit when you cry. Not as bad as I do—pale skin and red hair can be a nightmare when you want to hide tears or embarrassment—but enough that it's apparent something's up. I'll distract Vincent by asking him for a ride to Andy's. He won't say no—too much of a gentleman. Then you'll have a little time to compose yourself and prepare your mental script." Ceri pushed her fingers against her breastbone, feeling the feather against her skin. She was exhausted, but the waking nightmares hadn't returned. She stood and grabbed her purse.

"Thank you. You are such a great friend. I don't know what I would've done without you." Sandy stood and hugged Ceri, then dashed inside.

Ceri heard the lock engage on the bathroom door, smoothed her hands over her jeans, and went inside to intercept Vincent.

eight

When Ceri woke, she had a moment of disorientation. No matter how many times she'd woken in Andy's bed since being released from the hospital, it always took a moment for her to remember where she was and why. She scooted towards the edge of the bed. It was late—after six in the morning—and she had things to do, even if she hadn't figured out what those things were yet. She'd have to check her phone and email; something always came up.

An arm reached out and snagged her around her waist. "Not yet," Andy murmured. "Stay."

Ceri rolled towards him. He looked fast asleep. His arm was heavy, but she'd be able to slip out from under it easy enough, probably without even waking him.

As if hearing her thoughts through his dreams, his arm tightened and pulled her close until their bodies were pressed together, chest to chest and... Ceri bit her lip. She might wake him now if she left, but based on...other parts that were pressed together, he was waking up anyway.

This was not okay. Not only was this not part of their arrangement, not anymore, he was asleep and didn't know, nor did he consent to, what was happening. She wiggled a little experimentally to see if he'd loosen his hold, but all she managed to do was move in the exact right, or wrong, way to rouse his body even more.

Dammit. She didn't know how to get out of this gracefully without waking him. She rolled over carefully within the confines of his arm and lifted it off slowly and gently. She held her breath, but he didn't stir.

She slid out under his arm, then set it back on the bed. His silver eyes flew open. Oops.

"Where are you going?" His voice was rough and growly, as it often was in the morning.

"Bathroom. Shower. Clothes. Work." She ticked them off on her fingers, trying to affect distance and indifference. Ceri looked at her fingers as she counted, but her gaze was snagged by his body. He'd held her hand until she'd fallen asleep but must've gotten up sometime after that to get himself ready for bed. He was naked from the waist up—which she'd seen up close and personal—but he'd changed into lightweight pajama pants and, according to the evidence in front of her, nothing underneath.

Ceri licked her lips. This was not a situation she'd prepared to encounter.

Andy frowned for a moment, then looked down to see what'd caught her attention. He flipped the covers back up over his lower half, leaving only his glorious chest and shoulders on display. She'd always been a sucker for a great pair of shoulders.

"Better?" he asked. "I don't want to distract you too much from your task list."

"I'm good, thanks." Ceri turned away from him and headed to the bathroom, stopping to grab a change of clothes on the way.

"Let me know if you need help with anything," he murmured sleepily. "I can scrub your back if you can't reach."

Ceri slammed the door behind her in answer. She leaned against the wall opposite the door and resisted the urge to bang her head against it. This was a lot harder than she'd anticipated. She snorted, then shook her head at herself. Things were pretty bad when she was having to "TWSS" herself. She peed, turned on the shower, and stripped out of her flannel pajamas. The hot water and steam of the shower soothed the tension from her body and rejuvenated her. She never felt so at peace as when she was in water.

After washing and conditioning her long hair, she ran the soapy washcloth over her body and tried really hard to erase keep the picture Andy'd implanted in her mind. Her body didn't get the memo, and goosebumps rippled over her skin in the wake of the cloth, reacting to the fantasy of his hands soaping her back and the slight curves of her body.

She rinsed quickly and shut off the water. She had to figure out how to keep those kinds of unwelcome thoughts out of her head. She had to sever their tie completely and remember her reasons for creating space between them. When this was over—if it was ever over—and she was whole, body and mind, she'd go back to her empty house, her solitary life, and have to get used to waking alone, far away from the world's most glorious shoulders.

Ceri rested her forehead against the still-cool tile in the shower and took a deep breath. She was going to dry off, get dressed, and figure out today's agenda. She had the biweekly "psychics unite" meeting tonight, and since Paska'd said she couldn't skip it, she'd be there. Other than that, she didn't know of anything pressing.

She'd do some more research on psychics who'd been over-whelmed by the mind of another—there were more google results than she'd expected once she'd sifted through all the news articles debunking psychic powers, but so far, nothing useful. Maybe she should head home and grab her files on the Ruby Rose Killer, as the media had dubbed him in honor of the first piece of jewelry that'd disappeared. If she couldn't fix her mind, at least she could try to figure out what she'd missed about the case and why it was coming up now.

"Oh!" she exclaimed to the space that'd once held the bathroom mirror.

The door burst open, and Andy appeared in the doorway. "What's wrong?"

Ceri gasped and dropped the towel from her hands to cover herself. "Get out! Why are you in here?"

Andy backed out of view but didn't close the door all the way. "I heard you yell. I was worried."

She huffed and finished drying herself off. She could hear him out there, lingering. "What if the ghost is related to the serial killer?" she asked the slightly ajar door.

There was a long enough pause that Ceri wondered if she'd been wrong and he'd actually walked away.

"That's an interesting idea," he finally said. "I'm going downstairs to make coffee and breakfast. Join me when you're dressed, and we'll talk about it. I think you're on to something."

* * * ★ ★ ★ ★ ★ ★ * * *

She slammed the cover of her laptop closed and glared at the bar. Ceri was curled up in the alcove with her laptop and several pillows and blankets that had mysteriously appeared through no intervention on Andy's part, or so he swore.

Felicity appeared in the doorway. "Do you need something?" she chirped.

Relentless cheer and optimism were wonderful virtues, but if Felicity didn't tone down the sunshine, Ceri was going to jump across the table and strangle her.

"Can I get an iced tea and a Monte Cristo sandwich?" Ceri asked. She lifted her laptop off the table and twisted to shove the traitorous device back into her backpack. "And stay there until you can find some better information," she muttered to it. When she turned back around, Felicity was still standing there. Ceri raised her eyebrows at the server.

"You have a cool tattoo on your back," Felicity said. "Can I see the whole thing?"

"No," Ceri said.

Felicity's face fell, and a pang of guilt hit Ceri's gut. It felt like kicking a puppy.

She smiled gently and tried to soften her words. "I'm just not prepared to strip down in the bar, and there's no way to show it off without removing at least one item of clothing."

"That makes sense!" Felicity beamed at her long enough to move several feet past awkward. Ceri cleared her throat. "Um, my order?"

"OMG!" Felicity grabbed the order pad and fled.

Jezebel stepped gingerly into the alcove and slid in across from Ceri. "Did that woman actually say 'OMG?' I didn't know that was something people said outside of internet shorthand."

Ceri looked at the tall Black woman across from her. She'd never been able to pinpoint Jezebel's age, although until this moment, she'd assumed Jezebel was closer in age to Misty and Sandy than Ceri and Drew. But... "Internet shorthand? I didn't know anyone younger than a baby boomer said that."

"There are all modes and manner of speech in this world, Ceri. You of all people should know that. I've heard that sweet little Irish accent come out to play when you've had a couple glasses of wine." Jezebel set her bag on the bench and leaned forward. "But enough about turns of phrase. I have a favor to ask you. I know what you've been going through, and if you can't do this, I understand. Just say the word." She looked at Ceri with eyes wide and hopeful.

"I can't scry," Ceri said slowly. "I can't risk it, and I never see anything good anyway."

"Oh! I'm not asking you to scry. I would never, not now, not after..." Jezebel's voice trailed off, and her gaze shifted a little to the left of Ceri's.

"Not after you've all determined I'm broken *and* crazy?" Ceri asked in the driest voice she could muster.

Jezebel's gaze shifted even further to the left, and she cleared her throat. "Yeah. That. This is stupid. I can't believe I came here to ask for your help. I'm an idiot."

"As long as you're not asking me to scry, why don't you finish asking. I'll let you know if I can help, and we'll go from there."

"I don't really know who else I could run this by. Misty and Sandy don't have enough experience to answer the big things, and Morgana and Paska have..."

"Way too much?" Ceri supplied wryly.

Jezebel laughed, a deep belly laugh that brought a real smile to Ceri's face. "You've got that in one. I could go to Drew, but his stars are all whacked out this month."

"He told you his birth information?" Ceri was shocked. He guarded his origin details fiercely; even she didn't know his true age.

"He needed information, and his psychic bff was in a coma." Jezebel opened her messenger bag and pulled out a large manila folder. "I'm at an impasse that feels like a dead end, and I need help." She slid it across the table in front of Ceri and folded her hands expectantly.

Ceri narrowed her eyes at Jez but opened the folder anyway. It was filled with star charts covered in alchemical and astrological symbols. "I don't know what any of this means, and I don't know if I want to learn. Seeing meaning might be close enough to seeing."

Jezebel waved her concerns away. "I wouldn't ask you to see anything. This is just the background info. I'll tell you the rest, but first, I need your word you'll hear me out and give me the truest advice you can."

"Hi!" Felicity interrupted. She placed Ceri's iced tea on the table harder than was necessary and looked at Jezebel. "Oh my gosh, aren't you gorgeous! Do you want to see a menu?"

"Broken Halo Bitter and an order of fries." Jezebel reached forward and flipped the folder close.

"You got it!" Felicity whirled and bounced away.

"Is it my imagination, or does she speak primarily in exclamations?"

Ceri nodded. "Almost exclusively."

"I wonder how many people fantasize about punching her straight in the face?" Jezebel glared after the server, sliding to the edge of the alcove and peering out. "She is way too cheerful."

"Don't tempt me. It's been decades since I've been arrested for assault, and I really want to keep this identity's felony record clean." Ceri took a long sip of her drink. "Do you want to talk now, or wait for the drinks and food?"

"Let's wait. If she interrupts me to toss an exclamation point at me, even if she does come bearing alcohol, I might lose my mind." Jezebel started to slide back into the alcove, then paused. "Speaking of people who give me the creeps, who's the chick at the next table over? She looks like death personified."

Ceri carefully extricated herself from the nest of blankets and pillows and walked to the doorway. "Probably an early tourist or one of the newcomers who showed up after the Christmas Apocalypse. I've seen her around a lot. Always in the same all-black outfit, and always with her hoodie pulled down over her face like that. At least she's not wearing floral sundresses and chirping happily at everyone." Ceri returned to her nest and wrapped the blankets around herself. Without Andy by her side, she got cold too fast, and she ached. The feather might keep the monsters back, but it wasn't keeping her warm. She tucked her feet up into the blanket and forced a smile onto her face. "Since we have a bit of time, why don't we catch up? I haven't heard anything about your trip."

"It was just a typical business trip. I went on a six-week mystic journey with the so-called 'gods of my ancestors' to learn to read the sky intuitively instead of relying on birth dates and time zones. Hitchhiked back to Oracle Bay with some weird-ass ancient Greek oracles. I've never been to basic training, but I'm guessing it's easier than what I went through. I have so much crammed into my mind, I feel like I might go mad." Jezebel stopped at bit her lip. "Sorry."

"You don't have to apologize, Jez. Having centuries, maybe millennia, of knowledge crammed into your brain in six weeks is overwhelming. And if it was done in rough conditions without the fuel you need to thrive, it's got to be a lot. My brain overload doesn't lessen yours." Ceri reached out her hand and took Jezebel's. "There's no such thing as winning the pain olympics. Now, why don't you tell me what the problem is."

nine

Ceri stared at Jez, mouth slightly agape, deliberately ignoring the spread of paper on the table in front of her. "Are you serious right now?"

"So you see my dilemma." Jez pulled the scattered star charts forward, ordered them, and put them back into a neat stack. "And this is where you come in. I don't know what to do."

Ceri looked at the top chart, then at Jezebel. "You're going to have to spell things out for me."

Jezebel leafed through the stack and grabbed two charts, overlaying one with the other. The bottom chart was hand drawn on heavy parchment and looked like the traditional western star chart Ceri was used to seeing. The overlying one was printed on translucent paper that reminded Ceri of baking parchment. It had a sky map that had corresponding points on the chart underneath.

Jezebel fussed at the papers until their corners were perfectly square, then looked expectantly at Ceri.

Ceri shook her head. "I'm going to need a verbal walk through."

Jez crossed her arms. "This is someone's chart. I can see her traits, her strengths, her weaknesses, and her compatibilities. She's an Aries, Gemini rising, which surprised me when I found out. I was sure she was a Scorpio. She's so fiery but also private. And Scorpios are great matches for Pisces, and the sex can be explosively good. But she's not, and Aries and Pisces are not great matches."

"Okay, I think I understand. There is a woman in your life who is an Aries. You like her but found out your signs are not as compatible as you'd hoped. And now you need my advice on...?" Ceri had no idea where Jez was going with this.

"We went out on a date, and it was magical. Like, we connected at every level, then we started talking about our jobs. She was really interested in mine and gave me the relevant deets so I could draw up her chart before our second date. As soon as she told me her birthday, my heart sank. But still—even if we're not the most compatible, it could work." Jezebel shifted the top chart a little, better lining up a couple points to her liking. "But that's not all. I can take that basic astrological knowledge and apply it to my new knowledge of how to read the heavens themselves. And that's the real problem."

Ceri looked at the charts with more interest. "I am super interested in learning more about your new ability. Is it innate? I mean is it the same kind of magic that I hold or Misty holds, and you had to learn to tap into it, or is a learned skill?"

"Anyone could learn, the same way anyone can learn to read a palm or tarot cards. But the difference between reading the cards and *reading* the cards is the difference between reading a chart or the sky and being able to pull truth from the stars. It's magic, and it's mine." A satisfied smile crept over her face. "I never really felt like I belonged here with the rest of you. Your powers are all so extraordinary, and I was just good at making star charts. Nothing special. But now, I've learned this skill that few practice anymore, and even fewer can master." She looked back down at the chart, and the smile dropped off her face. "And that's why I can see that not only are we not as good a match as I would prefer, but she's destined for another. Another very much not me."

The gears clicked into place for Ceri. "And you want me to advise you on whether to go forward or back off?"

"Yes." Jezebel nodded. "That's what I need. I know what I *should* do—walk away now, so I'm not in the way of her destiny. But I know what I want, and that's to see where things go with her."

Ceri leaned back and thought about it. The answer seemed very clear to her—go for it! But she didn't want to give glib advice to anyone, much less a friend. She took a sip of her water with her eyes closed while working through the various answers she could give and the explanations that went with them. She took a deep breath, opened her eyes, and looked at Jez. "You say she's destined to end up with someone else?"

Jezebel nodded slightly and her eyes brightened with unshed tears.

"Did you have a good time on your date? You said it was amazing, right?"

"It really was. We started with an afternoon coffee, then went for a walk and just talked. Before we realized it, it was almost seven, and we were starving. So, we grabbed dinner and drinks. Then she remembered she had a bottle of wine open at her place that needed to be finished, so we headed back there. I didn't get home until almost ten o'clock."

"That was how many hours? Eight? Not bad for a first date," Ceri said. "I'm in awe."

"It was more like twenty hours," Jez said a little sheepishly. "But she makes a great breakfast. It's a good thing I'm not a vegetarian, because that might've ruined the morning vibe."

Ceri couldn't help grinning. "That's impressive, Jez. To recap: you went on a twenty-hour first date and had a marvelous time. You later learned that she is destined for another. If you didn't have that second piece of information, would you pursue this relationship?"

Jez nodded enthusiastically. "Absolutely, if only to get some more of her ham."

"I'm not up on the euphemisms the youths these days are using, and after hearing that one, I'd like to stay in the dark."

Jez laughed. "You're a dirty old woman. We had ham for breakfast, and she sent me home with a pound of bacon."

"Next question. If you pursued her, would even a positive chart guarantee you'd be together forever?" Ceri cocked her head to one side. She was genuinely curious, especially now that she had a strong suspicion who Jez was talking about.

"No, of course not. Even when things look clear, humans are still gonna human. No way around that."

"Go for it," Ceri said firmly. "If it's an immutable destiny, things will find a way. Maybe she'll walk away from you to be with someone else, or maybe she'll stay with you, destiny be damned. There are no guarantees she'll break your heart, but if you don't go for it, you'll never know. And maybe it'll work out. Or maybe you'll decide she isn't the one you want. But you need to try it to find out. A broken heart is better than a lifetime of wondering and regret."

Jezebel pulled the star charts back towards herself. "Are you sure? I don't want to ruin her future."

"I'm positive. It's kind of you to worry about Natalie's future romantic prospects, but you need to worry more about your current love life."

"I never said it was Natalie, so I don't know how you got that idea." Jezebel tucked the folder of star charts into her oversized bag.

"I didn't even need my psychic powers to make that deduction. Now go, call your girl, and tell her she's got some exciting love choices in the future, and you'd like to be one of them." Ceri made a shooing motion with her hands until Jezebel stood up.

"Thank you, Ceri. You always know the right thing to say." Jez flashed a bright smile and walked out of the booth towards the front door.

Ceri smiled and leaned back, brushing the feather with the tips of her fingers and allowing her eyelids to drift closed.

"Is it always like this?" Andy asked, sliding in across from her.

"Like what?" Ceri opened her eyes and regarded him sleepily.

"People coming to you with their problems and looking for advice." He reached out towards her but withdrew his hand before he touched her.

Ceri thought about it. "Yeah, it is. I'm the oldest one except the scary olds, and I guess I have a reputation for being a good listener and advice giver. I like helping, and it gives me all the best, early information. Plus, blackmail material."

Andy burst out laughing. "You have an exciting career ahead as an international blackmailing superstar."

"I'll buy you an island when I make it big," she promised.

"I'm expecting a very big island. Like Iceland. Or Australia." He grinned at her, and she couldn't stop her answering smile.

"No guarantees, of course, but I'll see what I can do."

"I was just seeing if you wanted to go home for a few hours before you have to go to your psychic group. You can obviously stay as long as you want, but you don't have to hang out in an only barely comfortable booth when you could be curled up in my big chair with a blanket and a book. I can be there in ten minutes if you need me. Less if it's an emergency."

"That sounds wonderful, although I might do a bath before blanket and book. I need some hot water to soothe away the knots in my shoulders and back." Ceri shrugged her shoulders up to her ears, then pushed them back and down, wincing as the tight muscles rebelled against her attempt at forced relaxation.

"I'll drive you home then if that's okay. I need to come back here for a while, but I'll be home in time to take you to Morgana's."

Ceri grabbed her purse and slid out of the booth, double-checking that her feather was still tucked safely against her side.

Andy offered his hand, and she accepted it gratefully and let him lead her out of the bar.

· · · · · ★ ★ ★ ★ · · · ·

CERI SANK DEEPER INTO THE TUB AND LEANED HER HEAD BACK ON THE SOFT bath pillow Andy'd produced out of the linen closet along with lavender bath salts, a bubble bath concoction that made the water virtually incapable of being reflective, and a tray that fit perfectly across the tub and was large enough to hold the feather, if she propped it up sideways. He'd then made her a cup of tea, drawn the bath for her, and left without a leer or a sideways knowing glance. She wasn't sure if her admonition had sunk in, or if this was a new tactic to create goodwill and to convince her to drop her guard and let him back into her heart.

Not that he's ever been in my heart, she told herself fiercely.

She pulled the plug with her toes and stood, letting the water sluice off her body. She felt more relaxed than she'd been in ages, and she tried not to get her hopes up that it was anything more than a temporary reprieve. She still had a couple hours before she needed to get dressed and head over to Morgana's, and she didn't want to spend any of that time thinking about any of the problems currently plaguing her.

Ceri dug through the bags of clothes she had scattered around Andy's bedroom until she found what she was looking for. She pulled on a pair of long, soft pajama pants and matched it with an even softer, forest green hoodie that looked like—according to Drew —she'd skinned a muppet. She added a pair of slippers—soft, of course—and snagged one of Andy's blankets from the bed before heading downstairs to curl up in the overstuffed chair with another cup of peppermint tea and *Lifestyles of the Witch and Ageless,* the newest paranormal cozy by Shéa Macleod.

The sound of the front door closing jolted her awake. She smiled as she stretched into awareness. She hadn't realized how much she'd needed a nap—it might have been the first time she'd slept deeply in months. It was better now that she was sharing a bed with Andy, but it was still sharing a bed and all the complications that came with it. Neither of them were terribly used to having someone else in their bed space, and because of the current—*and continuing into perpetuity*

—nature of their relationship, Ceri was jolted awake almost every time their skin touched. Almost every time.

But a comfy chair after a warm bath apparently hit all the right buttons. It almost made her wonder how efficacious the feather was. Could she go home? Paska said they should still spend time together, but if this was working...

"What's caused that crease in your brow?" Andy asked, walking into the living room and dropping onto the sofa across from her.

Ceri grimaced but decided that honesty was almost always the best policy. "I was thinking it might be worth seeing if I can sleep in my own bed tonight—if the feather is working well enough to keep the hell away."

If he was hurt, he hid it well. "That's an interesting idea," he said slowly. "And one we should explore. But maybe it'd be best if we did it in phases? You're more comfortable here where my essence is everywhere."

"Ew," Ceri interrupted.

A ghost of a smile flitted across Andy's lips. "Juvenile. Anyway, this house is part of me. Maybe it'd be better to start out with you sleeping here and me sleeping elsewhere for a night or two? If that's okay, then you can try sleeping at your place and see how it goes."

"Where will you sleep?" Ceri hoped her voice held only mild curiosity and not the barest hint of jealousy when she thought of him sharing a bed with someone else.

"Presumably, if you're here, your house is free."

Ceri held back a sigh of relief. "That sounds like a good idea. As long as you don't throw any wild orgies in my house."

"Tame ones okay, then?" he asked as a smile broke across his face.

"What's the point of a tame orgy?" Ceri asked. "Wild or nothing, that's my philosophy."

His smiled widened, and he waggled his eyebrows at her. "I'm intrigued to learn more about why you have orgy philosophies, and how you developed them."

"Whatever," Ceri said. "Who's being juvenile now?"

Andy rose to his feet and held out a hand to her.

She took it, but before she let him haul her to her feet, she asked, "Why are you ejecting me from my cozy nest?"

"You're due at Morgana's in an hour, and I assumed you'd want to eat, change, and take your hair out of the towel." He pulled her up and steadied her when she wobbled a bit on her feet.

"Are you serious?" Ceri grabbed her phone and swiped up to check the time. "Oh my god. I slept for almost an hour and a half. I never nap, and I certainly never nap that hard."

"You clearly needed the sleep," Andy said. "And you don't have to rush if you don't want to. They'll wait for you."

"They might wait, but Morgana will be irritated, and I do not want Morgana upset with me. Especially not now." Ceri pulled the towel off her hair and started finger combing it.

She headed upstairs, dragging the blanket behind her until Andy caught the trailing end and pulled it from her grasp. "I got this. Go ahead and figure out what you're going to wear."

Ceri hit the top landing at a near jog and pulled all her bags into a row in front of her. Her clothes were spread out among three different suitcases and a small pile on the chair in front of the vanity, and it made the ordinarily swift task of picking an outfit almost agonizingly long.

"I know you might only be here a few more nights if all goes well. But you should have space for yourself and your clothes. Why don't you take over the guest room? It can be yours while you're here. There's nothing in the closet or the dresser, and I can move that chair upstairs if you want. Or we can find you a desk. However you want it to be." Andy stood in the doorway with an expression that looked vaguely like horror as he regarded the piles of clothes on the floor.

"There's a bed in there, right?" Ceri asked absently. She grabbed her favorite pair of jeans, a silky, grey tank top, and an emerald-green hoodie—not the dead muppet one—with the Pour House logo on the back. She exchanged her slippers for her favorite pair of slip-on flats and stood.

"There is a bed," Andy confirmed. He turned his back while she stripped down to her panties and bra and started dressing.

"Maybe that's step one before we try sleeping in different houses?" Ceri suggested. "I can sleep in the guest room—still your house, but not your bed—and if I need you, you'll be right here."

"I'll be here as long as you want, whether you need me or not," Andy said. "Can I turn around?"

Ceri tugged the tank top in place. "Yep, I'm decent." She put the hoodie on and grabbed her shoes and the feather she'd carefully laid on the bed. "Wanna drive me to the wicked witch's house?"

Andy laughed and started down the stairs. "I'm so going to tell her you called her that."

"No, you won't. You value my skin too much to put me in danger, and you value your own too much to make me that angry." Ceri followed him into the kitchen.

"Do you want something to eat before we head over?" he asked as he grabbed the car keys from the hook by the door.

Ceri snagged her purse from the same hook. "No, there will be food. More food than I could possibly ever eat, in fact. Let's just get this over with."

ten

Ceri stood outside Morgana's front door, clutching the feather and holding a bottle of wine. She knew Andy hadn't driven away yet, and that he wouldn't until she was inside, but she still couldn't make herself do the perfunctory "knock and open" that was typical on gathering nights.

The door opened abruptly, and she gasped, taking a step back and almost falling off the front step. Before she'd even finished windmilling her arms for balance, careful not to drop either the wine or the feather, Andy was at her back, steadying her.

"You can stop glaring at me, angel," Morgana said. Her voice was dryer than a wooden god, and her vibe was way less Morticia Addams and more Mary Tyler Moore. "I didn't realize she'd jump so badly. No one here is out to hurt her."

"I'm fine, Andy," Ceri said, extricating herself from his arms and stepping forward. "You can go—I'll be fine."

Morgana rolled her eyes and huffed. She reached out and took the bottle of wine, then grabbed Ceri's hand and pulled her inside, firmly closing the door behind them.

Morgana looked Ceri up and down, an appraising look in her

eyes. "I may have been wrong to doubt you. If it turns out I was, I apologize."

As an apology, it wasn't the best she'd ever heard, but it might be the best one she'd ever heard from Morgana. "I'll take your apology as given, then. By the way, digging the new look. What's up with that?"

Morgana shrugged and smiled, sincerity flooding through her direct gaze so hard Ceri almost took another step back. "It was time. I've been a vintage, sexy goth for too long now. I thought I'd try something more...wholesome." She ran her free hand over her tweed skirt and flipped up the corner of her coral cardigan.

"Even the hair?" Ceri couldn't help but ask. Morgana'd had long, lustrous jet-black hair for as long as she'd known the woman, and now it was a shiny, light brown bob.

"Even the hair." Morgana's smile didn't falter, but Ceri could swear she saw gritted teeth behind the cheerful visage. "But enough about my reinvention. Let's get you into the sitting room, pour you a glass of wine, and make you a cheese plate. Then you can explain your feather, and Paska can tell us all why we're idiots."

"Sounds like fun," Ceri muttered, but she followed Morgana anyway. The second she stepped into the room, silence crashed over the psychics inside.

The silence lasted only for a few seconds, but it felt like an eternity in the spotlight before Sandy was handing her a glass of wine accompanied by a hand squeeze and a grateful smile. Drew made her a plate from the spread of cheeses, crackers, and meats on the sideboard, and Jezebel scooted over companionably and patted the space on the loveseat next to her.

Misty and Morgana watched silently with inscrutable expressions on their faces until Ceri was situated. She placed the feather across her lap, took a long drink of her wine, set it on the small table beside her, and piled cheese and prosciutto on a small cracker.

A burst of laughter made Ceri inhale in shock. Unfortunately, she was mid-bite and breathed in a chunk of aged, wine-washed goat cheese—a particular favorite of hers.

Paska slapped his knee and guffawed. If you'd asked Ceri ten minutes ago, she would've sworn she had no idea what a guffaw sounded like, but there was no other word for the laughter coming out of Paska's mouth.

When Ceri looked at him with raised eyebrows after she stopped coughing, he grinned and said, "Morgana and Misty look like they're studying an interesting but not particularly appealing specimen under a microscope, and Drew, Jez, and Sandy are bending over backward to accommodate the witch who helped them with their very personal problems so she doesn't know they still think she's losing her marbles. It's interesting, is all. I can tell you who here is coming around to admitting they were wrong and you are seeing a ghost, and I can tell you which of these self-important seers is a condescending jerk, if you want to know."

Ceri took a bite of cheese, chewed, and swallowed, and then took a long drink of crisp white wine. "I think I'll skip that bit of knowledge. At least for now."

Morgana sat in the large wingback chair with her back to the window. The chair looked exceedingly uncomfortable, burgundy velvet upholstery notwithstanding, but Morgana insisted on sitting there every time she hosted their biweekly meeting. She clapped her hands, and Ceri blinked. Morgana's prim new look was throwing her off.

"We are gathered here together to discuss three things. First on the agenda will be the summer festival. I would like to move that we all step back from being involved in ridiculous seasonal festivities. There are plenty of other people in the town who can take on that responsibility, and I, for one, refuse to be a part of planning any more." Morgana crossed her arms and glared. While her glare was usually intimidating, something about the cardigan made it...cute.

Misty rolled her eyes. "You say the same thing every year, and every year I tell you to sit this one out. In June, you're going to freak out and insist you need to be involved, try to change every decision that's been made by the committee, and pout if you don't get your way. While I'd love to suggest you step down for good as a festival co-chair, I know that's unrealistic. Why don't you just commit to being a part of it and having input from the beginning. Less stressful for everyone."

Morgana wrinkled her nose a bit, and Ceri bit back a giggle, imagining Morgana with a pair of chained librarian glasses.

"Fine. We'll table that until our next meeting." Morgana crossed her ankles and tucked her feet back. "Next on the agenda—"

"Why do we only have an agenda when we meet at your place?" Sandy asked. From the look on her face, Ceri guessed Sandy'd been dying to ask that question for the last six months.

"Because I'm the only one who cares about efficiency and ensuring we actually talk about the important things. Don't interrupt." Morgana's shoulders were so tight, Ceri's ached in sympathy. "Next on the agenda is Ceri. Is there a ghost? Is she going crazy as a byproduct of agenda item three? Paska says he has something to add to this discussion."

Paska stood and sketched a mocking bow towards Morgana. "First of all, I'd like to say—on behalf of everyone here—how much your new look is making you more approachable and less intimidating."

Ceri snickered a bit and noticed she wasn't the only one. No way was Morgana going to enjoy being called approachable and unintimidating.

"Secondly, I'd like to tell you to shove off with your phrasing. You worded it such that it seems a given she's either making it up or hallucinating. That is disingenuous and extremely unkind." He turned to encompass the entire group. "You should all be deeply ashamed of yourselves. You claim to disbelieve the existence of the ghost Ceri saw because you didn't predict its presence, but neither did any of you see enough to know her mind was unraveling because of the glimpse into eternity that burned its way into her cerebral cortex. And if you saw but didn't speak up, you're cruel beyond belief. If you didn't see but claim infallibility when something challenges your knowledge of what is and isn't, you're an idiot. So which is it? Drew? Why don't you tell us why you were willing to cut your vacation short to return to the bedside of your best friend, why you were willing to ask her for advice, why you've been searching for a way to help heal her mind, but you aren't willing to believe she saw something you couldn't?"

Drew looked at Ceri, then away so quickly she wondered if she'd imagined it. He didn't answer but squirmed under Paska's regard.

"Sandy, same question. Of all of us here, you're the newest to believe in yourself and trust in the abilities of others. But yet, you think you know all there is to know about the future and spirits?" Paska pinned her with a sharp stare, which Sandy met head on.

"I don't know everything, and I was probably wrong. Doubting Ceri's sight and trusting her to see to the root of my issues was hubris, and I should know better. After all, seeing and not being believed is all tied up in my namesake." She turned to Ceri. "I'm sorry. I don't understand, but I don't need to."

Ceri blinked. She hadn't expected Paska to do more than make everyone uncomfortable.

"I wonder if anyone else will be as sensible as the reader," Paska said. "What about you Jezebel? Are you still convinced Ceri's ghost was a coma hallucination?"

Jezebel tipped her chin up. "I don't know. I don't believe she'd be seeing ghosts the rest of us couldn't see, either with our eyes or our powers, but I am no longer willing to argue about it."

Morgana held up a hand. "You don't need to interrogate me. I was wrong, and I believe the scryer."

"So what about you, Mystic? You haven't gone to Ceri for advice as have most of the others here, but I suspect that's only because you were waiting to ask for what you need until tomorrow. And just so you know, the answers are, in order, 'Halloween, of course, and you're an idiot.' Ceri would've said the last two much more nicely and wouldn't have been able to answer the first question without a mirror, but now you know, and you don't have to bother her with your need and your skepticism." Paska fixed Misty with the same stare he'd pinned everyone else down with. "I think it's about time everyone here acknowledges how much Ceri gives you in terms of friendship, unerring advice, and her time, and look at how little benefit of the doubt you're willing to extend back."

Paska leaned back and crossed his arms over his chest. He caught Ceri's eye—she was still prying her jaw off the floor in surprise at his dressing down of everyone in the room—and winked broadly.

After a few moments in which most of the other people in the room—Morgana excepted—wouldn't quite look Ceri in the face, Paska leaned forward. "I hope you all feel like idiots now, and if you don't, you should. However, I'm willing to let you stew in your own stupidity and guilt for the next few minutes while I tell you exactly why you're ignorant."

Ceri eyed the open bottles of wine on the sideboard and wondered if she could refill her glass without drawing any attention to herself. It was soon apparent every eye was on her. Sandy, who was closest to the wine, grabbed the bottle of sauvignon blanc Ceri'd been drinking, and passed it to Jezebel, who handed it to Ceri.

"Thanks," she mumbled, not wanting to make eye contact with anyone, especially after Paska's lecture about their failings as friends.

"Keep that bottle, and maybe grab another. Tonight's going to be a long, difficult night for you." He eyed her with sympathy, and she gulped the wine, pressing her feather to her side.

"Is there anyone here who doubts Ceri's mind was damaged when she scried Andras the fallen angel?" Paska looked around the room for a moment, but no one moved. "And do any of you doubt that the reason she was damaged was because she saw eternity in his mind—an eternity that involved several millennia of hellfire, torture, and suffering, as well as the beginning and ending of all things?"

Sandy raised her hand, and Paska nodded at her. "What do you mean, the beginning and ending of all things?" she asked in a small, quiet voice.

Paska glanced at Ceri. She took a fortifying sip of wine. "I can see the creation of the universe—at least the creation of what we know as this universe. And I can see the destruction. I know how and when and why all things will cease to be. The knowledge contained in Andy's mind is... It's infinity. And maybe he can handle it because he was an archangel who fell and became a very important hell person before being killed brutally and finding himself here." She looked at Paska and took another drink of wine. He nodded at her encouragingly. "He was in hell for thousands of years. There was so much torture, and I see it all through his memories. He was tortured, but more often, he was the torturer. I can see every cruel thought, every dark desire, and every pained cry. I feel the despair at his connection to heaven being severed. Every day, I experience the devastation of finding out the love of his hellish life not only didn't return his affections, but betrayed him, leading to his second outcasting. And I have within me the death and birth of stars; things that even Andy doesn't register."

She stopped talking, took another gulp of wine, and stroked the feather in her lap.

"You never said." Drew's voice was shaky and uncertain, and he still wasn't meeting her eyes. "Why didn't you tell me?"

"Why should she?" Paska barked. "You clearly aren't trustworthy."

Ceri started to protest, but Paska quelled her with a look. She subsided into silence. Until Drew would look at her, there was little to say.

"Ceridwen Kenny had her mind pried open by eternity, but much of the more visceral memories are tied to hell. Is it any wonder that a mind like that would see a soul damned?"

Silence hung in the room after Paska's question. Ceri tried not to show the shock she felt at hearing his theory, but it made sense. The spirit was not beneficent, and she'd not seen ghosts before.

"From further discussions with both Ceri and Andras, it is apparent that this spirit, if not actively malevolent, is powerful enough to affect her physical world in ways that are harmful. And since we've all agreed that Ceri's mind is well enough to solve problems of our own making, I think we should also agree that her mind is well enough to recognize a motherfucking ghost when she sees one."

Ceri refilled her glass from the bottle next to her and drank deeply. No one was talking, and the silence made her feel even more uncomfortable.

"Okay," Morgana said brightly. "Now that we've all admitted, at least to ourselves, that we're terrible friends as well as profoundly stupid, let's move on to agenda item three, already touched upon by the wise and venerable Paska Cooper. Let's talk about Ceri's broken mind."

eleven

Ceri stood in front of the bathroom mirror—or at least where the bathroom mirror used to be. There was an outline in the wall showing where a mirror had once hung over the sink, and the gratitude she felt for Morgana who'd gone to the trouble to eliminate every reflective surface in her house even while thinking Ceri might be losing her mind was almost overwhelming. Or at least the cherry on top of the overwhelming sundae.

She pressed a cold washcloth to her face and breathed deeply. Despite Paska's warning that he was going to tell the others off, she hadn't been expecting that. Her hand drifted down to her phone. She could text Andy, and he'd be here in twenty minutes. She could text him she needed an immediate pickup, and he'd been here in three.

There was a knock at the bathroom door. "You should come out now," Sandy said softly. "I'm so sorry I didn't believe you at first, and I'm sorry I still called you for advice after I was so unkind."

Ceri opened the door and looked at the very young psychic in front of her. "Your problem wasn't stupid. No one's problems are ever stupid. I was happy to listen and steer you towards the truth you already knew. Did you have the discussion?"

Sandy nodded, and tears shone in the corners of her eyes. "You were right. Vincent was not only on the same page regarding timing, he was unequivocal in his support of me making decisions that are right for me and my body. I have an appointment for next weekend."

"Do you need me to go with you?" Ceri asked.

Sandy laughed through a sob. "Vincent is going with me, but thank you so much for offering. You are such an amazing person, and none of us deserve you."

Ceri shifted uncomfortably. "Everyone deserves people they trust. I'm glad I can be that person for so many people."

Sandy gave a watery smile and hooked her arm through Ceri's. "Ready to face the lions?"

Ceri grimaced. "Do you think Morgana's given up on her Stepford Wife impression yet?" she whispered.

"I don't know if I wish she'd return to the Morticia vibe or stay with June Cleaver. The new, gentler Morgana is a lot easier to talk to." Sandy giggled softly under her breath. "The first time I met her, she scared the crap out of me. And almost every other time since, to be honest." Sandy tugged lightly on Ceri's arm. "Shall we?"

Ceri sighed and let herself be led back to the rest of the psychics. After all, there was no way she'd fit through the small window in Morgana's bathroom.

CERI LOOKED DOWN AT THE DINING ROOM TABLE. WHILE SHE'D BEEN HIDING in the bathroom, the table had been transformed from "simple and elegant eating surface" to "new age table at the occult bookshop." Sandy's cards were atop a velvet cloth, Drew's crystal ball—real crystal, though, not a glass knockoff—was near the center. A teapot and two cups were at the ready, Paska's leather pouch of bone runes slouched next to the tea service, and Jezebel stood at the far end holding a cardboard poster tube.

The only psychic without an implement was Misty, and from the looks of things, her gloves were still on.

Misty intercepted her gaze and shrugged. "Given what happened to you, it seemed unwise to look directly into your soul. I don't have seven hundred years of experience to buffer my mind."

Ceri stuck her tongue out at the woman who called herself a palm reader to lend verisimilitude to her practice of reading a person's past, present, and future through touch. "I'm not that old, and you know it"

Misty laughed, and the mood in the room perceptibly lightened.

"What's the plan?" Ceri asked, eyeing the various tools of the trade. "Throwing my problem at the veil until something sticks?"

"You have a better idea?" Paska asked. He reached for his pouch made of leather of dubious origin and rattled the bones inside. "I've only been getting bits and pieces of the solution, even now that I know the whole problem, and when we've all tried individually, it's the same. However, the snippets aren't identical, which leads me to hypothesize that if we do this together, in one place, we might be able to stitch everything together into something comprehensive. Or at least comprehensible."

Jezebel opened her poster tube and removed a long scroll of paper. She thwacked it on the table, and it unfurled in one swift motion. "I'm going to need the exact date, time, and place of your birth."

Ceri drank her cup of lukewarm, too strong tea and watched Jezebel's pen dance over the chart in front of her. With the focus entirely on her and her splintered mind, she was a little overwhelmed. She touched the feather tucked against her for reassurance, then drained her cup when Morgana directed a hard look at her.

"Close your eyes and hold out both hands," Paska commanded.

Velvet and leather dropped into her hands.

"Normally, I don't like it when people touch my stones, but I think it's necessary right now," Paska grumbled.

Ceri bit back a snicker, but no one else did.

Paska laughed along with the others. "I know how to brighten a room, that's for sure," he said. "Concentrate on what you were doing, what you were thinking, when you scried Andras that first time. Hold on to as many of those memories as you can, and keep your eyes closed."

A moment later, the two pouches lifted out of her hands.

"You may open your eyes briefly, if you'd like," Paska said. "Just didn't want your gaze to get stuck on anything during a casting and pry open your mind any further."

Ceri's mouth dropped. The table had transformed from kitschy display to occult spread. A large tarot spread dominated the part of the table closest to her—it wasn't a spread she recognized, and she wondered if Sandy had designed it for the occasion.

Opposite Sandy's spread were three almost identical star charts, similar to the ones Jezebel had shown her earlier. One, on dark paper, had the traditional chart and astrological markings she was used to seeing; the second was on a paper that was translucent, almost like thin baking parchment, and had unfamiliar symbols divided into four quadrants and a fifth center section inside the planetary signs of the first chart; and the third chart was printed on a clear plastic sheet and covered in writing that looked like almost but not quite like Greek. "What is that, Jez?" Ceri breathed.

"Don't focus on anything," Paska said. "Glance and move on, then close your eyes again. Jezebel can explain once you've seen everything."

Ceri pulled her eyes away from the charts. To Ceri's right were a scattering of bone runes and several charred-looking sticks. At least she hoped they were sticks. She wasn't sure what else they might be, but when they were accompanying Paska's runes etched into human bone he stored in a leather-of-dubious-origin pouch, she didn't want to assume.

She turned her head when Paska growled softly. On her left was the empty cup of tea Ceri'd drained a bit ago. It was the least intimidating looking spread, but probably one of the most powerful, next to Paska's.

Finally, in the center was Drew's crystal focus stone. Someone had drawn chalk lines between each oracular aid, and the air fairly vibrated with power.

"Close your eyes," Paska said. "We'll tell you what's happening as it happens."

Jez huffed. Ceri felt her walk around the table until she was right next to Ceri's chair. "I hate narrating what I'm doing, but here goes. I'm the north point in this scrying because of the north star and all that. You saw I had three layers. When they're overlaid, they form a design—the golden ratio."

"Doesn't everything? Including the stars?" She was fascinated with how it all fit together, but still didn't see what Jez wanted her to see.

"Yes, of course. But this is three different charts. The bottom one is Oracle Bay."

"It's what?" Ceri asked. "How'd you manage that?"

"A little help from the town's archivist, and I was able to find out not only exactly when the town charter was signed, but nearly the exact time as well."

"Whoa. I didn't know it was possible to chart a town."

"The top chart is yours, and I apologize for Misty's age joke earlier. Now that we know you're three hundred and thirty-seven years old, we will be more careful about the taunting. Your chart is the traditional chart you're used to but with a few more details a typical astrologer wouldn't include, even if they knew about them." Paper rustled from the other side of the table.

"The middle one is Andy's. His is different because his soul is written in the heavens instead of the way you or I are related to the stars. I've overlain the three charts, with Andy separating you from our town, which is the amplifier and stabilizer of all of our powers."

"But what does it mean?" Ceri asked, rather impatiently.

There was another quiet rustle of paper. "On the Oracle Bay

chart, there are several points that I didn't initially understand, but now that I'm looking at the whole picture, I can see that they're us." Jezebel cursed under her breath. "I'm pointing at things, and it'd be a lot easier for me if you could see what I'm doing."

"No," Paska said. "Things are bad enough already. We don't need to make things worse because you are a visual storyteller, Jezebel."

"Ugh. Fine. There are a group of fifteen symbols in the center of the chart. They represent the mind, the future, and the spirit world. Those who have a connection to those things that are beyond human comprehension, the people who have seen beyond the veil. Each of us are represented here. Nine are the oracles I know about: you, me, Drew, Sandy, Misty, Russell, Zeke, Morgana, and Paska. Your symbol here corresponds with your sun sign on your chart, which is how I knew to align these two charts this way. But these six? I don't know who they are, only how old they are—kind of—and where they were born."

"There are six unknown oracles in town right now?" Ceri asked.

"As far as I can tell. The Andras chart—the middle one—has a very different symbol for him, although there are two others like that on his chart, so I don't think any immortal beings are on the town's." Jezebel's voice had morphed from frustration to barely contained excitement.

"Oooh, do you think the symbols represent a physical location?" Misty's voice was nearly as excited as Jez's.

Ceri didn't bother to hide her growing impatience. "Unless it's crucial to whatever it is we're doing right now to identify the mysterious six, can we table that for later? I'm tired of sitting here with my eyes closed."

"Of course," Jezebel said. "Anyway, the gist of it is based on the readings for you, the town, and your...demon friend, if we don't figure out how to heal the rift in your mind, the entire town will be sucked into hell along with you when your mind finally breaks."

Ceri gasped and her eyes flew open. Drew was behind her with his hands covering her face before she caught more than a glimpse of what was laid out on the table. "Real smooth, Jezebel," Drew muttered.

Jez huffed. "AND we can stop it, but it's going to take someone rooted in each plane to close the rift."

"I feel like I'm the AOTW on Doctor Who," Ceri said.

"The what now?" Sandy asked.

"Alien of the week," Drew said, hands still over Ceri's eyes. "What with the talk of closing rifts and everything, she's feeling a bit wibbly wobbly."

There was total silence for a second, then Drew bent down a little and whispered loudly enough for everyone to hear, "They're all just staring at us blankly. It's a shame we landed here among such uncultured swine."

Ceri grinned under his hands. "If I promise to keep my eyes closed, can you move your hands? Let's get on with this before we run out of time, and I drag you all into hell."

Drew took a step back.

"Like I was saying," Jezebel said. "We need someone connected to each plane, and fortunately, we're only working with three for this one, and not nine—or more—realms. We need someone grounded to earth, to Oracle Bay. Someone associated with hell, to keep the doors closed, and something...purer. I don't know what that means, exactly, but I know who's at the center of Oracle Bay right now."

"Who?" Ceri asked.

"You, of course," Misty said. "I own most of the town and manage the rest, but you're the quiet force everyone turns to."

"But since you're the subject of this, and not the force we need, we had to look further," Sandy said. "And that's where I come in. I laid out the cards in the same pattern as the symbols on Jez's chart, one for each of us, one for the six we don't know, and three for Andy and the others on his chart. Unless you want a deep dive into each card and what it means, I'll sum up."

"I'd love the abridged version now but want to hear all about the whole thing later." Ceri wished she had time now to dive deep into everything. The craft of her friends and the tools they used to dive into the future were fascinating.

"Perfect. Every single card I drew was Major Arcana, and that's a lot for an eighteen-card draw. I'm not really going to explain—just tell you which card goes with who in order. The Fool is one of the unknowns on Andy's chart, and I'm excited to learn who has that much faith and innocence and hangs out with a former demon. Paska is the Magician. I mean, duh, right? And Morgana is the High Priestess. Also not a huge surprise. But here's where things get interesting."

There was a pause, and Ceri bit her tongue to keep from huffing in impatience.

"Misty is the Empress, all that success, energy, and her ties to the earth. The Emperor—and the only card that was reversed—is another of the unknowns on Andy's chart. I'm less excited to meet an arrogant angel or demon or god."

Another pause, this time accompanied by the sound of drinking.

"Isn't the Empress some kind of fertility card?" Misty asked.

Sandy sighed loudly. "Yes, but no. Moving on. Andy is Strength— fire, virility, and confidence, and Jezebel is Justice."

"Damn straight I am," Jez interjected.

"You're the Hanged Man, Ceri. You're buffeted by forces you can't control, and you're fighting too hard. You need to surrender to it, trust in us, even if we don't deserve it. You need to decide what you're going to do, what you're going to fight for. It's a water card, and it's so perfectly you right now."

The lump in Ceri's throat that never seemed to go away entirely reappeared. She cleared her throat. "I will."

"Death is Russell—also a duh, I think. He deals in death, in endings and beginnings, and in being a bridge. I'm Temperance, which is hilarious since my dad is literally a wine god. Drew is the Moon—and dude, you need to get a grip on that anxiety and insecurity. You are awesome. Zeke is Judgment. That's everyone here." Sandy sounded exhausted, and Ceri knew it was hard for her to pull so much at once from the cards. It took energy to glance beyond what most people saw. "The six that I don't know are the Lovers, the Chariot, the Hermit, the Wheel of Fortune, the Star, and the Sun. We don't have a Hierophant, which is interesting for this town. There's also no Devil, no Tower, and no World. Don't know what that means, but that's it." She took a deep breath.

"We should work together like this more often," Misty said. "It's fascinating."

"So as far as I can tell, the centers linking everything together are Andy—which we knew, you and Drew, which we suspected based on Morgana's earlier prediction that she didn't share with anyone but Andy until today, and whoever these two other symbols represent on Andy's plane. That's five people, which is symbolic, of course."

"Find me a number that isn't symbolic, and I'll eat your cards," Morgana said. There was a beat of silence, and she added in a very chipper and un-Morgana like voice, "Kidding, of course! I merely meant that there are many significant numbers throughout cultures and history, and since none of us do numerology—although we might want to think about recruiting at a later date—that's irrelevant to the here and now."

"With those two readings, we have the beginnings of the story," Paska said. "We know where, we know what, and we kind of know who."

"And that's where I come in." Morgana's voice was smooth—it usually was—but smooth like cream or a springtime pond, and not the smoothness of dark velvet at midnight Ceri was used to. "At first, I thought I'd learn nothing new from your leaves than I'd seen from mine, but as I contemplated, two new symbols became obvious. One was a bridge connecting what I'd seen before—a shark surrounded by flames. It may be obvious to some, but sharks can be omens of death, and the flames likely represent hell in this picture. They are especially significant because you use water to scry most often, and hell is trying to claim you. Fire and water are enemies but can also balance." She cleared her throat. "The bridge, as I mentioned before, leads from the fiery death to wings. They reinforce that the figures Jezebel and Sandy weren't able to identify will be crucial to the solution and lead us one step closer to figuring out who they are."

There was a dramatic pause that lasted long enough for Ceri to grow impatient again. "Just tell me, Morgana. Please." Even with Morgana-lite, she didn't want to antagonize her if it was possible.

"They're winged creatures, likely angels—or fallen angels, like Andras." Smugness radiated from her voice.

"Didn't we already know that?" Ceri asked. Everything in her mind was confusing enough without being able to see, either literally or psychically.

"We knew they were likely immortal or divine beings," Paska said. "But Oracle Bay's been host to a lot of those lately. There aren't a lot of winged creatures, though, that would be part of this solution."

Ceri mulled it over. "Okay, then. Angels or demons. Got it."

"And that's my cue," Paska said. "Andras is connected to these other beings that will be crucial to saving you and saving the town. You are connected to him, to Drew, and to Oracle Bay. So now we're up to what on our reporter's checklist?"

Ceri rolled her eyes, even though she knew no one could see.

"Don't be rude, Ceridwen," Paska chided. "We started with where—Oracle Bay, of course. We already knew the why, but now we have confirmation—you're intrinsically connected to this town in ways probably you didn't even realize. Jezebel gave us the what— the town being sucked into hell. Sandy told us the who—you, Drew, Andy, and two others. Morgana showed us the nature of the others, and we can see the connections between you all. So what remains?"

"Um...when?" Sandy offered. "But shouldn't we have a how? Aren't the questions who, what, when, where, and how? Why isn't on that list."

"Hush girl." Paska didn't sound offended, though. If anything, he sounded proudly amused. "You're right, of course. We're lacking when and how. I would like to posit that 'when' will be Ceri's breaking point. And that seems like a very important date we want to stay ahead of."

Ceri heard people walking around the room, and it was almost enough to make her open her eyes again. "Little narration for the woman who is obediently keeping her eyes closed?"

Paska chuckled, his laugh dryer than the bones he'd scattered on the table. "I cast the runes you're used to seeing, but I also threw the bones."

"Are they real bones?" Sandy asked.

Ceri was so glad Sandy was still a relative newcomer and felt comfortable asking all the questions Ceri wanted to but didn't feel she could.

"Yes. The runes are carved pieces of bone. The runes themselves are etched into the polished bone and then stained with blood and ink to make them easier to read," Paska replied absently.

"Makes them grosser, too," Jezebel said.

"You're not wrong. Nothing like disconcerting people who know what they're looking at. And the bones, as I called them, are also bone. Fingers, to be exact."

"Erghhh," Sandy said. Her gag reflex was so pronounced Ceri felt hers trying to rise in solidarity.

Oh no, Ceri thought frantically. *Was it too early for morning sickness?*

"Please excuse me a moment," Sandy said. "Continue on without me. I'll be back after the finger bone discussion is over."

Ceri heard her quick steps exit the room, then the sound of the back door opening and closing.

"Huh, never took her for the squeamish type," Paska said.

"Men are so blind," Morgana muttered. "But never mind that. Go on with your 'when,' old man."

"The bones and runes have scattered and crossed. Oddly enough, they fall into a spiral pattern, one that matches everything else we've looked at today. Time counts down to the center, and we are very nearly there. Days maybe. No more than a couple weeks at the outside. We must act, and act now, to save you and our town." The hardness in his voice startled Ceri. She was used to him being stern, exasperated, crotchety, avuncular, but she'd never heard him afraid before.

"Now it's up to us to find the last key to the puzzle," Drew said. "I'm at the center—as are you, Ceri. And Misty and I are going to find the how. This is the only part we can't see right now. There's no way to lay out ahead of time what's about to happen."

"What is going to happen?" Ceri asked. Paska's fear and the direness in Drew's voice were teaming up and sending ripples of goosebumps across her body. She grasped her feather tighter and tried not to think about hell or demons or the end of the world. "Didn't we already have an apocalypse this year? Isn't there a rule about that?"

"This isn't an apocalypse," Morgana said. "This won't affect anyone outside of Oracle Bay. In fact, if we issued an evacuation command, it'd likely only be you and the town. That's hardly enough to qualify as the end of the world."

Ceri bit her lips hard enough to draw blood in order to keep back the scream rising in her throat. "What if I leave, too? Will that help?"

"It might save the town, although that's not a guarantee. But it won't save you, and it won't save anyone around you." The fear was gone from Paska's voice now, and only steel remained.

Drew's voice took over again. "My ball is the center of the table and will take everything we've learned and pull it together. We considered having you come forward and touch it to direct the visions, but decided it was too risky. Instead, Misty agreed to do so."

Ceri gasped. Misty was even more wary of using her powers now than she'd ever been. Something about what she'd seen and experienced when trying to save her boyfriend from an angry goddess whose mother was masquerading as a particularly fertile goat had made her more cautious, and Ceri couldn't remember the last time she'd seen Misty without her gloves on. The question of whether Misty ever took them off—and if she should ask Joseph what kind of things she saw in bed—implanted itself in her mind, and she had to hold back the giggle that threatened to escape. She knew it'd be tinged with hysteria, and she didn't want to have to explain her prurient imagination.

"I'm back." Sandy's voice was quiet, and Ceri jumped. She hadn't heard the tarot reader return. "Let's finish this up before Andy breaks down the door and demands we return Ceri."

"He wouldn't…" Ceri's voice trailed off. He very much would.

"I don't know what's going to happen when Misty touches my ball, so be prepared for anything," Drew warned. "I'll tell you what I see as I see it. We can worry about interpreting it later."

"I'm taking notes," Sandy said. "We don't want to miss anything."

Ceri braced herself on the chair and nodded.

The room exploded in light.

twelve

Ceri shook her head, trying to break out of the daze she was in. A cool hand touched her forehead, and someone pressed a glass into her hand. She took a tentative sip, then started gulping down the ice water.

"Can I open my eyes?" she asked when the cup was empty.

For a moment, no one answered, then she felt someone take her hand. It was Drew. "Sweetheart, your eyes are open."

Ceri blinked rapidly, but nothing changed. "Oh my god. I'm blind."

"You're not blind." Paska's rough voice was right beside her, and she startled again. "You're holding your feather in front of your eyes so close that you probably can't see anything else."

"What happened?" she asked, dropping the feather to her lap. When she did, the whiteness surrounding her field of visions disappeared—and only a glowing silver feather remained. As she watched, the glow slowly disappeared. Magic feather, indeed.

"I think we can all agree that Misty touching Drew's balls was explosively successful," Jezebel said with a snicker.

Ceri's lips curved upwards in an answering grin.

"I think we can also all agree that we were too powerful together, and Misty's hands should never come near my balls again," Drew said. "We'd destroy the world with our passion."

"Do you remember anything?" Sandy asked.

"There was a flash of light and then... That's it, actually." Ceri's shoulders slumped a bit. She blinked back the faint prickle of tears.

"That's all I remember, too," Misty said. She sounded like she was on the ground.

"Why don't we head back to the sitting room," Sandy suggested. "It's more comfortable, and we won't have to worry about Ceri getting drawn into any of our divination tools."

Ceri stood and swayed a bit, then closed her eyes against the waves of dizziness and exhaustion that washed over her. Drew's hand at her elbow steadied her, and she let him lead her to the couch.

Misty groaned. "I don't want to get off the ground. The ground is comfortable and never betrays me by tipping over."

"C'mon, Misty," Sandy cajoled. "I'll help you up."

Misty didn't answer, but based on the grunts of effort from the two women, she let Sandy haul her to her feet.

"I feel drunk. Like college drunk," Misty said. "The world is spinning a bit, and if Sandy lets go of me, I'll probably run into a door."

"Wanna hear a funny story about Misty and college?" Drew asked.

"Don't you dare, Drew Hardy?" Misty gasped. "That was told in confidence."

"That was told as an amusing anecdote in an effort to assuage my humiliation after my debut—and only—karaoke experience. You were trying to make me feel better by recounting an embarrassing story of your own."

"I was hoping it'd catch on and Joseph and Bill would volunteer, but no such luck," Misty muttered.

"I want to hear the story," Ceri said as Drew helped her to the loveseat, then sat down beside her. Someone handed her a glass— this one was wine instead of water, and equally welcome. She didn't want to hear what Drew and Misty had seen, not really. At least not yet.

"We have time," Drew said. "We can't talk about it until Morgana comes back anyway."

"Where is she?" Ceri asked, realizing for the first time that was the only voice she hadn't heard. She opened her eyes and looked around the room.

"Liquor store," Paska replied. "She suddenly felt the need for something stronger than wine, and she doesn't keep anything else in stock. Either that, or she's making a run for it. Could go either way with her."

"Story, then," Drew said. There was a long pause while he looked at Misty with one eyebrow raised.

"Fine, you can tell it," Misty said. "It was a long time ago, and it was pretty funny."

Drew stretched beside her and spread his arms across the back of the loveseat, lightly brushing her shoulders with his arm. She leaned into him and waited for the story.

"You must remember that Misty had never before been out of Oracle Bay for more than a few nights at a time. She knew she could see things no one else could see, and she didn't want that ability. So, she decided to leave to go to college. And for some reason, the school she chose happened to be the same one a certain goatherd we all know and love attended." Drew's voice had dropped into the rhythmic cadence he always used when he was telling stories. It was captivating.

"He's not a goatherd," Misty muttered.

"Semantics," Drew replied, waving away her criticism with a hand. "Misty will tell you it was mere coincidence. She wasn't following him, and she didn't know how she ended up at the same party as him on one fateful November evening in Corvallis. She was still young—barely nineteen—and was giddy with the lack of power she experienced so far from her home. She'd taken to dancing with strangers, holding hands with attractive young gentlemen of her acquaintance, and finding other ways to let down her guard and dull her senses."

"I cannot believe I agreed to this," Misty said. "I forgot how ridiculous you make every story, like it's some kind of grand tale."

"This is a grand tale, my lady," Drew said, then continued. "On this particular evening, Misty had consumed a couple cans of fine, college-priced lager, but never developing a taste for cheap beer, quickly moved on to the next substance offered her. An hour or so later, she was feeling decidedly mellow—stoned, I believe, is what you'd call it in today's parlance. And that's when a certain young man—not the goatherd earlier referenced—declared his intent to leave. He stated he had room for two additional people in his car, and after a glance at the goatherd—who was paying rather more atten-tion to a comely senior than to Misty, our heroine volunteered to take the ride."

Ceri felt the mood in the room shift from the nervous tension that'd been present when she woke up to a more relaxed conviviality. She looked around. Misty was rolling her eyes and looked torn between embarrassment and delight at the retelling of a college story. Sandy was leaning back, twirling her dark hair around a finger, and sipping a glass of wine. Jezebel was sitting in Morgana's chair and looking sternly around the room in an expression that was so reminiscent of Morgana that Ceri had to bite back a laugh—she didn't want to interrupt Drew's storytelling. And Paska was... Paska was staring at her with a gaze so intense that she shivered under the force of it.

The minute he noticed her noticing, he smiled, and the weight dissipated. She blinked rapidly, then turned her attention back to Drew.

"Our heroine was, as you'll recall, in an altered state of being, ran out of the house with the other two passengers in an effort to secure a place in the front passenger seat. Typically, this space is secured by inexplicably yelling 'shotgun!' However, in this instance, the contenders forewent the traditional shouting in favor of a footrace—a time-honored method of finding a victor, and much safer than a duel, particularly for the inebriated."

"Oh my god," Misty muttered. She dropped her face into her hands to hide her reddening cheeks and self-conscious grin.

Drew smiled and sat a little straighter. He was coming up on the grand finale.

"Our heroine is such a force of nature that one might be forgiven for forgetting she is quite small in stature. The other contenders were not as vertically challenged, however. And this is where Misty realized she would have an advantage. For between the three passengers and the vehicle they were aiming for was a large sign with a ground clearance of approximately five feet. She saw her chance, and she went for it, knowing the behemoths would have a natural advantage of longer legs but would have to go around the sign. Misty ran straight ahead, confident in her ability to win the day."

"Um," Sandy said. "How tall are you, Misty?"

"Five three," was Misty's muffled response.

A laugh ran around the room as the punchline became apparent.

"As you have already intuited, our heroine was approximately three inches taller than the bottom of the sign. She'd been running as fast as she could—"

"Which fortunately, wasn't very fast," Misty said into her hands. Her shoulders were shaking in laughter.

"And smacked her forehead against the bottom of the sign. Her legs continued on a little longer than the upper part of her body, and she ended up flat on her back gazing up at the stars in confusion—and no little pain." Drew looked around the room to ensure every eye was on him before finishing. "She soon popped back onto her feet—we all can look back on the resilience of our teen years, those of us who can remember them, anyway, with envy at her ability to stand so soon after—and continued the rest of the way to the car, where she secured her rightful spot in the front passenger seat. The other contenders had collapsed in laughter and were unable to continue. Thus, our heroine proved that much like the fabled race between tortoise and hare, persistence can win the day when speed does not." Drew stood and bowed with a flourish.

Ceri rolled her eyes but applauded enthusiastically.

Drew sat and looked around. "No standing ovation today? I must be slipping."

"I hope you're happy now, Drew," Misty said, finally dropping her hands into her lap.

"Immensely. And if anyone else has embarrassing anecdotes they'd like me to recount in dramatic fashion, you know where to find me." He put his arm around Ceri and pulled her close. "I know more than a few about Ceri, but I'm leaving her alone today."

"Much appreciated." She leaned her head against Drew and, for a moment, forgot why they were here and what would be revealed when Morgana returned.

As if the thought had conjured her, the front door slammed open, and Morgana yelled, "Someone better have an excellent explanation for what's out here. I dislike practical jokes, and this is not funny."

SEVEN PSYCHICS STOOD IN A ROUGH CIRCLE AROUND THE ENVELOPE THAT HAD been left in the middle of Morgana's front stoop with "Agatha" written in a spidery scrawl across the center.

Paska crouched down and picked up the envelope. He turned it over—it was sealed with dark red wax and stamped with a fleur-de-lis. He broke the seal and shook the contents into his hand.

"Is it jewelry?" Sandy asked, shining her phone's flashlight at it and catching the sparkles of the facets with the beam of light.

"It's a pendant," Ceri said. "A red enamel flower—enamel was popular in the twenties—with a diamond solitaire in the center. If you flip it over, it'll be easier to see, but I'm willing to bet it's an Oriental poppy."

Paska gave her a sharp look. "Same vintage as the tiara, then?"

Ceri nodded. "This was the missing item from the second victim."

"Oh," Drew said. He pulled Ceri closer as his body went on high alert. "Is this the ghost? Or something else? What is going on?"

"That is an excellent question," Morgana said darkly. "Is there a note?"

Paska reached into the envelope and pulled out a single sheet of paper. He glanced up at Ceri. "I assume Agatha was the name you used at the time, and this is very much meant for you?"

Ceri nodded. "I was Agatha Collins then. What does it say?"

Paska held the note out to her. Ceri read it, and the pressure returned to her chest, along with the dizziness that'd been a near-constant companion since getting out of the hospital.

"What is it?" Drew asked, slipping an arm around her.

"It just says, 'I wonder if you'll find me this time before I start picking flowers from this garden.' It's signed with a sketch of a five-petal flower. Which is the flower on the third piece of jewelry."

Paska took the letter back from her outstretched hand and tucked it and the pendant into the envelope.

"Should we give it to the police?" Sandy asked.

"No," Ceri said at the same time as Misty and Drew. "They haven't been particularly helpful lately, and now that Drew is finally not a murder suspect, I don't want to draw their attention with trophies from a hundred-year-old murder spree. I don't know what's going on or why, but I don't think this is a matter for the cops."

"Agreed," Paska said. "If we thought a serial killer was in Oracle Bay, it might be a different story. But until we know more, let's keep this close to our respective chests. Tell your partners, of course, but caution them to keep it to themselves."

"Who needs a shot?" Morgana asked, leading the way back into the house.

Ceri sat down again, declined the whiskey, and refilled her wine-glass. The new item had interrupted the evening and the promised big reveal from Misty and Drew. Her eyelids drooped. She was exhausted, and she could see the beginnings of hellfire in her peripheral vision. She didn't know how much longer she'd be able to stave off the waking nightmares without Andy by her side.

"Let's just get to the point so we can all go home and sleep," Drew said, interrupting the rapid-fire conversations and suppositions about ghosts and serial killers and the possibility they were related, and whether it was all part of Ceri's mind-rift.

The room quieted, and Paska nodded. "Excellent suggestion. I take it we do not need a recap as to what had occurred up to the point when Misty touched Drew's ball?"

"I'm good," Ceri murmured. "I got your reporter's questions down."

Misty and Drew exchanged a look, and he nodded at her.

"It was terrifying," Misty said. "If that's what you see, what you're dreaming about, I'm impressed you're still standing." She shuddered.

Drew took up the thread, but with none of the grandiosity he'd used earlier. "It was like being pulled along in a tunnel at top speed. There was fire flickering everywhere, but the tunnel itself was a featureless white tube."

"But the screaming..." Misty's usually tan face paled, and she knotted her hands in her lap.

"The tunnel widened into an enormous room—no walls or ceiling in sight. You were in the center," Drew said. He took Ceri's hand and squeezed lightly. "A circle of flames danced around you, but when I looked closer, I realized it wasn't dancing flames. It was people. People burning and dancing in a circle."

His narration was disjointed and that, more than anything else, drove home how disturbing the vision had been.

"This is where I started to black out," Misty admitted. "But a circle of water formed around the flames, enclosing them but not quenching them?" She turned towards Drew, and he nodded.

"It was weird. Not the weirdest thing, of course, but it was weird." He paused and looked down at where his hand was entwined with Ceri's. Then he looked her in the eye. "I am so sorry about everything. I've been a terrible friend, and you deserve better."

"Just tell me," she said, trying not to let fear take hold.

"Two figures stepped into the center to stand by your side. A creature made of fire and ash—Andy, presumably, and another made of what looked like some kind of faceted quartz the same color as my ball. That was likely me." Drew took a deep breath. "The dancing fire people started spiraling in, closer and closer until the heat was nearly unbearable. The water that encompassed the flames was faltering, and you were melting."

"Like the wicked witch?" Ceri asked. It was a weird thing to latch onto, but it kept the terror at bay.

"Exactly like," Drew confirmed. "Then two pillars of white reached out and took your hands and pulled you up. They touched your head, and for a moment, everything stopped. The fires stopped moving, the water stopped receding, and the dull roar I hadn't noticed until then disappeared. It was still and silent. Then your head exploded." He said the last so quickly, Ceri blinked and had to rewind the sentence in her head and play it back several times before it registered.

"My head...exploded?" It was ludicrous, and she was positive she'd misunderstood.

Drew nodded. "And then everything fell away, and Andy and I were standing on Main Street in Oracle Bay, looking down at you."

"Oh, okay, then. That's good, right?" Ceri asked. It wasn't good. If it had been good, Drew would've been more specific. But she had to ask.

"Only in the sense that the town existed, because you..." he trailed off and squeezed her hand. Ceri watched him blink back tears.

The room was silent—a near impossibility for seven adults—and it was not helping Ceri's calm.

"Well, it was just a vision, after all. I guess that means we need a couple angels, right? Who else would be giant pillars of light capable of exploding my head?" She interred as much bravado into the question as she could, trying to get anyone else to say something. To make a noise. The silence was unbearable. "Somebody say something!" she yelled.

"Finding a couple angels is the next step," Paska agreed smoothly. "But that is a step for tomorrow, I think. I took the liberty of sending a message to your young man. He'll be here shortly to retrieve you. Do you want to take the jewelry with you, or shall I hold on to it? I can keep the other piece, too, if it'd make you more comfortable."

"Thank you, Paska. And yes, please keep the stupid jewelry. Maybe tomorrow I can figure out what's going on." Ceri bit the insides of her cheeks to hold back the tears. She was tired and scared and losing the fight against the visions of hell that threatened to return. "We can figure out everything tomorrow."

Ceri set down her wine and stood. She wobbled a bit but didn't know if it was the wine, the fear, or the exhaustion, but whatever it was, she needed to be somewhere else as soon as possible before she lost it. The sound of a car door slamming outside brought a smile to her face, and she took a step forward, then turned back to the room. "Can someone tell him?"

"Tomorrow," Paska promised. "Tonight, just rest."

Ceri smiled her thanks again and started towards the door.

"Look out!" Sandy yelled.

Ceri stopped in her tracks and turned to look back at Sandy. A large object fell three inches in front of her and crashed to the ground. She looked down. Morgana'd had a macabre photo of a crumbling castle on a boggy island hanging over the doorway. Now it was on the floor, the glass shattered, and the silver backing reflecting her face.

A thousand shadowy hands clutching ghostly daisy chain bracelets of topaz and diamond reached out from the reflections in the prisms of splintered glass. Ceri felt herself getting closer, falling into glass and shadow. She reached her hand out and was yanked back into the room and turned around so her back was towards the doorway.

She closed her eyes, collapsed to the ground, and burst into tears.

thirteen

The heated argument in the kitchen pulled Ceri out of her ball of misery. She unfolded herself from the loveseat Drew'd helped her to when she'd collapsed and followed the angry voices through Morgana's house.

Morgana was leaning against a wall, her unwrinkled sweater set giving no indication of the turmoil of the evening. Paska was on a kitchen stool next to her. They each had nearly full pint glasses of what looked like whiskey. *Guess your alcohol tolerance goes through the roof once you hit a thousand,* Ceri said to herself.

The only other people in the room were Andy and Drew. She vaguely remembered hearing the rest of the psychics say their good-byes and filter out immediately after Andy burst through the door, stinking of sulphur and sending sparks of anger from his fingertips. There weren't any visible scorch marks in Morgana's kitchen, so at least he'd controlled himself somewhat.

She focused on her best friend and her...other friend and tried to figure out what they were arguing about.

"You can't use her as a guinea pig for all your stupid psychic experiments!" Andy said heatedly. There might not be burns on the kitchen counters, but his shirt had smoking holes.

"It wasn't stupid, it wasn't an experiment, and no one else could've done it except Ceri," Drew replied in a voice Ceri recognized as the carefully controlled patience he used on particularly stupid tourists. "Unlike you, we are trying to figure out how to fix this problem so Ceri can go back to living her normal life."

"What do you mean, 'unlike me'? Are you trying to imply I'm not doing everything I can to help her?" The kitchen was filling with smoke.

Morgana opened the windows and turned on the exhaust fan, then returned to her whiskey.

Paska caught sight of Ceri and held out the bottle towards her. A smile ghosted across her lips, and she padded over on bare feet to stand between him and Morgana. She took the bottle, noted that it was nearly empty, and took a drink. She shuddered, half in discomfort, half in pleasure, when the heat of the Irish whiskey hit her esophagus.

Paska grinned at her and dipped his head. It looked like respect, but with Paska, it could mean anything.

"I'm not implying. I'm stating that the only help you're interested in giving Ceri is help to your bedroom where she'll be tied to you and dependent for as long as you can keep her there." Drew's voice was no longer calm, and if he'd had any hellfire in him, he'd be smoking, too.

"You know nothing, *Solomon Paine*."

Drew took a step back, and his skin took on an ashen cast.

Andy plowed ahead, either oblivious to or not caring about Drew's reaction to the odd name that she suspected was the original he never talked about. "You're so set on following your own path, meeting your own needs, that you can't even see what *she* needs. You and the rest of your conjuring friends are using her. You call her a liar, tell her she's crazy, but you still seek her out to solve all your petty problems. You don't care about her unless it gets you something you want." Andy's fist hit the countertop so hard the granite cracked.

"I'll be billing you for that, Andras," Morgana murmured.

"Put it on the tab," he snarled without turning around.

"You call me selfish?" Drew spit out. "Have you told her you know who can help? Or are you waiting for her to decide to fall in love with you before you tell her you know how to seal the rift that will keep you and your past out of her mind?"

Ceri gasped. Her hand flew to cover her mouth.

Andy and Drew whipped around to stare at her. They were wearing almost identical guilty expressions, but she only had eyes for Andy.

"Is it true? Do you know how to fix me?" she whispered.

"No." He shook his head decisively. "But unlike what this charlatan said, I have been exhausting all my sources trying to figure it out, and I've been doing it without subjecting you to further harm."

"Further harm?" Drew turned back towards Andy. "Is that what you think we're doing? At least we're allowing Ceri to be part of the process. She knows what's happening on our end and doesn't have to ask for status updates. You didn't even give her the courtesy of telling her there was anything to update."

Paska walked forward and stood between the men before the argument could pick up steam again. "I think you've both had more than your say tonight. Morgana and I allowed you to release the pressure that's been building in each of you, but you're done now. It's evident you both care deeply for Ceridwen, although maybe not as much as you care for yourselves based on the posturing you're doing while ignoring the fact she's swaying on her feet and looks likely to collapse in exhaustion at any moment."

Ceri saw the moment when Andy and Drew really took her in as someone more than the subject of their argument. The bravado leached from their frames and anger melted into concern. Andy reached her side first, and Ceri didn't miss the resentful glare Drew leveled at him.

"We can finish this later," Andy said—he apparently hadn't missed Drew's hard look, either. "But I think we can both agree that right now, the top priority is getting Ceri home and in bed. She's tired."

Drew nodded stiffly and took a step back. "Agreed. Later."

Morgana pushed herself off the wall and drained her pint glass. "Both of you missed Paska's point. Your top priority shouldn't be taking care of Ceridwen. Your top priority should be giving her the agency to decide for herself what she wants to do. Both now, when she is exhausted, and always. Don't make decisions about her or for her without her input. You might think you're championing this woman you both love, but you're making her small, and that's something that should never happen to any woman."

Ceri smiled at Morgana who nodded back gravely.

"But really, dear, you probably should get some rest," Morgana added. "You look like you're about to fall asleep on your feet. Besides, I am tired of having people in my house, so it's time for all of you to leave."

Paska chucked Ceri gently under the chin. "I'll be by tomorrow to grab the other item. Will you be at the Pour House?"

"Probably in the afternoon," Ceri said. "I'm going to sleep in, then go home for a bit, but I'll head over to the pub for lunch."

"See you then." Paska walked out of the house without another backwards glance.

Drew looked at Ceri. "Ceri—"

She held up a hand. "Tomorrow? Can we meet for coffee, or are we still avoiding the good stuff?"

Drew smiled a little ruefully. "We could get them to go and walk down to the water."

Ceri shook her head at him. "I guess that'll do for now, but you need to make things right with Bill, or I'll do it for you. How does ten sound?"

"Perfect. I'll see you then. I love you, Ceridwen Kenny." He held out his arms, and she stepped into them.

"Love you, too, Drew Hardy," she murmured into his shoulder.

When she stepped back out of his arms, he met her eyes and held them for a moment. She knew what he was asking—knew he was worried about her, knew he didn't want her to leave with Andy. She nodded. "It's okay. Promise."

Drew closed his eyes, then smiled sadly at her before walking out of the house.

Ceri held her hand out to Andy. The instant his skin touched hers, a cool shield descended over her mind. It didn't block out the hell waiting on the other side, but it put some distance between her and hell and tempered the flames licking at the corners of her awareness.

"See you later, Morgana," Ceri said over her shoulder. "Thanks for the whiskey."

Morgana didn't reply, just turned her back to Ceri and busied herself cleaning up the kitchen. They were clearly dismissed.

Ceri and Andy were halfway down the hall towards the front door when it burst open. A lanky white man strode into the room.

"Am I too late for the meeting?" Russell asked. "I just got back to town tonight and saw your message."

Morgana turned around, probably to tell him off, but before she could say anything, Russell made a noise that has half-laugh and half-choking cough. "Are you wearing...pearls?"

Morgana didn't reply with anything besides an icy glare that was tempered by her cardigan, bob, and necklace.

Russell snickered, then looked at Ceri. His eyes drifted up to fix on a spot about six inches above her head. "What's with the ghost army you're leading, Ceri? I'm a necromancer and a medium, and even I have to say that's creepy as fuck."

Ceri curled up in the blanket Andy had brought her when they'd arrived home. To his house, not home. This was *not* her home. He was in the kitchen making her a cup of tea.

"Do you want to put your pajamas on? I can bring them down for you," he called.

"No. Wait. Yes. But I can get them myself." Ceri shifted the blanket aside and uncurled her legs.

"Don't be ridiculous. I'll grab them—and my own. You stay cozy." Andy darted up the stairs and returned a couple minutes later in his soft flannel pajamas pants she knew for a fact he'd purchased specifically to wear to bed once she started spending the night here after… After everything.

He handed Ceri her favorite light blue pajamas. The long pants were almost impossibly soft, and the matching tank top was light-weight, super soft, and attractively cut. Not that *that* mattered.

"Thank you." She pushed the blanket—also soft, she was consistent in her creature comfort needs—to one side and stood.

"You can change here if you want. I'll be in the kitchen and won't come out until you tell me I can." Andy started towards the kitchen.

"That's very sweet, but I'm going to use the bathroom. Because I have to use the bathroom. I drank a gallon of wine and too much whiskey at Morgana's." Ceri stepped into the small half-bath tucked behind the stairs. When she emerged in her pajamas, a cup of peppermint tea was steaming next to the big chair she knew Andy favored, and he knew she coveted.

"Do you need anything else?" Andy asked. He looked uncertain and hesitant, two looks Ceri hadn't often seen on his face. "I don't want to crowd you, and I don't know how much space and time you need to process everything that happened tonight. I can leave if you want me to."

"Please stay," she said. "I don't want to talk yet, but I really need you here. I'm tired, and thing are pushing in on the edges of my vision."

"Of course. What do you need?"

Ceri looked around the room, but her eyes settled on the over-sized chair. It was too intimate, but right now, she didn't care. She needed his arms around her. And if she was going to be honest with herself, it was as much for her comfort as it was to drive away the darkness. "Can I sit on your lap? It's okay if you don't want me to. We can sit on the couch or something, but I need to touch you, at least for a little while."

It might've been her imagination, but she thought she saw him swallow.

"Yes. The chair is fine." He walked over to the chair, set the glass of whiskey she hadn't even noticed him holding next to her tea, and moved the blanket. He opened his arms, and she walked into them. She sat on his lap, hesitantly at first, but then settling in when he wrapped the blanket around them and pulled her into his chest. "Good?"

She sighed and nodded. "Good. Thank you."

She didn't know how long they sat there while her tea grew cold, and he sipped his whiskey in silence. Her eyes were drooping closed when he finally spoke.

"Do you want to talk about anything? Do you want to know what I've been doing?"

"Yes. Both. But not now. Not tonight. I'm so tired of talking." She rested her head on his chest and listened to the slow, steady rhythm of his heart.

She was so close to sleep and knew if she didn't move now, he'd have to carry her to bed. She shifted, trying to rouse herself enough to walk up the stairs, brush her teeth, and crawl into bed.

His arms tightened around her for a moment, then loosened.

She tipped her head up towards him to say goodnight but was caught in his silvery-grey gaze.

Her lips parted, and his eyes tracked the movement.

"Ceri," he said. "You're exhausted, and you had too much to drink."

She slipped one hand around his neck, traced the tendon standing out into his hairline, and curled her fingers into his silver hair. "I don't really get drunk, not anymore. You know that. One of the perks of age. I can't drink like Paska and Morgana, but I can hold my liquor."

Andy groaned softly as the fingers of her other hand trailed along his jawline. "You will not be happy about this tomorrow. Please don't do anything you'll regret. I don't want you to regret anything we do together."

Ceri knew he was probably right—she wouldn't be so blasé about this in the full light of day—but right now, she needed more than his arms around her. She needed him. She didn't know if her need was giving into the attraction that'd only gotten stronger since she'd started sharing a bed with him again, the stirring of feelings she'd pushed away for centuries, or the desperation of knowing this might be her last chance to feel this kind of connection before her mind and body were too far gone for intimacy.

"Just a kiss," she breathed. "That's all I need. Please, Andy. Help me chase the monsters away." She brushed her thumb over the curve of his bottom lip.

He inhaled sharply and pulled her close. "I will stop the second you tell me to. Nothing will happen without your explicit consent. And I'm telling you right now, I'm not consenting to anything besides a kiss." Then he crushed his lips to hers with a passion and force that stole her breath.

She parted her mouth for him and moaned his name as he plunged his tongue into her. "Andy, please." She shifted on his lap until she was straddling him, then pressed her breasts against him.

His hands ran down the length of her body and stopped at her hips. She tried to rock forward, but his hands held her back.

"Just a kiss," he said, the regret in his voice clear. "If you want to go further tomorrow in the clear light of day, we can talk about it then. But not right now."

Ceri knew he was right, knew that her exhaustion and fear and need to use him to chase her nightmares away was clouding her mind, but right now, she didn't care. She wasn't ready to let go. She felt safe in his arms. Wanted. Needed. And more than anything, she felt worthy of his want.

Andy stood, spilling her off his lap. He caught and steadied her, then stepped sideways.

When the heat of his body left her, the energy drained from her. She stumbled backwards and blinked, then yawned so big she thought her jaw might dislocate.

"Do you want me to carry you upstairs?" Andy asked, still well out of arm's reach.

She shook her head. "I can make it."

"I'll give you some time to brush your teeth and get into bed before I come up. There are a couple things I need to do downstairs before going to bed." He turned back towards the kitchen and walked stiffly across the room.

Guilt and a bit of embarrassment stained Ceri's cheeks. She'd spent weeks pushing him away, and then put him in a position where he had to do the same to her. She went upstairs without another word, finished getting ready for bed, and briefly contemplated sleeping in the guest bed. But she wasn't yet sure if she'd be okay without him close. It'd been a long day, and her mind was more tired than usual. She spritzed her pillow with lavender mist, fluffed it up a bit, then crawled under the covers with her back towards where Andy would eventually lay.

When she heard him coming up the stairs, she closed her eyes. Ceri willed her shoulders to untense and her body to slide into the relaxed posture of someone asleep.

"I know you're awake," Andy said quietly. "You don't have to pretend with me. I'll leave it up to you whether you want to talk about what happened earlier. I won't bring it up unless you do. And I'm not going to start something when we're in the same bed."

Ceri didn't answer. Embarrassment was taking hold again, and with it, the anger of rejection. If he really wanted her, why had he pushed her away? Her shoulders tensed again, and she heard him sigh.

A few minutes later, the bed dipped as he climbed in beside her. "Do you need me closer?" he asked.

She shook her head mutely and closed her eyes tighter, willing sleep to overtake her.

"Goodnight, Ceridwen," he whispered. "I hope you have lovely dreams. I know I will."

The light clicked off.

Ceri opened her eyes and stared into the darkness. Fear was creeping in again without his hands to drive it away. She had weeks, maybe only days, left, and she didn't want to face the last few days alone. Her breath hitched in an almost-sob.

An arm wrapped around her and pulled her close. "I'll hold you close and keep your nightmares away. Sleep, Ceri. You're safe here."

Ceri took a deep breath and relaxed into his arms. This felt altogether too comfortable. She was in deep trouble.

fifteen

The steam from Ceri's second cup of coffee enveloped her face, and she inhaled the sweetly bitter aroma of the quad shot Americano she'd liberally dosed with sweet cream. A caramel latte with extra foam was cooling next to her on the bar that ran the length of the bank of windows that made up the west wall of Caffiend Dreams.

Ceri took another sip and looked at her watch. It was almost ten-thirty, and Drew's coffee was going to be stone cold when he got there. She wrinkled her nose at it in consternation. Drew was a punctual person, and he was always where he said he'd be when he was supposed to arrive. Thirty minutes late was weird.

She looked over at Bill. There was a long line, and he was the only one behind the counter right now—the woman he'd hired to work the morning rush was nowhere in sight. Bill saw her looking and rolled his eyes at her.

"I'll make him another one when he deigns to show up," he called. "And if he doesn't show up soon, I'll leave you in charge so I can find him and drag him out of bed." Bill turned back towards the customer he was helping and took his order for two iced half-caf vanilla lattes.

When he moved to the espresso machines, Ceri walked up to the counter with her drink and grinned at him. "It might be more efficient if I rouse him. I'm not confident you'd manage to drag him out of bed without a significant delay."

"I am shocked!" Bill poured the foamy milk into the cup and handed the drink across the counter. "I have nothing but the purest intentions."

The tall Black man taking the coffee from Bill laughed uproariously, and Bill shot him a mock glare. "Don't be rude, Bryan. Everyone knows I'm an angel."

Bryan snickered again. "Just because he yells 'oh god,' doesn't make you a deity."

"Just for that, I'm charging you double for the coffee," Bill shot back.

Bryan grinned. "Send Gabrielle the invoice."

"Right, because what I want to do is get your sister mad at me. I guess I'll have to let it go this time. Now get out of here before the ice in your coffee melts and you think of more ways to malign my character." Bill pointed at the front door, the sparkle in his eyes belying his hard-nose tone.

The door swooshed open, and the sound of two bodies colliding reverberated through the coffee shop.

Ceri whipped around in time to see Drew hit the ground and Bryan's iced lattes sail through the air, upend, and land in Drew's lap, splashing the black-clad woman walking out of the coffee shop with her beverage. She was everywhere. Ceri glanced at the other people in line. She knew most of them and saw them on a near daily basis when she was working on Main Street. It wasn't weird to recognize people in a small town; she was letting the nightmares affect her too much.

Stunned silence descended on Caffiend Dreams as ten people stared at the coffee-soaked tableau in front of them.

Bill recovered first and walked around the counter with a handful of rags. He hauled Drew to his feet and handed him a clean towel to blot the coffee stains off his linen slacks.

Felicity stepped out of line—Ceri hadn't even noticed her without the constant exclamatory sentences—and went into action. She took the rest of the rags from Bill and started mopping the coffee from the floor.

"If you were that angry about the insult, Bill, you could've just said so instead of trying to take me out." Bryan shook his head. "I wish now you'd sent the invoice to my sister."

"Maybe next time. Right now, why don't I make you another drink?" Bill walked behind the counter, washed his hands, and started remaking the lattes. He barely looked at Drew and hadn't even asked him how he was. This was not good.

"Hey, man," Bryan said. "I am so sorry about that. Send me the dry-cleaning bill, and I'll take care of it."

Drew laughed and ran one coffee-soaked hand through his short, light hair. "It's my fault. I was late to meet Ceri and wasn't watching where I was going. I'm the one who should apologize."

"You might be right, but it's not me you need to apologize to. Save that for the lady you kept waiting." Bryan grabbed his replacement coffee from Bill and walked out of the shop after a long pause and a cautious glance outside.

Felicity walked up to the counter with her handful of wet rags. "Wow! That was something else, wasn't it? You don't always get that kind of excitement when you walk into a building!"

Bill eyed her warily, and she smiled brightly.

"If you tell me where to dump these, I'll get out of your way!"

"Hand them to me, then hold on—let me get your coffee order in as a thank you. And if you're ever looking for a new job, let me know."

Felicity giggled and fluttered her eyelashes at Bill, who was completely oblivious to her charms.

Ceri moved towards the wall, hoping Felicity wouldn't see her, but it was too late.

"Hi, Ceri!" Felicity walked over and hugged the shorter woman.

Ceri tried not to shrink back but wasn't sure how successful she'd been. "Oh hey. How are you?"

Drew dropped heavily into the empty seat next to Ceri's purse. She walked towards him, trying to get out of Felicity's sphere, and pushed the now-lukewarm latte at him.

Felicity followed and looked at them brightly.

Ceri was saved from having to do anything further when Bill called Felicity over. She took her coffee, waved enthusiastically at Ceri, flinging droplets of coffee around, and left.

Ceri sat next to Drew and waited, arms crossed, for an explanation. Bill'd been joking around about getting Drew out of bed and now barely looked at him? She fixed Drew with a gimlet stare. "Something is going on."

"Let me get another coffee, then we can go for our walk, and I'll tell you all the ways I've failed as a human being lately. But before I get into that, I need some caffeine." Drew stood, drained his coffee, and tossed the cup into the garbage.

Bill was in the middle of several orders and didn't glance over at Drew and Ceri, but two fresh coffees were on the counter nearest them.

Drew grabbed his and took a drink, then winced. "Thish ish very hot."

Ceri looked at the other one with deep suspicion. It didn't look like another quad shot Americano, which was probably good. She didn't need a third one that morning. But what else...

"Unsweetened latte, heavy on the foam, low on caffeine," Bill said without turning around. "I'm cutting you off, young lady."

"Thanks, Bill." Ceri grabbed her cup and followed Drew out of the coffee shop. As soon as they were out of earshot, she turned to her friend. "I was just getting used to convivial cups of the good coffee again, and now you two are barely speaking? What is going on with you?"

Drew sighed. "This isn't about me. This is about you. I've been a terrible friend lately, as both Paska and Morgana pointed out last night. Let me make it up to you." He slung an arm around her shoulders and pulled her close.

The motion shifted the feather she'd tucked under her sweater, and the wispy edges of each downy barb brushed against the side of her breasts. She shivered, then blushed.

"Are you cold?" Drew started to shrug out of his jacket, but she shook her head.

"No, I'm fine. Just a shiver." She took a sip of her drink, hoping the motion would be enough to hide her flush. "And we can talk about how you're a terrible friend after you tell me what's going with you and Bill. Did you talk to him about your fears?"

Drew nodded but didn't say anything as he led her down Main Street, left at the first—and only—light, and towards the less popular but equally beautiful bay side of Oracle Bay. The tourists always wanted the ocean, and Ceri didn't blame them. There was a reason her house was on a bluff overlooking the ocean just outside of town. The sound of the waves crashing against the rocks at night made her feel safe and warm, and the lighthouse sweeping the coast to warn off stray ships was her comfort nightlight. Add in the occasional foghorn, and she was in her happy place.

Drew sat on the first bench they walked by. She was panting from the walk and was glad he didn't want to go further.

He pulled the lid off his cup, blew gently on the steam rising from the froth, and took a small sip. "This is so good," he breathed.

Ceri sat next to him. "Yes, the coffee Bill makes is amazing. We love the coffee. And I love you. You know I have your back no matter what, so spill. What happened?"

"I don't deserve you," Drew said.

"What? What does that have to do with Bill and coffee and your relationship?" Ceri was not connecting Drew's dots the way she usually did. A hundred years of friendship usually had them on the same page, but right now, she wasn't sure they were even in the same book.

"You unreservedly have my back, no matter what I've done wrong. You didn't even ask before throwing out your support." Drew's shoulders slumped.

Ceri swallowed her sigh of frustration. She loved this man, she really did. They'd been friends since he bumbled his way into a case she'd nearly wrapped up in LA in 1913, and close friends since reconnecting in San Francisco in the late 40s. They'd spent over sixty of the last eighty years living in the same town—occasionally as roommates—and except for five years at the end of the twentieth century when they'd gone their separate ways before Drew found his way to Oracle Bay and called Ceri to join him, they'd spoken to each other almost every day.

But when he got into a sulk, he went all out.

"Drew, I cannot manage your guilt right now. Feel your feelings however you need to, but don't ask me to do the work to reassure you or make you feel better. You know we're friends, and that I'm not going to hold your disbelief against you, but it hurt. A lot. And I can't tell you it's all okay just so you can move on confident that an apology fixed things. You said you're sorry. I said I'll forgive you. I'm hurt, but I'll get over it. Now that that's out of the way, let's move on." Ceri smiled encouragingly at him. There weren't very many men she'd feel comfortable being so blunt with, but Drew had been on the receiving end of her lectures about not making women do his emotional labor enough times that she was confident he'd recognize what he was doing and take a few steps back.

"Ugh. You're right. I'm sorry again. But I'll deal with those shortcomings on my own time. Thanks for being my friend for so many years. I truly am hashtag blessed." He grinned at her, his too beautiful eyes sparkling in amusement.

"Whatever. I'm the best, blah blah blah. Now, are you doing to tell me what's going on between you and Bill, or am I going to have to threaten to tell all of your embarrassing stories, accompanied by either ukulele or a triangle—I'm still deciding—at the Pour House's next open mic night?" Ceri held up her coffee in one hand and tapped the index finger on her other against the cup. "Ding!"

"Fine. Although hearing you perform at open mic night would almost be worth the humiliation." Drew crossed one leg over the other and leaned back against the bench. "I didn't even know they had open mic nights. When did those start?"

Ceri shrugged. "They don't, but I'm sure if I cajole Brandy and tell her all about my performance piece, she'd set it up for me right before the karaoke debut."

Drew shuddered. "I know I've been a jerk, but you don't have to be cruel."

Ceri laughed. "Mood lightening is over now. Spill."

Drew leaned forward and planted his elbows on his thighs as he looked out over the water. "I did what you told me to do. I talked to him. I told him I was afraid our paths would diverge when he aged and I didn't. He told me I was a shallow jerk too obsessed with appearances. So I tried to explain that it wasn't me, it was him."

"Ouch. You'd think after a couple hundred years of talking to people, you'd have figured out how to be a little smoother." Ceri shifted sideways on the bench so she could see Drew's face as he talked.

"Once I explained that I was more worried about him wanting someone who looked his age, it did not get better. He said I'd once told him that fifty years wasn't enough for us, but it was better than nothing, and if I was going to back out now just because he was going to die someday, then I should just leave now."

Ceri took Drew's empty cup and set it down on the ground, then scooted close to him and wrapped him in her arms. "Do you want to leave him now?"

Drew reared back and glared at her. "Of course not! I love that jerk."

"Okay then. I think you know what to do." Ceri dropped a soft kiss on his cheek and returned to her end of the bench.

"I do?"

"You do. You go home with a large bouquet of his favorite flowers, or an artisan cheese plate, or a bottle of expensive Scotch. Something he loves but wouldn't buy for himself. You grovel. You tell him what you just told me—that you love him. Leave out the jerk part. And then you say you know there are no guarantees in life or in love. Even if you were the two most ordinary men in the world, you might not grow old together for any number of reasons. But even with all the caveats and limitations and footnotes and disclaimers, there's no one you'd rather face the uncertainty of the future with. And also, Oracle Bay might get sucked into hell later this month, so who knows! Maybe you will spend the rest of both your lives together."

"Ha. Very funny." Drew was patting his pockets frantically.

"What's wrong? Are you missing something?"

"Looking for a notebook and pen to write down everything you said so I can read it back to Bill tonight." Drew smiled at her.

Ceri shook her head. "Maybe paraphrase a bit. Reading from a cue card might not seem very spontaneous and genuine."

"You're the boss." Drew leaned back again and put his arm around her shoulder. "You really are the best friend, you know?"

"I know." Ceri rested her head on his shoulder and looked out over the deep blue of the bay.

"What's going on with you and Andy?" Drew's voice was casual, but it didn't fool Ceri.

She narrowed her eyes at him. "You know what's going on. I scried him when we were getting a little worried about errant goddesses and coming apocalypses. Apocalysii? That shouldn't have a plural. Anyway. I scried him. It was too much. My brain broke a little. We had a fling. I ended it. My brain broke a lot. Now I sleep in his bed so my nightmares don't destroy me and carry one of his feathers under my clothes so I can go out in the daytime without holding his hand."

"That was a lot of very short staccato sentences. That means you're hiding something, and the something you usually hide from me is feelings. Do you have them?" Drew reached out and tapped the top of her slightly pointy ear. "Did you kiss him?"

"Stop it." She batted his hand away and tried to decide which question had a less perilous answer. "Of course I have feelings. I'm a human being. I feel all sorts of things. Right now, I feel irritated with you."

"Are you in love with him?" Drew asked bluntly.

Ceri opened her mouth to say no, then closed it again, before opening it again to emphatically deny it.

"You look like a fish, and this close to the shore, you don't want to do that or you'll end up on the menu somewhere." Drew pursed his lips and regarded her. "You're usually an excellent liar, so this salmon impression means one of two things. Either you aren't in love with him but want me to think you are. Or, and this is where I'm putting my money, you are one hundred percent head over heels in love with your fallen angel and you didn't realize you'd fallen so deep until I asked you right now."

Ceri closed her mouth again. She stroked the rachis of the feather through the thin material of her sweater and didn't meet Drew's eyes. She knew her feelings for Andy had been growing, but she wasn't ready to think about how much. She wanted him, but love was too far. Not now, when everything was about to end. "You can't tell him. You can't tell anyone."

"I won't, of course. Even if you hadn't asked me not to, it seems like declarations of love would be more appropriate coming from you than me. But at least tell me why you don't want him to know."

Ceri bit her lip and looked at her lap. "I don't want to."

"I know you don't. You've spent three hundred years running from even the suggestion of a relationship, so it makes sense you're not wanting to dive in now—especially not now. But don't pretend that's all there is," Drew said.

"Fine. You want to know?" Ceri snapped. "He's been pushing for this, and I keep pushing back. I don't want to be a weak woman who gives in after I've been asked enough times."

"That's fair. Absolutely. He shouldn't be trying to wear you down. Do you need to stay with Bill and me instead for a couple nights? We can talk to Paska and work something out with the magic feather." Drew caught her chin and turned her head until she had no choice but to meet his gaze.

The thought of not staying with Andy curdled something inside her gut. A moment later, she recognized the feeling as the first fingers of panic. "No!" She took a breath. "I mean no, that's okay. He's not pushing like that. He's actually very polite, mindful of my privacy needs and all that. He set up his second bedroom for my stuff, and there's a bed in there and a computer desk. And a lock on the door." And the vanity table she adored. "But he seems to think I need to hear about how much he cares for me a lot. And when I was in the hospital, he told them he was my husband. And sometimes he makes suggestive comments." Ceri wrinkled her nose and grimaced. As soon as the words had come out, she realized how prim they sounded. Drew was going to have a field day with that.

He surprised her by nodding. "If you don't want the innuendo, I'll talk to him and let him know it's making you uncomfortable. I know you're not a prude—and if I know, he definitely knows. But just because you're open to conversations like that sometimes doesn't mean you are all the time."

"Ugh. Now who's lucky to have the best friend in the world?" Her phone buzzed in her purse, and she reached in and silenced it without looking. "That's probably Paska or Morgana wanting to know why I'm not at the Pour House yet for the big ghost hunt."

"This conversation isn't over—you'll still have to explain a few things about your feelings, but you've caught me with this abrupt conversational turn. What big ghost hunt?" Drew's front pocket dinged politely to notify him of a new text.

"Russell is back in town. He seems to believe I'm leading an army of ghosts around, and today we're going to try to find out why."

"And you didn't open with this?" Drew practically shouted at her.

Ceri threw up her arms in surrender. "The last twenty-four hours have been pretty intense, Drew. And you distracted me this morning with your uncharacteristic lateness, dramatic entrance into the coffee shop, and frosty interaction with your fiancé."

"Fine. I'll give you that, but still... An entire army of ghosts? That's sounds too ominous to sidestep." Drew stood and pulled his phone out of his pocket. "It's Morgana wanting to know why you're not where you're supposed to be."

Ceri rolled her eyes and opened her purse. "I'm twenty minutes late. I'm sure I have ten texts from her, one terse message with nothing useful from Paska, and a missed call from Andy. I'm surprised he didn't show up to make sure I'm okay, actually." She looked down to grab her purse and dropped it. A large, sparkling ring rolled onto the ground.

Drew picked it up before she could caution him not to and examined it. "I'm not a jeweler, but I'm guessing by the size, the five white petals of something I don't recognize, the amethysts and the diamonds, that we're looking at another trophy—number three to match last night's drawing."

Nausea twisted her stomach, and Ceri nodded. "It's white jade. It's the third one, and the second in two days. I don't like this."

Drew's lips were set in a grim line. He tucked the ring into his pocket, picked up her purse, and pulled her close. "We're a ten-minute walk to the Pour House. Can you make it, or should I call Andy to give you a ride?"

Ceri looked around, but they were alone. "Let's walk, but don't leave me, please."

"Not a chance, Ceridwen. I'm right by your side."

sixteen

Russell, Morgana, and Paska were settled into their regular booth when Ceri and Drew walked through the door.

Andy was at the bar, and he waved at her cheerfully. Heat stained her cheeks. He'd woken before her and had been downstairs when she'd gotten up. She'd dawdled over her morning routine, taking a longer shower than usual, until she heard him leave.

When she'd gone downstairs, she'd found breakfast and a note waiting for her.

Heading to the bar to check the tanks and go over the books with Brandy. See you there at 11:30. I'll have your lunch order in. —AS

And now he was waving at her like nothing had happened. Like last night, she hadn't thrown herself at him like a lovesick teen, forcing him to be the responsible one. She was being ridiculous—he hadn't rejected her. He just hadn't taken advantage of the situation, no matter how much he'd made it clear it was what he wanted. But still, it stung a little too much.

"Are you okay?" Drew asked, jolting her out of her thoughts.

"Fine," she said tightly. From the knowing smirk he shot her way, he clearly didn't believe her. "Let's go get this ghost talk over." She strode over to the table in long, deliberate steps. She was a strong, independent woman, and she didn't need anyone to take care of her.

"You're late," Morgana said.

"I was busy," Ceri replied, sliding in next to Russell and across from Morgana.

Russell shifted away from her slightly. He was focused on something just behind her.

"Seriously?" she asked. She stood and walked around the table to sit next to Morgana, leaving the spot next to Russell for Drew.

"There are dead people floating behind you. They look angry. I don't like it." He didn't sound disturbed; he sounded intrigued.

"It's not been a walk in the park for me, either. Especially since they're following me around, and not you. And I don't think anyone really believed they were there until you showed up." Ceri tried not to look at Drew when she said that but couldn't help sneaking a glance.

"A lot of profoundly stupid people in this town," Paska said placidly from where he sat nursing a beer in the back corner.

Ceri took a deep breath and looked at Drew.

He met her eyes for a long moment, then reached into his pocket and slid the ring across the table.

Paska raised an eyebrow but didn't say anything. He slid the ring into his pocket. A resigned look appeared on his face, but before Ceri could puzzle out what he was thinking, she heard the reason for his sudden change in demeanor.

"Hey guys!" Felicity set six waters on the table and pulled out an order pad. "I have Ceri's order in already, but what can I get for the rest of you?"

Paska held up his glass. "I'll have a pitcher of the lager."

"Awesome, Mr. Cooper! How many glasses do you want?" Felicity's smile lit up the entire alcove.

"How many mouths do you think I have? I've got my glass." Paska's voice dripped with disdain.

"Iced tea and a bowl of the clam chowder," Morgana said.

"Nothing for me," Drew replied.

Felicity's gaze fell on Russell, and her face lit up. "Hey! You're new! My name's Felicity, and I'll be your server! What's your name?"

Russell's eyes widened in what looked akin to horror. "Um. Russell. My name's Russell. And I'll have whatever beer Andy recommends. Oh, and uh, a steak sandwich and fries."

"You got it, Russell!" Felicity took one more look around the table before turning and heading back to put in their orders.

"What is wrong with her?" Russell whispered. "She's so happy."

Ceri cocked her head and regarded Russell. "She's a walking exclamation point, but I don't think there's anything wrong with her."

"You're not wrong, Russell," Paska said as he drained his beer. "Something about her gives me the creeps."

"If Morgana feels the same way, I have a theory," Drew said.

Morgana glared at him, then nodded slightly.

Drew grinned expansively. "Until Morgana's makeover, the three of you were the gothest psychics in town."

"Is gothest a word?" Ceri asked.

"It is now." Drew waved her question away. "Anyway, Felicity's excessive cheer threatens the darkness you all shroud yourselves with in the name of cool."

Morgana's glare became a glower.

Drew laughed. "Morgana, I know you're just as scary as you were three days ago, but your glare is a lot less effective when it's accompanied by a sweater set and pearl earrings."

Morgana took a deep breath, and Ceri held hers, waiting for the explosion of temper. Then Morgana exhaled slowly, smiled almost as brightly as Felicity, and said, "Good. I am trying to appear less intimidating."

Ceri stared at Morgana, trying to come up with something to say in response to the most preposterous statement she'd heard in the last year.

She was saved from having to think of something by Felicity's return.

"Here's your pitcher, Mr. Cooper. I brought a couple extra glasses in case you decide to share!" She winked at him.

Paska smiled tightly but didn't reply. He took the pitcher and refilled his glass.

"And for you, new Russell, I have Mr. Sterling's newest! It's a..." She tipped her hand towards herself and peeked at her palm. "... Pearly Gates Pale Ale! Isn't it so fun that all the beer names have references to heaven and hell? I just love that!"

"Thank you," Russell said without looking directly at Felicity.

"And I have a beer for you, too, Ceri! This one's an Irish Red!" Felicity beamed at Ceri and set a reddish amber beer in front of her.

"What's the name of it?" Ceri asked, taking a tentative sip.

Felicity's brow furrowed. "What do you mean? It's an Irish red."

"Don't all the beers have heaven or hell themed names?" Ceri asked. She knew she was being a jerk, but she couldn't help it. She might not be in the running for gothest psychic in Oracle Bay, but the girl's aggressive cheer was making her cranky.

"Oh no," Felicity whispered. "I forgot."

Before Ceri could tell her not to worry about it, Felicity raced back to the bar.

"Now she's going to come back more than necessary," Morgana said. "This is already less private than it should be for these kinds of discussion."

Paska nodded. "The demon should not open until four, so we can meet in private during the day."

Brandy appeared in the alcove with a large tray. "Are you going to pay what we're losing by staying closed over lunch for paying customers and serving the only people in town who I never get to charge?" She put a Monte Cristo sandwich in front of Ceri and set Russell's and Morgana's food in front of them, then narrowed her eyes at Ceri. "I don't know what you said to Felicity, but she's too upset to wait on you anymore today."

"I didn't say anything mean," Ceri protested. "I just asked her what the name of my beer was."

Brandy rolled her eyes. "She shows up on time almost every day and only spills on you, which are great qualities in a server, but wow, is she a lot. My teeth ache after a day working with her. It's Redemption Irish Red, brewed in honor of red-headed Irish women all over town."

Warmth curled in Ceri's chest, and a small smile formed on her lips. "Thanks, Brandy."

"You're welcome. And thank you." Brandy picked up her tray.

"For what?"

Brandy winked. "Love working for a happy boss. He lets me do whatever I want. We're four weeks and a KJ hire away from Thursday night karaoke."

"I haven't..." Ceri's voice trailed off. She didn't know how to say she wasn't making Andy happy in a way that wouldn't sound like denial or innuendo. Instead, she smiled and nodded.

"I like her. I kept trying to hire her away from Andy to co-manage the Sleeping Inn bar with me, but she was stubbornly loyal to Andy. And I guess it's paid off for her if she's in charge now." Russell took a huge bite of his steak sandwich and groaned in pleasure. "Was it her idea to add lunch? If so, it's the third best decision she's ever made."

"What are the other two?" Drew asked. He was eyeing Russell's steak fries with unconcealed avarice.

Russell scooted his plate further away from Drew. "Get your own food, Hardy. Her second-best decision is to add karaoke. I love karaoke with a passion that cannot be described."

Drew groaned. "Not another one of you. I already know I'm not going to see Bill on Thursday evenings once this starts up. He, Joseph, and Misty will have a permanent table staked out so they can sing in front of strangers for fun."

"Jezebel will be right there with them," Ceri said.

"Count me in," Russell said. "What about you, Ceri? I'm not even going to ask the old folks—they probably don't even know what karaoke is."

"I will come and watch," Ceri said. "But you couldn't pay me enough to sing."

"No," Morgana said shortly.

At the same time, Paska replied with an enthusiastic yes. "It's modern bardic tradition."

"It's not," Morgana said. "It's not even close."

"Fine. But it's still fun." Paska refilled his glass. "Can we get started? I'd like to get through the ghost discussion before I run out of beer and have to talk to that woman again."

Russell finished his sandwich, wiped his mouth with his napkin, then pushed the plate with a still-heaping pile of fries towards Drew. His expression sobered, and he looked at Ceri. "Paska caught me up with what's been going on with you, and while I can't pretend to understand even a fraction of what's happening, I agree with his assessment that you're more susceptible to and aware of the departed because of the connection your mind has with hell. But you only saw one?"

Ceri thought back and chewed her lip. "I thought it was only one, but maybe it was only one at a time. They're shadowy—I don't really see any features, except for the first time."

"What was the first time?" Russell leaned forward and eyed her like she was a particularly interesting specimen under a microscope.

"When I was waking up in the hospital."

"When she was coming out of a coma," Drew said.

Russell nodded. "That makes sense. Just about anyone could see a spirit when they're hovering between life and death, sleeping and waking. A lot of this is still new to me, so I might not get everything exactly right. But I *think* what probably happened was that one or more of these ghosts happened upon you while you were in a coma and latched on. So when you woke up, they came with you. That, along with your too-open mind, is why you can see them when no one else can even sense them." He leaned back and tapped his chin with his index finger.

"Why'd they latch onto me, though?" Ceri asked.

"That's the question we need to answer," Russell said. "They can affect the physical world, so they're already too powerful. I can help them move on, of course, but I'd rather not force the issue. It's always easier when they leave of their own accord. And quite often, lingering spirits have unfinished business to take care of. Can you tell me what you saw last night when Morgana's creepy photo fell off the wall? We can use that to start a conversation."

"A conversation?" Ceri asked. Her memory of it was a little hazy. She'd felt compelled to look deeper, but she wasn't sure if she'd seen anything except for broken glass before Drew had turned her around.

Russell reached under his seat and grabbed a large backpack. He grinned, pulled out a long, slim box, and plunked it in the middle of the table.

"A Ouija board? I would've thought you'd have moved onto something more..." Ceri searched for the right words but realized there weren't any.

"It's a tool, and one I'm familiar with. We all have ways to focus our energies, and this is mine." Russell didn't sound offended, but Ceri cringed anyway. "It's an easy way to open a conduit for speech, and something tangible to hold on to mentally, so I don't accidentally put too much power into the spirits I'm talking to. You only raise the long-departed from the dead three or four times before you learn your lesson."

"I have a lot of questions, but they'll hold," Drew murmured.

"I'm not sure I saw anything... No, wait. There was a dark figure holding out a broken bracelet. It was in all the pieces of glass—like a funhouse mirror." Ceri shuddered at the memory.

"A bracelet?" Paska asked. "Was it part of the collection?"

Ceri felt the color drain from her face, and her head swum. She'd speculated that they were connected, but speculation and confirmation were two very different things. "Yes, it was. Does that mean...?"

"It certainly eliminates one of our issues," Paska said.

Ceri shook her head before Paska even finished his sentence and said, "It does not! It might connect two of them, but it doesn't make either the ghosts or the serial killer trophies go away."

"And regardless of how much the spirits can affect the material world, they cannot carry items from the past to the present and hide them in purses," Russell said. "They are likely connected, but the dead are not leaving trinkets for Ceri like enthusiastically macabre ravens. The spirits might give us the answers we need to find the person or persons who are tormenting you, Ceri, and for that, we'll need to talk to them."

"Small Medium at Large!" Drew shouted.

Four pairs of eyes turned towards him.

He shrugged and said, "Misty isn't here, so I am fulfilling her role in helping Russell come up with a name for his new business."

Morgana nodded thoughtfully. "It's too clunky, but I like the direction you're going."

"I'm not opening a new business," Russell muttered. "There is no way I'm taking people's money and talking to the spirits of their dead relatives to find out where the wills are hidden. I'm doing this for you, Ceri, because we're friends. But I am not for hire."

"How much has Misty been bugging you about this?" Drew asked while Russell set up the board and moved the planchette to the center.

"I've gotten a dozen texts from her since she found out I was home. Her current favorite, based on the number of times it's been at the front of the lists of names she's sent, is 'Happy Medium.'" Russell looked at Ceri. "Paska told me you're avoiding all seeing right now, out of an abundance of caution. But I'm going to need you to participate in this. The spirits are attached to you, and although I can see them, they'll respond better to you. I'm not in the mood to pour energy into a conversation if it's unnecessary."

"It should be fine," Ceri said, placing her hands on the planchette across from Russell's and willing her words to be true. She couldn't handle another deep dive into hell—not now when her emotions were already all over the place—but if this confirmed they had two problems instead of three, it might be worth it. She took a deep breath and smiled at Russell. "This isn't looking into the future. It's just a conversation."

"One moment," Drew said. He stood and waved towards the front of the bar.

"If Felicity shows up because of that, I will find someone to haunt you for the rest of your life," Russell said.

Drew grinned and mock-shuddered. "Perish the thought. I was getting Andy's attention. If Ceri's going to open her mind to something, she might need backup."

"He's been such a good boy, staying away this long," Morgana said. "He deserves a treat."

Andy growled as he walked into the alcove. "I'm not your dog, witch." He folded himself into a chair, blocking the doorway, and looked at Ceri. "You okay with this?"

She nodded. "Glad you're here, but I'm okay." Ceri looked at Russell. "Okay, tell me what to do."

seventeen

Ceri stared at the board, waiting for something to happen. It'd been almost ten minutes since she'd invited the spirits hanging around to speak. But whether they were shy, unwilling, or unable to communicate, the result was the same. No movement from the planchette, and not a sound from anyone else in the alcove.

Ceri heard rattling dishes and glasses from the main dining room, the low murmur of voices, and if she listened hard enough, the waves crashing against the pier. But no ghostly winds or bean sídhe screams. Nothing otherworldly at all. Impatience competed with relief at the spirits' reluctance to communicate.

"Hey boss, I'm going on break!"

Ceri jumped, sending the planchette skittering across the board. Goosebumps raised on her arms, and she shivered.

Felicity was in the doorway immediately behind Andy and staring at the Ouija board with wide eyes.

Andy closed his eyes and took a deep breath. Ceri watched him school his expression into his usual mask before turning around. "You don't have to tell me—just make sure Brandy or Zeke know. I'll handle this table for the rest of the day, so you don't need to let me know when you get back, ether." He turned back to the table without waiting for a response.

"Sorry," Felicity mumbled, backing out of the alcove without taking her eyes off the Ouija board.

"I'm going to put a door here," Andy muttered. "If you charlatans are going to continue to use this space for your chicanery, I'll need to keep the nosy customers away if I want to keep them."

"It's fine," Morgana said dismissively. "We are the town *charlatans*. Everyone expects us to have the tools of our trade with us, and team meetings are a common thing among mundane humans, are they not?"

Ceri nodded slowly. "I think so, although I've never worked in such an environment. Has anyone here? Russell? You're the youngest."

Russell shook his head. "I waited tables until I dropped out of college, then started bar tending."

"I was an accountant for a while in the nineties," Paska said. "It was interesting, and we had a lot of team meetings."

"Interesting?" Ceri asked skeptically.

"You can do a lot with a computer and access to money," Paska said. "I made a lot of money."

"You probably could've helped Vincent out last year if you'd shared your embezzlement experience," Ceri said.

"My experience with white collar crime and computers is out-of-date and would have done no good. I looked into it." Paska moved the planchette back to the board.

Russell was staring at Paska with what looked like horrified fascination. "You stole money from your employers?"

"They were unethical, and many worthy charities received generous and anonymous gifts when I left that job. I have no guilt," Paska said. "Now why don't you try again, Russell. If you want to learn more about the crimes I've committed in my life, we can reserve a couple weeks some other time."

Russell tore his eyes away from Paska. He glanced at the board, positioning his fingers on the planchette, then looked up at Ceri. His mouth formed an 'O.'

"What?" Ceri twisted around. A shadow shifted behind her. "It's not the right shape," she whispered.

"They're here and they're ready to talk," Russell said. "You have to invite them to speak."

Ceri hesitated. She wasn't sure she really wanted to hear what they were saying, no matter how important Russell thought it was.

Andy's hand settled on her leg. He squeezed her knee, and the pressure shot confidence through her, straightening her spine. She placed her hands on the planchette and said, "If you want to talk, we want to listen. Tell me why you're here, why you're following me."

The planchette started moving. Russell lifted his hands and propped his chin on his folded hands to watch.

R. E. V. E. N.

Ceri jerked her hands away, but it kept moving.

G. E.

"If you want to keep using the Ouija board, we can stick with that, but if you'd prefer something more direct, I can offer a couple options. Say no to stick with the board, yes to hear more options."

It's like a telephone answering tree, Ceri thought. A hysterical giggle rose in her throat. She dropped her hand to Andy's. He turned his palm over to take hers. She held on in a death grip.

The planchette slid to the *yes,* then back to the center.

"Excellent. Thank you for trusting me. Option one is you can take temporary possession of my body and speak through me. That's the easiest for me, but the hardest for you. You won't be able to take control, and you'll be subject to my will. You won't be able to get a foothold. The second option will be to allow me to push enough life energy into you so you can take on a semi-corporeal form and speak that way. It won't cost you anything, and you'll be in your former body, even if it's just for a bit. It'll only last as long as I have the energy to maintain it. You'll need to speak quickly and tell us what's so important that you're hanging around Ceri now." Russell leaned forward and fixed his gaze on a point over Ceri's shoulder. His eyes were hard, and his face was grim. "If you do not tell me why you're here and what you want in the time I give you, I will force you to move on. You'll get no closure, and no choice. If you're open and honest, I'll help you move on when your business is done. Say yes if you understand."

Once more, the planchette zipped across the board to the *yes* before returning to the center.

"Only one of you will be able to speak, so designate someone now, and make your choice. Do you want to possess me, yes or no?" Russell rubbed his left temple, and Ceri realized he was hoping they'd say no.

No.

"Do you want me to give you the energy to speak with your own voice?" Russell sat up straighter and put more confidence into his voice.

A couple hundred years of telling fortunes to disbelievers and telling cops when they'd screwed up an investigation made the move recognizable. Russell was playing the ghosts. He was using body language to steer them the way he wanted while still maintaining the appearance of choice.

Yes.

"Whichever of you will be the spokesperson, come forward. The rest of you need to fall back. If my energies are divided among you, none of you will have enough to speak." Russell paused, presumably waiting for the ghosts to shuffle into position. He closed his eyes and took a deep breath.

Ceri watched in fascination. She'd seen a little of this earlier in the year when Russell'd done something similar to Martha so she could get Adriana to confess to the Main Street murders, but that'd been a lot more theatrics and a little more ritual.

He opened his eyes, and Ceri gasped. They were unfocused and milky white. Light streamed from his hands, creating an ethereal river between his glowing hands and the rapidly forming figure standing next to her.

Ceri pushed away from the spectrally lit form beside her. Andy hooked an arm around her waist and pulled her onto his lap.

The ghost's features swirled and settled until it looked human. A slightly translucent human, but human, nonetheless.

"You're..." Ceri leaned forward and peered at the face of the young woman in front of her. "You're Laura Taylor. I've only seen pictures, but that's who you are, right?"

"Who's Laura Taylor?" Andy whispered.

"She's the first victim of the Ruby Rose killer," Ceri said. "It is all connected, isn't it?"

The ghost nodded, then looked at Russell, one imperious eyebrow raised.

"You should be able to talk now," he said. "It might take you a moment to get used to it, but you're good to go. Remember, though, be quick."

Laura smoothed her hands over her short, dark dress and down the lines of her body, and a smile spread across her face. "It's been a long time since I've seen myself, you know? I still look good." She stumbled forward and huffed in irritation. "Alright, alright. I'm getting to it."

Her voice was breathy and girlish, which somehow matched her wide-eyed ingenue appearance. It was hard to determine colors and hues, but Ceri knew her fashionable bob was jet black, and her skin was the light brown of a white woman who spent time in the Los Angeles sun. A white woman who wasn't Ceri anyway. Ceri had two skin colors: paper white and bright red.

"You've already figured out who I am, so you probably know why we're sticking around. I don't care as much about revenge as some of the others, but I want people to know what happened to us." She paused and lifted one hand to the hollow of her throat. "We were murdered!"

Ceri pursed her lips and wondered if Laura was the best choice to speak for the crew. She hadn't thought much about the case in the last half century—you can't hold on to failure forever when you live several lifetimes—until the last couple of weeks, and she hadn't read through all her old notes. But she was pretty sure she remembered Laura's notes. "You were an actress, weren't you?"

Laura smiled at Ceri. "I was! Did you ever see me?"

"I wasn't so lucky," Ceri said. "But I remember your name."

"I was just about to make it big when I was cut down in the prime of my life." Her tone turned mournful, and Ceri knew she had to do something to jolt her into action or they'd run out of time to find out what was going on.

"Laura, you don't have much time. I know why you haven't moved on, but why are you here in Oracle Bay, and why now? I haven't seen you around before." Russell pulled Laura's attention back to him.

"Oracle Bay?" She wrinkled her nose.

"That's where we are now. This is where Ceri is." Russell pointed at her.

"Agatha," Ceri said. "Agatha Collins. That was my name then."

"We're not here for Agatha or Ceri or whatever her name is," Laura said. "Helen recognized her when she wandered by searching for a way out of hell and followed her back. When we realized who she was, we tried to help her see. Helen didn't know she was a witch when she hired her to keep her from being murdered—not that it worked—but we can see it now." She turned towards Ceri. "We tried to make you see, but you won't look. Why won't you look?"

Ceri stared back at the ghost and leaned back into Andy. "What do you mean, you tried to make me see?"

"The mirrors, and the glass. You keep hiding from us, hiding from the truth. We just want to make you see before it's too late." Laura's voice vibrated with frustration, but it was threadier than it'd been a minute ago.

"We're running out of time," Russell said. His voice was steady, but sweat was beading on his brow. "Say what you need to say now."

Laura looked at Russell. "You're in danger. Everyone here is in danger." Laura's voice was tight, urgent. She looked between Russell and Ceri, then fixed her gaze on Russell and pointed at Ceri. "You have to stop her before she destroys everything."

"Who?" Andy demanded. "Stop who?"

"I brought another pitcher for Mr. Cooper!" Felicity announced, walking into the alcove with a full pitcher.

The air in the alcove dropped, raising goosebumps on Ceri's arms, and Laura blinked out of existence.

Russell's head snapped back and bounced off the wall behind him. "Fuck!" he bit out. "That hurt."

"I am so sorry, Russell! Do you need ice? Another beer? If you come back to the kitchen with me, I can make sure you're not injured!" The look Felicity raked over Russell looked less clinically concerned and more carnally interested.

"I'm good. You just startled me." Russell folded the Ouija board and put it and the planchette back in the box. He kept his head turned away from Felicity.

Ceri watched Felicity go into a full pout, but Russell didn't turn around.

The server smiled, but it looked almost forced this time. "Okay, then! Anyone else need anything?"

Andy stood, sliding Ceri off his lap and back into her chair. He towered over Felicity and stared down at her.

She met his eyes. The longer he looked at her without speaking, the dimmer her smile got. When it'd completely fled her face, he spoke.

"Did I or did I not tell you explicitly that I'd be managing this table for the rest of the day and that there was no need for you to come back here?" His voice was so quiet, Ceri had to strain to hear him from her position behind him.

Felicity's lower lip trembled and tears filled her large, expressive eyes. "I f-f-forgot." She blinked and tears trailed down her face.

Ceri's irritation about-faced into sympathy.

Andy growled wordlessly. "Fine. Try to remember next time, okay? And I'll talk to Brandy about switching up your tables. This table isn't that great anyway. No one ever tips."

Felicity bobbed her chin and ran away.

Andy took a deep breath, then sat again. "My apologies," he said to Russell who'd finally turned around. "Are you okay?"

Russell sniffed and touched a finger to his nose. "It's bleeding, isn't it? That always happens when the gate is shut from the other side. You can't just go around scaring spirits that way."

Ceri giggled. Every eye at the table turned towards her.

"What's so funny about that?" Russell demanded, dabbing at the blood with a bar napkin.

"She scared the ghost," Ceri said between bursts of laughter.

"And?" Russell bit out.

"Usually ghosts scare people." Another gale of laughter claimed her.

Andy sat next to her and slid an arm around her waist. Ceri looked up at him and saw his lips twitch. "She's not wrong," Andy said.

"Children," Morgana huffed. "As we are unlikely to get anything else today, I am going to return home. I have a photo to reframe and hang, not to mention a cracked countertop to replace and several scorch marks to get out of the drapes."

"Send me the bill," Andy said.

"With interest," Morgana said. She swept out of the alcove.

Paska was looking at the table. His brows were knitted tightly together. Andy grabbed the pitcher Felicity'd set down and filled Paska's glass.

"Something was odd about that encounter," Paska said finally. "But I can't put my finger on it."

"A lot was weird about it, and I'm the person who can talk to the dead," Russell said.

"Of course. You're very young. When you're as old as I am, it takes a lot more to register." He took a long drink of his beer, reached into his pocket, pulled out a flask, and took a pull from that before tucking it back into his pocket.

Ceri grabbed her forgotten beer and took a sip.

"Do you like it?" Andy asked. "I made it for you."

A thrill ran up her spine. "It's wonderful. Thank you." She didn't quite meet his eyes.

"The serial killer is a woman," Paska said.

"What are you talking about?" Drew demanded. "He was a man, and he's been dead for decades."

"How do you know?" Paska asked.

Drew sputtered for a moment. "The murders were a hundred years ago. It'd be impossible for him to be alive."

Paska raised his hand into the air. "Raise your hand if you were alive at the turn of the last century. What about the one before that? And the one before?"

"I saw the turn of the 17th, 18th, 19th, and 20th centuries," Ceri said. "Drew, you're not as old as me, but you've seen a couple go by."

"I've only partied like it's 1999," Russell said.

"Me, too," Andy said. "I was in hell, though, for the previous ten thousand years."

"Not impossible, then," Paska said. "You should well know by now, boy, that there are few things that are impossible. You've met gods and angels and demons, and you have the hubris to think you know what's impossible and what's not?"

Two angry red spots formed on Drew's face. He exhaled forcefully, grabbed one of Paska's "sharing" glasses, and filled it. "You're right, of course. There's no reason a serial killer couldn't be still alive. But a woman?"

"Drew's right, Paska. The chances of it being a woman are very, very low. Why do you think that?" Ceri took a sip of her beer, then reached into her pocket for her phone. She pulled up a browser and started typing.

Paska licked his lips. "What do you think Laura was warning us about?"

"Me," Ceri said without looking up from the pages of results that'd come up. "She was warning us that I was about to destroy everything. Which we already knew, so not helpful, Laura." She selected the first link and bit back a gasp.

"I don't think so." Paska shook his head. "Russell will know better than I do, of course, but I don't think a group of ghosts would grab onto someone they vaguely recognized, state they're here for revenge, and be focused on a town they'd never heard of getting sucked into hell. Would they even know that was going to happen?"

Russell was shaking his head forcefully. "Until this very moment, I didn't know we were getting sucked into hell. Do we have a time-line on that? It's possible I left a few items at my aunt's house that I urgently need to retrieve."

"Don't worry, we're going to stop it. Probably. The real question is, how would ghosts from Ceri's past end up here if they've not been attached to her the whole time?"

"If she'd had the missing jewelry, that would explain it. But unless she's a total sociopath who's planting old serial killer trophies to get attention, I don't think that's likely." Russell didn't even glance at Ceri, for which she was grateful.

"You didn't ask, but I'm still stating for the record I hadn't seen any of these pieces until recently. They'd all been taken before I was hired." Ceri glanced up at Paska before turning back to the phone. "Do you think we should've shown her the jewelry?"

"I was going to before the server chased her away." Paska looked at Russell. "Keep going. What other explanations might there be? Nothing will be too weird to consider."

"Drew was there, right?" Russell asked. "In LA at the same time? Maybe it was him."

"I wasn't, and it wasn't," Drew said. "And what would be my motivation to hold on to my murderous tendencies until now? Ceri and I have been friends for over a hundred years. Why wait?"

Russell tapped his fingers on the table. "Because you were waiting for her to be off-balance already? I don't know. It wasn't you.

Or if it was, you didn't have the ghosts following you around before. Unless your trip to Mexico was a front to go dig up the trophy jewelry and bring it and the ghosts home with you, I don't see a way you'd be responsible."

"Thank you?" Drew leaned back and crossed his arms. "Would you have seen them before? I mean, you weren't very open about what was going on, and you're clearly more confident now. Have your abilities changed? Are you more sensitive now?"

"I would've. I can see all the spirits in town, and a lot of them want to chat. I'm better able to channel my energy now, which makes me more powerful, but it hasn't changed my perception. They weren't here before." Russell creased his brows and massaged his temples.

Ceri held up her phone. Once she was positive she had everyone's attention, she said, "There have been other murders in the last century—three sprees every twenty years—that followed nearly the same pattern. Seven kills. All women. And all on the west coast. And they all had a piece of jewelry stolen. None of the reports are very specific about what jewelry, but I think we can hop to a conclusion here. It's been twenty years since the last ones." Fear clenched in her stomach, and the note she'd gotten last night seemed like even more of a threat this time.

"I cannot think of a way seven spirits would've found Ceri, latched onto her, and pulled themselves forward if they weren't already close. She was only in a coma. Her spirit wouldn't have wandered too far away, especially not as tethered to Andy as she is."

"So they're not something out of hell? Not damned souls who found me when I was between life and death?" Ceri wasn't sure if that was better or worse. Probably worse. Everything was always worse.

Russell stood, still rubbing his temples. "I have a headache and can't think straight. I'll let you know after a nap and several Tylenol."

Ceri narrowed her eyes. He was playing them the same way he'd played the ghosts earlier. "You're messing with us," she accused. "What aren't you saying?"

Russell looked at her. "I am exhausted, Ceri. I do have a headache. And I don't know what to think. My mind keeps jumping to one conclusion, but it doesn't make sense to me."

"You might as well tell us now," Andy said. "That'll save me the trouble of making you do it later."

Russell blanched slightly, then looked at Ceri. "Your fallen angel is a little scary."

"Someone had to fill the space Morgana vacated when she started wearing pearls," Drew muttered.

"Fine." Russell sat down again. "I keep fixating on one thing, although I don't think it's much more likely than Ceri or Drew being responsible. If the killer is still alive as Paska said—and Laura's words could certainly be interpreted as a warning about the murderer as much as about Ceri's plan to destroy the town—she's recently arrived in Oracle Bay, and she brought the trophies and the ghosts with her."

eighteen

"We're not getting anywhere," Ceri muttered into her beer. She was taking Paska's advice—she was choosing to interpret it as advice, anyway—to walk the fine line between using alcohol to numb and overusing and having a third beer. "Two days of too many things, and we're in the same place we were before."

"That's not true," Andy said. "I might not have agreed with the way your friends managed things yesterday evening, but we know a lot more now than we did yesterday at the same time."

"I guess that's true. I had no idea I was about to pull the entire town into hell before I flip the calendar page again." Ceri nodded.

Drew tipped his chair back and balanced it against the wall. "I'm going to take off pretty soon if you're okay, Ceri. But I agree—there's so much we know, but it doesn't feel like enough. I want to *do* something." He tipped back his glass and finished the beer. "Something besides drinking three pints of beer at noon, that is."

"You young people are so impatient," Paska muttered. "We have two separate issues—now that we know the ghosts and the serial killer are intrinsically linked."

"Now that we *suspect* they're linked," Ceri corrected.

"What's more likely, girl? That the serials killer's victim's ghosts arrived in town around the same time the serial killer's trophies started appearing in your life? Or that the ghosts hitched in with either their jewelry or the woman who'd killed them?" Paska's tone was withering, and the look he directed at Ceri made her cringe. He didn't look angry. Just disappointed.

"Fine. Two issues. Two huge issues. Although, I guess if I suck the town into hell next week, the second one will be moot." Ceri took another drink of beer, then a gulp of water. "But why now? And why leave the jewelry?"

"Intimidation," Paska stated bluntly.

At the same time, Andy muttered, "She's threatening you. Trying to make you feel helpless before she...what did the note say?"

"Starts picking flowers," Paska supplied. "Which is obviously threatening to commit murders here—like you said, it's been twenty years."

"When we figure out how to fix everything and the day is saved, I'm going to give my liver a break for at least a month," Drew muttered, refilling his glass again.

"Can we damage our livers irreparably?" Ceri asked. She was trying to deal with the imminent threat—the second imminent threat—she'd brought to Oracle Bay, and right now, light-heartedness was the only way she knew how. She and Drew looked at Paska.

"So far, so good," he said. "Although I haven't had lab work done in a couple decades. I don't know what kinds of questions might arise, so I avoid it altogether. I have theories if you want them."

"You have theories about everything," Drew said.

"I've lived a very long time and had a lot of time to think." Paska shrugged. "Let's put the serial killer issue on the back burner for now. I want to hear what Andy's learned from his inquiries and how it meshes with what we learned last night. Your mind, Ceridwen, is the more pressing issue for us, even if the town wasn't at stake."

Andy glanced down at her. "I've been making calls to some old friends, and a couple are coming to town to see what they can do."

"What kind of friends?" Paska asked. "Fine feathered friends?"

Andy tilted his head and regarded Paska through narrowed eyes. "Are you mocking me?"

"Not at all!" Paska held his hands in front of him. "But if our seeing last night was correct—and it was—we're going to need an angel."

"Two, actually," Drew said. "Two columns of white light to save the town."

"I wonder if that means they have to still be committed to Her in their original angelic capacity, or if an angel who's stepped down from her service but not fallen will suffice. The friends coming to town are one of each." Andy looked at Drew with brows raised.

Drew shrugged. "I don't know. All I can tell you is that I saw twin columns of light reach into Ceri's brain."

Andy needed to know the rest of the vision. They might not have a future together, but even a present couldn't rest on lies for very long. "Tell him what happened next," she said softly.

Drew shot her a sharp look.

"What do you mean?" Andy asked. "What happened next?"

Drew kept his eyes on Ceri as he answered. "In the vision Misty and I shared, you, Ceri, and I were surrounded by flames wreathed in water. Ceri began to dissolve, but two pillars of white appeared and pulled her back into herself. They placed their hands on either side of head, pushed through her skull, and time stopped." He took a deep breath and looked at Andy. "Then her head exploded."

CERI PROPPED HER FEET ON ANDY'S DESK IN HIS OFFICE ON THE SECOND floor of the brewpub and tipped his chair back. She had a bodice-ripper—one she'd never read—a cup of chamomile, and one of Andy's soft, worn work shirts. The chair wasn't as comfortable as the one at home, but it was closer to Andy, and she needed that for both of them right now.

A crash vibrated the ceiling of the office, and she winced. He'd been on the roof for almost forty-five minutes, stomping around and occasionally smashing something large and heavy with a bellow of anger.

Drew and Paska had excused themselves almost immediately after Drew'd told Andy the rest of the vision. Andy'd started smoking, and the booth filled with the stench of sulphur. Ceri'd pulled Andy upstairs and away from the bar patrons, hoping that he'd be able to calm down. He was working on it, but not in the way Ceri'd hoped. Instead of joining her for some deep breathing meditation, he was breaking things and yelling incoherently.

So she tiptoed downstairs and grabbed some tea, then made herself comfortable with the book she'd found in his bottom desk drawer.

"Are you okay with this?" Andy yelled at her from the doorway.

Ceri grabbed a sticky note from his desk and tucked it into the book to mark her place. "Am I okay with a couple angels exploding my brain? Are you even serious with that question? Of course I'm not. I don't want to die, and I don't know how I could possibly live through a brain explosion. But I also know how prophecy works. It's not a straight-line destiny. What Drew and Misty saw was the most likely scenario with events as they are now. It doesn't account for changes or decisions made. It also isn't necessarily literal. After all, he saw the angels as bright columns of light, himself as a humanoid many-faceted quartz stone, and you as a figure of ash and fire. Maybe the explosion was the angels blowing up the rift in my mind to seal it?"

"I don't like it," he growled.

"I'm not asking you to support exploding my brain. I'm asking you to keep an open mind—not as open as mine, obviously—and be patient." Ceri leaned forward and reached out a hand.

He hesitated for a moment, then stepped forward and took it.

"My mind is that open, you know. I see everything you see all the time. But my brain was created to encompass it all. When you touch me without your guard up, I can see what you see, feel what you feel. The only difference between what you're experiencing and what I live with is the pain. I don't feel the same pain you do. For me, it just *is*."

"For me, it's unending horror. How can you live with that?" Ceri squeezed his hand and pulled him forward.

"The same way you live with your three hundred and seventy years. You have triumphs and failures and regrets. You let them go. They're still there, and when you focus in, they hurt. But overall, it's in the past and separate. It's the same for me. It's millennia of memories, and most move to the background with age and effort. Your mind just wasn't ready for an eternity to take root." He pulled her to her feet, spun them around, and sat, pulling her into his lap.

"I feel like my mind is exploding already," she said, leaning into his chest. "It might be a relief, actually. Especially if it saves everyone else."

Andy's body tensed under hers, and Ceri grimaced. That had not been the right thing to say to get him on board with welcoming the angels who may or may not be exploding her mind.

"I didn't mean..."

"It's okay. I've felt the weight of your pain through you, and I know how heavy it is. It's natural to want it to end." His pause went on long enough for Ceri to turn to look at him. He grimaced at her. "I don't want you to end, but I can't ask you to indefinitely push through the way you feel right now."

"Thank you." She leaned back against him and closed her eyes. She'd been spending altogether too much time in his lap in the last twenty-four hours, but she didn't have the strength to protest right now. Besides, it was nice. Comforting. Nothing more than that. Regardless of what she'd refused to admit to Drew earlier and what she was not going to admit to herself ever, the relationship she had with Andy would never be platonic. She wanted him too much for that to ever work. She might tell herself that last night had been a moment of weakness, a desire for closer connection. That she probably would've kissed any available person who'd ever shown even a modicum of attraction to her. But it wouldn't be true. It'd never been true. She wanted him as much now as she had the first time they'd fallen into bed—maybe more now.

"What are you thinking about?" Andy asked, absently stroking her hair. "Your pulse picked up just now."

"Stop listening to my blood," she retorted. "It's creepy."

"Well, when you put it that way, of course it is. But I wasn't listening. I can feel the vibrations of your heart throughout my entire body." He shifted slightly and grabbed the book she'd been reading. "Thinking about this book? There are more than a few scenes to bookmark in here."

Ceri's jaw dropped. "You've read it?"

"Why do you think it was in my desk? I don't keep romances around in case you show up to read them." Amusement laced his voice. He held the book in both hands, arms wrapped around her, and paged through it. "Want me to read a couple passages to you?"

"No. Stop it." She wiggled, and he released his hold. Ceri stood up and walked to the other side of the desk to sit in the extra chair. "Don't do that."

"Okay." He put the book down again and looked her in the eyes. "What do you want to do now?"

Ceri tried to hold his gaze, but her eyes kept dropping to his collarbones, the broadness of his shoulders, the way his t-shirt stretched across his chest, and the smattering of burn holes on his abdomen. She licked her lips and tried very hard not to think about what she wanted to do next. Even if she was willing to admit there were still unresolved feelings and mutual attraction between them, she knew what Drew and Misty had seen—she was going to die soon. It wasn't fair to give him hope now and break his heart in a few days.

"I didn't mean that." Heat roughened his voice, and answering flames kindled in her. "I was talking about the next steps for everything else. Finding the serial killer who's been stalking you, figuring out how the angels can save you without destroying you. Keeping you safe until we can make both of those things happen. What do you want to do?"

Ceri took a deep breath and focused on a point over his head and far away from the tense and release of his shoulders as he bent over and rummaged through his desk. "I don't know. I want it to all be over—I want to sit at home in my clawfoot tub full of bubbles and lavender bath salts reading a romance novel and drinking Champagne without worrying about whether I'm going to see a monster in the mirror or find antique jewelry in my purse. I want to reopen my shop and help people find what they're looking for. I want nice evenings out with my friends without something dire hanging over our heads. And I want to watch you do the opening number at karaoke next month."

Andy's head shot up sharply. "What was that?"

"I want to get through a couple months without murders or psychic interference from gods and monsters?" Ceri asked. Did he not know about Brandy's plans?

"I heard that one—although knowing the group of charlatans you hang out with, it seems unlikely you'll collectively be able to stay out of trouble that long. No, it was the one right after that. Something about singing. About me singing." A wisp of yellowish smoke rose into the air.

"It was nothing. Please don't start smoking again. I can't handle another sulphur-filled room," Ceri begged, clasping her hands in front of her and giving him her most wide-eyed, pleading look.

"I do not sing. Ever." He ducked back down, then made a victorious sound. He straightened and put a half dozen paperbacks on the desk in front of her. "I knew they were here somewhere. If you haven't read these, you can have them. I don't have a bathtub as nice as yours, but you're welcome to take these with you anytime. I've read them already."

Ceri sorted through the stack. Of the six, five were new to her. "Thank you. I might have to take a bath when we get home, just so I have an excuse to read one of these." If he wasn't going to entertain the idea of participating in karaoke, she'd let it go. For now, at least. There'd be plenty of time to jolly him into it later. If there was a later.

"Are you ready to go now? I don't have anything else to do today that I need to do here. The ordering I need to do for the brewery can be done at home. And it's a weeknight, so we're not expecting big crowds that'll need my help. Brandy and Zeke have everything well in line." Andy stood and looked down at her. "Or if you want to be alone, I can drop you off and come back here to finish my work."

"I'm ready to go any time, and wherever is easier for you to work is fine with me. I don't need to be alone in the house. Just the bathtub." Ceri grabbed the five books she hadn't read as well as the one she'd started while waiting for Andy.

"Does my temper bother you?" Andy asked.

The change of subject was abrupt enough to make her do a mental U-turn. "What?"

"You said you didn't want the smell of sulphur in here, that you'd had enough of it. It happens when I'm angry, so I wondered if it meant you'd had enough of my temper." Andy was very carefully not meeting her eyes, and the space between his brows was tight.

Ceri thought carefully about what she wanted to say. This wasn't a good time to get the words wrong, but the silence was stretching out too long, and his face was getting more and more pinched. "I am wary of men who can't hold their tempers. Everyone gets angry, and it's unfortunate that your anger comes with an olfactory accompaniment, but there's nothing wrong with that." She paused and considered whether she should even say anything further.

"But?" he prompted. "I can see you have more to say."

She gritted her teeth and pushed ahead. "But when anger turns into aggression, it bothers me. You occasionally react to anger by becoming too possessive or controlling or the way you did earlier—stomping around and smashing things. I don't like that. I wouldn't say it frightens me, but it makes my adrenaline surge. Everyone loses it occasionally—I've indulged in my fair share of crockery-breaking tantrums. It's when it happens often enough to become a noticeable pattern instead of a surprising anomaly."

Andy nodded slowly. "And my temper is a pattern."

Ceri smiled at him gently. "A bit. You keep extra shirts everywhere in case you burn through what you're wearing. Morgana is going to invoice you for damaging her counters and her drapes. Why do you think Drew didn't want to tell you about the rest of his vision?"

"Are you afraid of me? Is that why you ended things?" He finally looked up at her, and the desperate hurt in his eyes made her choke on her inhalation.

"I'm not afraid of you, Andy." She stepped around the desk and took his hand. "I worry about your reaction to things I know you won't like. I hate weighing whether to tell you something against the probability that you'll lose your temper and burn a hole in the sofa. But that's not why I ended things."

"Why, then? You like me, you're attracted to me, and we enjoy each other's company. Why did you walk away?"

"I don't do long-term. I told you that from the beginning. It's not who I am, and it's not who I want to be. I'm not interested in relationships, especially not with men. I don't usually get involved with people I have to see every day, either. It just complicates things." Ceri dropped his hand and picked up the books. "Will you take me home, please?"

Andy laughed roughly and ran his hand through his silvery white hair. "Complicated just scratches the surface. When was the last time you were in a relationship?"

Ceri pinched her lips together and walked into the hallway. She didn't mind that she hadn't spent longer than a couple months with any one person in over three hundred years, but other people were not so sanguine about her long and storied history as a single lady.

"What? Fifty years? A hundred?" Andy pushed open the back

door leading to the employee parking lot and held it while she walked through with her stack of books.

Ceri waited for him to unlock his car, then climbed in and buckled her seatbelt.

Andy got behind the wheel and started the engine. "I'm dropping it now. You clearly don't want to talk about it, and it's none of my business. It makes me feel a little better about myself, though." He looked at her with a broad grin before glancing behind the car and pulling onto Main Street. "I might be vastly superior to every other man you've spent time with, but at least none of them succeeded where I failed."

Ceri rolled her eyes, and a grin snuck out from between her tightly pursed lips.

"What do you want for dinner tonight? I can grab something from the Pour House kitchen later, or we could go out. I haven't had fish and chips in a while, and the Codfather just reopened for the season." Andy turned left down the small residential street that led to his house and pulled into the driveway.

"Fish and chips sounds good. I was also thinking it might be nice to go to the Sleeping Inn for dinner. I need crab cakes in my life as soon as possible." Ceri opened the door and breathed a sigh of relief that he wasn't going to ask more relationship questions. At least not now.

"Why don't we do the Codfather tomorrow for lunch, and the Sleeping Inn tonight?" Andy suggested. "Unless you have lunch plans tomorrow already."

"I do," she said. "I'm having fish and chips with a friend, then we're going to walk down Main Street and see if the new owner has a reopening date for Title Wave yet."

"I'm more interested in the other side of their business. A cocktail bar is exactly what Oracle Bay needs so people can stop telling me to serve cocktails." Andy snorted. "I have beer. I have wine—although not as much as I used to since the wine store is closed; I hope someone takes over that space soon. And I have hard liquor, various mixers, and the desire to serve zero drinks that require shaking or stirring or garnishing."

"You're missing the valuable market of people who just need a martini from time to time," Ceri said.

"I'm really not missing anything," Andy said as he unlocked the house and opened the door for her. "Are you going to take a bath?"

Ceri pulled her phone out of her pocket and looked at the time. "It's only three. What time do you want to leave for dinner?" She winced inside at how very domestic that sounded.

"Seven? I have a couple hours of work to do and need a shower before we head out again." He kicked his shoes off and set them on the rack by the front door.

"Perfect. Unless you need something out of the upstairs bathroom, I'm heading up to immerse myself in the hottest bath I can manage." Ceri looked at him expectantly, and he shook his head.

"It's all yours. Although if you wanted that glass of bubbles to go with your bubble bath, I can bring that up in a little while? I promise not to look when I hand it over." His grin was mischievous, and she shook her head at him.

"I'm not sure you're trustworthy," she said severely.

"Add extra bubbles to your bath, then I won't be able to see anything, even if I'm tempted to peek."

"I'd love a glass of bubbles, but if there's nothing cold, don't go to any trouble on my account." Ceri grabbed the book she'd been reading earlier and set the rest down.

"Your account is never any trouble. I'll be up in about twenty minutes with your drink." He bowed, then walked into the kitchen.

Ceri walked upstairs, stripped, grabbed a towel, and turned on the water.

The Sleeping Inn's dining room lights dimmed, blanketing the space in an intimate atmosphere.

"I wonder if Russell will come back to work here," Ceri said as they waited to put in their drink orders. "Oh! I can't believe I let him get away with that!"

"I'm not following," Andy said, not looking up from his perusal of the menu.

"Russell said karaoke was the second-best decision Brandy had ever made," Ceri said.

"I am not singing."

"No, this is about something else—this time anyway. Third on the list was the food menu she added. Which I would've put first, but it wasn't my list." Ceri paused when one of the bartenders came to take their drink order. The Sleeping Inn might not be a cocktail bar, but they did alright in that department. She ordered a greyhound, and Andy requested a Hendricks martini with a twist.

"I'll put these orders in. Your server will be back with your drinks in a few minutes. In the meantime, here are a couple menus to glance at." He tipped an imaginary hat at them and sauntered away.

Ceri raised her eyebrows at him. "A martini seems awfully fancy for someone who doesn't want a cocktail menu at his bar."

"I didn't say I didn't enjoy drinks that require a bit more work—just that I don't want them on my menu." He returned to his examination of the menu. "What was the best decision Brandy ever made, according to Russell?"

"That's just it! I don't know. We got sidetracked before we could ask, and he didn't volunteer it. Now that I've remembered, it's going to drive me bananas until I see him again. Maybe I should text him." Ceri reached into her purse for her phone, then withdrew her hand before grabbing it. "Or maybe I'll just wait until I see him again. I don't want to be weird. I don't know him very well, and he did just get back to town and have to perform an emergency seance. He probably needs a nap and a martini before getting text-bombed by the weird, haunted woman."

Andy shook his head at her, then moved his menu aside for his martini.

"Are you ready to order?" The server's voice was husky and rich and oddly familiar.

Ceri examined the server—trying to be surreptitious—while Andy ordered. She didn't look familiar, but there was something there. She was a white woman with a strong face that was almost severe, black hair that was pulled back tightly into a low bun at her nape, and brown eyes so dark that there was no real line between her iris and pupil. And she was wearing all black. It wasn't a hoodie and jeans, but...

"And for you?" the server asked, interrupting Ceri's examination.

"Do we know each other? I feel like I've seen you before." She wasn't sure how to ask explicitly if the server was the woman in black she'd seen all over town for the last couple weeks.

The server shrugged and glanced down at her order pad. "I don't think so, ma'am. I'd remember your hair. Besides, I just got to town a couple weeks ago. I'm staying with my aunt."

Ceri pursed her lips and steadfastly ignored the ma'am. It was a term of respect and not a commentary about her age. She smiled up at the person she couldn't quite place and ordered. "I'll have the crab cakes and the spring salad, please. And a glass of something white. Do you have any recommendations?" Ceri perused the wine list, looking for local makers.

"I haven't tried everyone on here yet, but the chardonnay we have by the glass is really delightful and should pair with the crab. It's from Cairdeas Winery in eastern Washington near Lake Chelan. Their winemaker is superb, although I heard she's leaving them to start out on her own." The server's face lit up, and Ceri smiled and leaned forward. She loved watching people talk about things they were passionate about.

"I'll have that, then! If it generates that much excitement, it must be good." Ceri handed her menu to the server.

"Why don't we get a bottle?" Andy said. "I'm in the mood for a little wine tonight, too. Thank you."

Ceri turned her attention to Andy and gave up trying to place the server's face—she probably just looked vaguely like someone she'd met at some point in the last three hundred years. She was too young for it to be a long-lost acquaintance, and if she was the hoodie-wearing woman, maybe Ceri had caught a glimpse of her face at some point. "Wine? I'm appalled, sir. How are you going to show your face in the brewery tomorrow?"

Andy grinned at her and drained his martini. "If you don't tell anyone, there doesn't have to be any shame at all. We can make this our little secret."

Ceri laughed. "So many secrets in Oracle Bay."

"There are, you know. Gossips might think they have the upper hand, but how many people know that the weirdness in January was a wine god stirring up mischief and not just the murders? Or that the secret to the amazingness of McEwen's farm is because he had a goddess hiding in his immortal goat? There are a lot of things that stay hidden here." Andy reached across the table and brushed her forearm with his long fingers. "It's probably true, however, that everyone in town knows your secret."

Ceri's skin was burning where Andy touched her, but it wasn't from hellfire. Things were getting out of hand if a casual touch like this was enough to stoke the flames. "And what secret is that?" she asked a lot more flirtatiously than she'd intended.

"That you're the kindest, most insightful woman in town. That you're too selfless by far. And that you have the most amazing dimple just above your left—"

Ceri's face was flaming, and she snatched her hand away from him. "Andy, you are the worst," she hissed under her breath. "And no one knows about any dimples anywhere on my anatomy." Her embarrassment didn't bank the fires his touch had ignited, though, and she put her hand back on the table.

Andy looked at her, down at her hand, and then straight into her eyes. He took her hand in his, but didn't close his fingers, as if he was waiting for permission or a rebuke.

Ceri didn't know what she was doing, but the tightrope on which she'd been balancing since the Autumn Bazaar was wobbling, and she had to decide which way to fall. And she was definitely falling fast. She closed her fingers over his hand. A bubble of panic rose in her chest, so she gulped down the rest of her cocktail to push it back.

"What are you doing?" Andy asked. "I don't want to walk back through the door you slammed in my face if you're going to throw me out again when you don't need me anymore. Sometimes I feel like there's still this connection between us—more than what I forced on you last fall. But other times, it's like you meant every word when you told me we'd never be anything more than friends."

Ceri didn't know how to reply, so instead, she squeezed his hand gently and smiled at him. "I don't know. Everything is so weird. I feel like time is simultaneously running forward out of control and plodding through molasses. I don't know what I feel right now, other than grateful you're here with me. Not at the restaurant." She paused and took a breath. She hadn't planned on talking about her feelings tonight. It was just supposed to be dinner with a friend. "And maybe something a little more than gratitude. I don't know."

The server set down two glasses and pulled the cork out of the bottle. She poured a little in each glass and waited for them to approve the wine.

"Oh, this is good!" Ceri said. "It's rich and full without being too oaky. There are times I want some oaky Chard, but not with my crab cakes. Thank you so much for this recommendation. And I'm sorry, I didn't get your name?"

The server finished the pours and set down the bottle. "I'm Joanna. It's only my second day, so I'm glad you liked my recommendation." Her smile lit up her face and turned her severe features into something breathtaking.

"You said you were staying with your aunt?" Ceri asked, trying to find the end of the string that was niggling at her recall. In her periphery, she saw Andy open his mouth, then close it again. She knew he'd been about to reel her back in from the third degree she was about to give Joanna. He might not have said it—which was good, because then she'd have been mad—but he was right.

"I am so sorry, Joanna," Ceri said. "I am being nosy and obnoxious. I try not to be a bad customer and didn't do a great job on that today. Thank you for the wine, and I hope you love it here."

Joanna exhaled deeply, and Ceri recognized it as relief. She really had been out of line.

"Your food will be out soon. In the meantime, enjoy your wine. If you need anything else, just give me a wave." Joanna's smile had tightened, and tension was vibrating in her jaw as she walked away.

When she was out of earshot, Ceri said, "I cannot believe I was quizzing her like that. Maybe I've lived here too long and am turning into one of the gossipy old ladies that are in every BBC murder mystery show. Thanks for letting me know."

"I didn't say anything. And I can't say I'm not as curious as you. She doesn't ring any bells for me, but if you think you know her, I'm curious." Andy let go of her hand and took a drink of the wine.

When he didn't return his hand to hers, she dropped it into her lap. "I think she's the woman in the black hoodie I've been seeing around town. Maybe she was scoping out all the businesses looking for a job or something. And you might not have said anything, but you wanted to. I'm glad you didn't, but your expression pulled me up short. Maybe the gossip mill in town isn't running as well since Martha died. She was the one who knew everything and delighted in sharing it."

"Of course, she got a lot of her gossip by illegally bugging people's homes and businesses, and then she was murdered," Andy said. "So please don't try to fill those shoes. You charlatans are scary enough without eavesdropping."

"I might be a sideshow huckster, but at least I've never been kicked out of hell." She stuck her tongue out at him.

"Pretty sure that risen demon is about the best thing there is. I was kicked out of hell for being too good for that world." Andy crossed his arms over his chest. He tipped his head back a little and looked at her down his long, perfect nose.

"Okay, demon. If you say so." Ceri took another sip of her wine, then moved the glass out of the way for Joanna to set down her crab cakes and salad and Andy's braised rabbit with spring vegetables.

Once Joanna was out of earshot, Ceri leaned forward and looked at Andy's food. "That looks amazing. I'm almost regretting my order now."

Andy took a bite of the rabbit and smiled. "There are a lot of benefits to not living in either heaven or hell, but top of the list has to be the food and drink. This is amazing." He put another bite on his fork and pointed it at her. "Want some?"

Ceri leaned forward and took a bite, never letting her eyes leave his. She leaned back and licked her lips. His eyes followed the movement of her tongue, and she thought she saw a flash of yellow-orange flame. "That is really good. The crab cakes have a lot to live up to now."

"I'm going to expect a bite in return, you know," Andy murmured.

"Of course. We must be fair." Ceri stabbed a generous portion of lightly fried crab onto her fork. "Oh my god, this is so good. It melts in my mouth." She loaded up her fork again and held it across the table.

Andy circled her wrist with one hand to hold her steady and took the bite she offered him. "That is really good. It's been a long time since I tasted anything that delicious." He let go of her wrist and leaned back. And he smoldered.

Ceri hadn't been aware that people could do that in real life, but Andy was definitely smoldering. And his smolder was catching parts of her aflame. The man was a fire hazard and should come with a warning label.

The rest of the meal was playful banter interspersed with heated glances and casually intense brushes of skin against skin.

By the time they were getting ready to leave, Ceri's skin felt too tight and the thoughts swirling in her head were less about the hell she saw in her nightmares and what would happen when the angels came for her mind, and more about whether Andy could make her see god tonight.

"Ready?" he asked. He stood and held out his hand.

"I don't know," Ceri replied. She wanted the inevitable next part of the evening—she wanted *him*—but did she want the after? If she tore down the remaining barriers between them and fell back into his bed in the figurative sense, it'd be hard to walk away again. She didn't want to hurt him, and even more, she didn't want to hurt herself. Romance was fine for a while, but it was only a thin candy shell, and there was usually nothing underneath. But wow, did she want him. She put her hand in his and let him pull her up.

He didn't step back as she stood. They stood facing each other with barely enough room between them for the holy ghost, should the spirit take time out of chaperoning middle school dances to check on two very old people. The heat of his body permeated her clothes and warmed her skin.

"If you're not ready, we'll slow down. I don't want to lose you because I put my libido over your comfort." Andy's arm slid around her waist, then dropped to grab her purse from where it hung on the back of the chair. "But never mind that now. We have to get out of here right now."

Ceri tipped her head up at him in confusion. "What? Why?"

"It's too late," he sighed as his eyes went from heated to resigned.

"Little premature or something tonight?" she teased as she tried to figure out what the issue was.

"That would be so much better than what's about to happen." His teeth were clenched, and the tendon in his jaw vibrated.

Ceri watched him take a deep breath and exhale. The tension and apprehension sloughed off his body with the force of his exhalation. One more deep breath in and out, and the mask he wore most of the time fell into place. He grinned—it was genuine looking, if not warm —and turned around, dropping his arm from around her waist.

"Boss! It's so funny to see you here! I mean, not that it's funny ha-ha. But it's weird to see you somewhere besides the Pour House. Of course, I know you don't live there and you must eat sometimes, but isn't it cool that we ran into each other? I saw Ceri at the coffee shop, and now you're both here!" Felicity's bright tones crashed into them, and Ceri took half a step back from the force.

"Hello, Felicity," Andy said. "We were just on our way out. It was lovely to run into you."

"Don't let me push you out the door! Why don't I buy you a drink while I wait for my niece to get off work?" Felicity grabbed Andy's arm in an attempt to tug him towards the bar.

"Joanna!" Ceri said, snapping her fingers. "That's why she looked so familiar. She has your eyes, and her voice is just a huskier version of yours."

"You met my niece? Isn't she the bees' knees?" Felicity exclaimed.

Ceri smiled at the woman and wondered if she knew her cheer

pushed a lot of people away. "We'd love to, but like Andy said, we're on our way out. Have a nice evening. Please tell Joanna she was a fabulous server, and we hope she loves our little town."

"Oh, I will!" Felicity beamed at them, and Ceri realized she was going to keep beaming until she and Andy walked away.

Ceri turned, pulling Andy with her, and waved over her shoulder. "Bye! See you later!"

Once they were out in the cool spring air, she relaxed. "I know she's just a cheerful person, but it grates on me."

"I have never wanted to fire someone for being too happy, but she is exuberant." Andy's voice was clipped with none of the earlier playful heat they'd generated.

"I think she's just...happy. It gives me the heebie-jeebies, but some people are just..." Ceri shook her head, then shuddered. "Cheerful."

Andy laughed and held out his arm. When she looked at him, his mask had once more fallen away. "Let's get out of here. We can figure out what comes next when we're far away from Felicity and have locked all the doors and windows."

She slipped under the arm he held out and pressed herself into his side. She might not know what she was doing, but she knew what she wanted. And right now, all she wanted was him.

The front door closed behind them. Andy slid the deadbolt home, kicked off his shoes, and looked down at her.

Ceri saw the question written on his face and knew there'd be no walking back from where she was about to go. She slung the handle of her purse on the hook near the door, toed off her flats, and hung her jacket next to the purse. Then she took a step back, away from Andy. She saw the moment he thought she was distancing herself from him. A flash of hurt so quick she wouldn't have seen it if she'd not been staring at his face. She didn't want the hurt to last any longer than it already had. She crossed her arms, grabbed the hem of her shirt, and pulled it over her head, then tossed it on the ground. Her jeans were next, but her hands were too shaky to unbutton the fly.

"I don't know why I'm so nervous," she said. "It's not like I haven't done this with you before."

Andy's flash of hurt had morphed into an expression of shock—wide eyed and perfectly still—but his hands were shaking almost as much as hers. "Maybe it's because..." His voice was rough. He cleared his throat and started again. "Maybe it's because it's been a while since we've been so free like this, or because it feels like more now than it did then."

Ceri nodded vigorously and gave up on unbuttoning her jeans. "Although I'm stuck in my trousers, so I guess this is all we have tonight."

Andy made the growling noise he always did when he was aroused. He stepped forward and pulled her into his arms, running his hands along the bare skin of her torso, then sliding up to cup her breasts. "You're not wearing a bra."

"I don't like them that much, and generally no one can tell when I'm not. Besides, I wanted to see the look on your face when you realized." She grinned up at him, then gasped when he pinched her lightly. "And I'm still wearing these jeans. A little help, maybe?"

"I think we can find a way to get those off." Andy's hands didn't make the downward journey to help with her button. He seemed preoccupied with the bare skin on the upper half of her body. "If you're sure this is what you want."

Ceri took a deep breath. She'd been dancing around it all evening with him, and a little with herself even when she realized how much she cared for him. But now she had to stop dancing, stand in front of him, and lay herself bare. "I've walked away from so much in my life in the name of independence and keeping my heart whole. It's never been a very difficult decision. Until now." She took a half step back so she could get his shirt off, too.

Once his chest was as bare as hers, she pressed herself against him, wrapped her arms around his neck, twining her fingers in his short, silver hair, and pulled his head down for a kiss.

It started slowly enough. They explored each other's mouths leisurely, taking their time the way they hadn't last night. But the languor didn't last. Ceri hooked one leg around his hip in an effort to get closer. It was the kind of move you could only pull with someone who you were familiar with.

Andy reached around to steady her and hold her against him, then lifted her into his arms and walked forward until her back hit the wall.

"We should go upstairs," he murmured against her mouth

"Boring," she replied, raking her fingernails along his back. She could feel the faint ridges of skin where his wings were when he made them appear, and she knew the effect that would have on him. She held on to him while his wings sprang forward and a slivery light illuminated the room.

"Maybe boring, but the things I have in mind for tonight need a large area to work in and a comfortable place for you to lie down." He dropped her legs and set her down.

Ceri's knees wobbled a moment before she steadied herself. She reached out and ran a single finger along the edge of one of his feathers, just to watch him shudder in pleasure. "Fine. This time. But only because I need to brush my teeth."

"I'll meet you upstairs in two minutes, and you'd better have found a way to out of those jeans before I get there." He fixed a stern look on his face and shook his finger at her. "Or else."

"Or else what?" Ceri widened her eyes in mock innocence and twirled a long strand of red hair around her index finger.

"Or else you'll need to be punished." The wicked glint in his eyes sent anticipatory shivers down her spine.

"Gasp! Oh no! I hope it doesn't come to that!" She grinned, pulled him close for one last kiss, and ran upstairs. "Don't take too long! I don't want to have to start without you!"

As soon as she was in the Andy's room, she managed to unbutton her jeans and peel them off. Her underwear followed. She walked into the bathroom.

She washed her hands and splashed a little cold water onto her face and wished desperately for a mirror so she could see how she looked. She walked out into the middle of the bedroom and eyed the huge bed that took up most of one side of the room. His room looked less cluttered now that she'd stowed most of her things in the spare room. And that reminded her...

Ceri cocked her head but didn't hear Andy coming up the stairs yet. She had just enough time to find it. She headed into the spare room and opened the top drawer in the bureau to dig the lacy teddy she'd shoved back there just in case she had occasion to wear it. Instead of the scrap of lavender silk and lace she was expecting to see, there was a bracelet with a chain of diamond daisies with golden pearl centers and emerald leaves between each flower. She'd bought it for herself a few years ago—daisies were her favorite. But she hadn't been able to find it on her last trip home to pack more stuff to bring here. Underneath the bracelet she thought she'd lost was a knife, although knife seemed too innocuous a word for what she was seeing. The polished wooden handle held a foot-long serrated blade. It was covered in dried blood that had flaked off a little in the drawer.

She couldn't take her eyes off it. She'd never seen the knife before, but she knew instantly what it was. Every single victim of the ruby rose killer had been dismembered by a serrated blade. And although this piece of jewelry wasn't from one of the victims, Ceri didn't need to call on her past as a private investigator to make the connection. Whoever was doing this had either skipped the last three victims on their way to the grand finale, or she hadn't found them all. Her stomach clenched and nausea roiled through her at the thought of coming across three more grisly reminders that she was being stalked by a hundred-year-old serial killer and the sudden fear that real murders would start now that the symbolic ones were over.

She was frozen in place. Cold sweat had sprung onto her brow, and her vision swam. Her mind was racing, unable to slow down, to think, to let go of the scream bubbling in her throat.

Andy's footsteps sounded on the stairs. "Ready or not, here I come!"

Ceri giggled at the entendre, but her laughter dissolved into hysterical sobs.

Andy's footsteps quickened, and in seconds, he was in the doorway. "Ceri, we don't have to do this if you don't want to, if you're not ready." He stepped forward and set down two whiskey glasses half full of deep amber liquid. His gaze snagged on the drawer she was staring into.

"That's my bracelet," she whispered. "I thought I'd lost it."

Flames erupted from him, and the stink of sulphur filled the air. He slammed the drawer shut, picked her up, grabbed the whiskey, carried her across the hall.

She sat on the edge of the bed wrapped in the blanket he'd draped around her shoulders and sipping on the fiery liquid. Her sobs had finally quieted, and now they were mere hiccups between sips.

Andy was pacing back and forth, sparks flying with each step. He hadn't said a word since he'd picked her up and carried her out of the room. He stopped, looked down at her, and said, "I'll be back in a second. I'm just going to get you some clothes."

"I don't want them," Ceri said. "I don't want anything from in there. What if whoever is doing this touched them? Touched my stuff? I can't." She started shaking again.

Andy knelt beside her, took the glass of whiskey, and pulled her into his arms. "Shhh... It's okay. Of course you don't want any of those things. There's a pair of your yoga pants in my bottom drawer—they got mixed in with the laundry. And your t-shirt you had on earlier is still downstairs. Let's get you dressed and get out of here."

"Where will we go?" Ceri asked, scrubbing a hand across her tear-stained face. "I don't want to go to my house. What if..."

"We are not going to your house," Andy said. "First, we are going to the Pour House because it's a public place, it's *my* public place, and from there, we'll figure out what we're going to do next."

Andy grabbed her yoga pants from the bottom drawer, handed them to her, then pulled out a duffel bag. He packed a few t-shirts, grabbed their toiletries from the bathroom, and then aimed a kick at the wall so hard it splintered the drywall.

"Are you okay?" Ceri asked, looking at his bare foot now covered in plaster.

He took a deep breath, and the sparks disappeared. "I'm sorry. I shouldn't have lost my temper like I did tonight. I don't understand why no one saw this coming or how to prevent it."

Ceri stood and let the blanket slide back down onto the bed. She had to think, had to explain. It was the only way to keep fear from overwhelming her. "There's a lot going on at any given time. The possibility of the entire town getting sucked into hell is big enough to overwhelm anything else that might come up. Add to that how screwed up my aura is, and it's no wonder no one can see anything else that's going on with me. And it's not like anyone wants to look into you. Unless you want an entire group of oracles in your bed every night." Her voice had barely wavered. Three centuries of perfecting dissociation was really coming in handy; she almost felt clinically detached from everything.

Ceri took his hand and pulled him close. "Can we get out of here?"

He held onto her tightly for a moment, then let her go. "Let's do that before I accidentally burn the house and all the evidence down."

He carried her down the stairs despite her protests that she was capable of walking the distance herself. While she found her shirt and put it back on, he grabbed her purse and walked into the kitchen. She was about to protest when she realized what he was doing, and a wave of gratitude washed over her, pushing the tears back into her eyes and making her sag onto the couch.

Andy returned from the kitchen with her phone and the slim wallet that held her driver's license and a single credit card in his hands, and a grim line slashed across his face. "I texted Paska. He'll come over and pick up everything and do a sweep of the house to make sure there's nothing else. There are seven, right?"

Ceri nodded. "But I've only had four delivered."

"Five," he corrected with a hard set to his jaw. "And based on what is upstairs, I think there are a couple others that haven't been found yet. That felt final."

"Will you check my jacket pockets?" she asked softly.

Andy nodded, dropped the duffel bag, and reached into the pockets. He picked her jacket up off the hook and handed it to her. "Nothing here. I don't want to get in either of our cars tonight, so I'll carry you to the Pour House."

Ceri started to protest, then thought better of it. She was exhausted—physically and mentally—and didn't want to walk the mile in the dark right now. It didn't matter who saw her being carried. The whole town knew she was living with him, although most didn't know why.

She followed him outside and stood numbly, waiting for him to pick her up. Instead, he handed her his shirt and the bag. "What?" she asked, staring down at the shirt she just realized he hadn't put back on yet.

She looked up at him. His wings were spread wide and fluttering a bit, stirring up what little dust there was from the two days of dry weather they'd had.

"We're not going to walk," he said tersely. "We're too vulnerable on the ground. Besides, what's the point of these magnificent wings if I don't take every chance I get to carry my favorite human around?"

Ceri smiled wanly and walked into his arms. He scooped her up, and she wrapped her arms around his neck, burying her face in his chest in anticipation of the quick launch into the sky she was now strangely used to.

A bright light exploded around them, and Andy jumped back several paces.

Ceri dropped the duffel bag and curled into an even tighter ball in Andy's arms.

"FEAR NOT!" a voice boomed, reverberating in her brain and body like the sky had turned the bass up too high. "I COME IN PEACE AND WITH GOOD NEWS!"

Andy's body tensed around her, then relaxed minutely.

"Barachiel," he said flatly. "Your timing leaves something to be desired."

"By my clock, I'm right on time," the angel said cheerfully. "You're going to want to take a few steps up and brace yourself."

"For what?" Ceri asked, not looking towards the still-blazing light.

The earth jolted, knocking Andy forward and onto his knees.

twenty-one

The ground stopped moving after what felt like hours but was more likely less than a couple minutes. The town had gone dark. The only visible lights were the lighthouse in the distance and the incandescent angel in front of her.

He was glowing, almost too brightly to look at. His features were soft behind the unearthly light, but she recognized him from his last visit.

Andy set Ceri on her feet and flexed his shoulders. "You'd better have an excellent reason for that entrance," he snarled at Barachiel.

"I've wanted to do that for a long time," the angel said with a delighted grin on his face. "I never get to say 'FEAR NOT' anymore. It was one of the most enjoyable things about living in a time when we randomly showed up at births and deaths and events that would one day have historic significance. Now, I'm not supposed to appear in a column of light with my wings out anymore. Sigh." He sighed loudly with his last word.

Ceri felt some of the tension drain from her body and numbness replace the shock. She could feel herself shutting down. "That wasn't good news," she accused.

The angel shrugged. "It was. The good news was that I am here."

A klaxon blared, breaking the silence of the night.

"What's that?" Barachiel asked, turning around and bumping into Ceri with his wings. She felt him shudder, and his wings folded up and disappeared before she could blink.

"Tsunami alert," Ceri said, pulling out her phone. "I'm going to text the others, but we should probably get to higher ground."

"No need to worry," Barachiel said. "There will not be a tsunami tonight. The earthquake was the only portent scheduled for today. Were you two going somewhere? Can I come?"

Being in Barachiel's presence was a little like being buffeted by an actual tsunami. The ground had washed out beneath her, and she was sputtering for air.

"We were going to the Pour House," Andy said, his voice still terse. "And I suspect there'll be a lot of clean-up to do, both there and around town."

"At least we know no mirrors fell off the wall and broke in the house!" Ceri said.

Andy slipped an arm around her and pulled her in close. "Silver lining," he agreed before looking back at Barachiel. "If you dim your light, you can come with us, although I don't know how exciting things will be with a bunch of broken glass and no electricity."

"I'll take care of it," Barachiel said. "See you at the bar!"

Ceri watched his wings flare out as he launched himself into the sky. "He's going to take care of what?" she asked.

Andy grabbed the duffel bag from where it'd hit the ground and picked Ceri up. "Possibly the town's power outage. Probably the mess in the bar, although with Barachiel, it's hard to say. One of his primary purposes in life is to bring joy to people, although he includes himself near the top of that list, and what brings him joy can go in a number of different ways." He followed Barachiel into the sky, although at a much slower pace.

· · · · · ★ ★ ★ ★ ★ · · · ·

ANDY LANDED ON THE ROAD JUST AROUND THE BEND FROM THE POUR HOUSE and out of sight. The bar was dark when they arrived, and several dozen people were loitering outside. Most were on their phones, scrolling through news and social media sites and announcing updates as they came in.

Brandy and Zeke were in front of the door. Ceri couldn't read the expression on Brandy's face—she was either extremely angry or really freaked out. Ceri was positive that the latter feeling would cause the former, though. Brandy loathed not having control of every situation.

Zeke was leaning against the door, looking as placid as ever. Ceri didn't really get him, and since he showed very little interest in being part of the group, she usually didn't try. Now she wondered if he would've been able to steer them in the right direction a little faster, what with his connections to the god who cast her disobedient children into the hell that was now trying to claim Ceri, and with her, the entirety of Oracle Bay.

"Everything okay?" Andy asked when they were in easy conversational distance.

"Other than the giant freaking earthquake knocking out power and breaking who knows how many bottles and glasses? Peachy." Brandy glowered at nothing in particular.

A flash of light came from inside the bar, briefly illuminating the parking lot.

"What was that?" Brandy demanded. "If there's someone in there right now, I will haul them out and tie them to the bottom of the pier during the next low tide. Right over the most barnacled portion."

Ceri blinked. She'd never heard Brandy lose her temper before, and if she'd been a demon, she'd have sulphur smoke rising from her.

Zeke put a hand on her shoulder. "It's fine. Nothing to worry about."

Brandy turned her glare on him, but under his unwavering certainty, her anger lessened. A little.

The streetlights blinked three times, then came on and held steady.

A cheer rose from the small crowd in the parking lot as Main Street lit up again.

Andy walked forward and raised his voice a little. "Looks like we missed out on the big one again! I'm going to head inside and look around to make sure it's safe in there, but once I give you the all clear, you're welcome to come back in. You can grab your stuff and head home if you'd like, but if you decide to stick around, the first round is on the house."

The cheer for free drinks was considerably louder than the one for the restoration of electricity.

"Brandy, why don't you hold the door? Zeke, Ceri, come on in with me." Andy pulled open the door and ignored Brandy's protests. "You're staying out here because you're scarier than Zeke and can keep the crowd back until I say it's safe."

Ceri followed Andy through the door, then gasped. The room was spotless. No broken glass, no spilled drinks. The wooden floor gleamed, and the bar glowed in the warm light of... "Have you always had chandeliers?"

Andy sighed. "This is why Brandy got to stay outside. Barachiel! I think you got a little carried away. The chandeliers need to go."

The angel walked into the middle of the room. His expression looked suspiciously like the beginning of a pout. "The lights you had in here before weren't as pretty, and they weren't bright enough."

"They weren't supposed to be bright. It's a bar." Andy crossed his arms.

"Ugh. Fine." Barachiel snapped his fingers, and the chandeliers disappeared. "Anything else you'd like to complain about?"

Andy looked around, and apparently satisfied with what he saw, nodded. "Looks good. Thank you, Barachiel."

The angel beamed.

"You might want to dim yourself, too," Zeke said laconically. "The humans will be coming in soon."

Barachiel huffed, then blinked off.

Ceri closed her eyes, saw the red afterimage on her eyelids, and waited until it was barely visible before opening them again.

Barachiel stood in front of them, looking almost like a regular, mundane human being. He was wearing dark jeans, a tight pink t-shirt, flip-flops, and a beret.

"Um." She looked at him, then at Andy. She had no idea how to criticize an angel's fashion sense. "Nice clothes?"

He beamed at her, and the rest of the tension from the evening melted away. He was so beautiful, so warm. She never wanted him to stop smiling at her.

"Knock it off," Andy said.

"I was just taking the edge off her tension. If she'd tightened up any further, she was going to pull a muscle." Barachiel dialed back his smile.

The almost overwhelming peace she'd felt rolled back but didn't disappear completely.

"I almost forgot," Barachiel said, reaching into his pocket. "I found this on the floor near that back alcove area." He held something out, but Andy snatched it from his hand and shoved it into his own pocket before Ceri saw what it was.

From the look he gave her, the look that made her feel like he was making sure she was still here, still safe, Ceri knew what it was. "Six," she said.

He took his hand and looked around. "I think we can let the people back in. Hopefully no one will wonder why it's cleaner after the earthquake than before."

"We can get them all very drunk and make them hazy," Zeke suggested.

"I don't think that'll work on Brandy, though. Even if she agreed to drink on the job, and even if we could pour enough beer into her to get her that drunk, I don't think she'd forget." Andy let go of Ceri's hand. "I'll let her know she can get back to work, although I think we'll close tomorrow so everyone can have a day off."

Andy went outside, and Ceri stared after him. She was still numb from the events of the evening. Her emotions had ping-ponged all over, and she wasn't sure how much longer she'd be upright. If anything else happened, any more stressors appeared, she was going to scream.

The bar's customers streamed back in, and almost everyone stayed for their free beer and loud, boisterous conversations about the second earthquake that year—and how unusual that was.

Ceri made her way to the back alcove and tucked herself away, trying not to think about *why* Oracle Bay was experiencing a two-hundred percent increase in annual earthquakes. The stress was wearing down what little defenses she had, and now that Andy wasn't at her side, flickering flames invaded her peripheral vision. She didn't have her feather—she must've left it at Andy's when they packed up and left. And she couldn't dwell on the portents, as Barachiel had called them, that meant she was almost out of time before she was destroyed and the entire town with her.

Her breaths got quicker and shallower, and her chest felt like it was being compressed in a human-sized vise.

Barachiel sat down across from her and smiled in what looked like sympathy. "I'm not as good a buffer as Andy—he's been to hell, and it's his mind you inserted yourself into—but I'm better than nothing. I'm not going to hold your hand or touch you, but my presence should help a little."

Ceri looked across the table at him. He was beautiful, and when he relaxed into his "I'm just a regular human, nothing to see here" persona, his beauty didn't overwhelm. "Are all angels gorgeous?" She hadn't meant to ask that, but she'd wondered about it since she'd started meeting so many.

Barachiel smiled, although this time it didn't seem to affect her tension, which was almost too bad, really. She didn't usually like to have her emotions manipulated, but today seemed like an excellent time to make an exception.

"If you're asking if they're all as good-looking as me, sadly, the answer is no. Even among angels, I stand head and wings above the rest." He beamed at her, then looked around and drummed his fingers on the table. "Do humans drink and eat because they need something to do with their hands? I don't usually sit at tables to talk to mortals, and I find myself having trouble sitting still."

Ceri grinned, and the darkness receded from her vision almost completely. "We eat and drink because we have to to live, and sometimes because it's enjoyable or comforting or celebratory or ritual."

"I have no need of sustenance or ritual, nor anything else. It's much like sex, isn't it? Survival and ritual." Barachiel nodded thoughtfully. "There could be no other reason to..." He shuddered and trailed off before finishing his sentence.

"Um." Ceri wasn't sure how to reply to that, so she changed the subject. "You didn't tell me about the others. Allowing even that they couldn't possibly be as good looking as you, are they all the western ideal of beauty?"

Barachiel tilted his head and considered. "I have obtained a phone now, and the nice person at the phone store helped me set it up. They were confused about my relative ignorance about human machines and customs but helped me get a phone number so I can text people and make phone calls. I haven't yet, because I don't have anyone else's number, but they also helped me get Twitter, which is a 'social media and news app,' according to the phone person."

Ceri was having trouble following his thoughts from beginning to the end, but trying was enough to keep her distracted. "You're on Twitter? Please tell me that's not where you get your news."

Barachiel waved a hand in the air. "I care little for what most humans think of as news, and as yet, Twitter does not seem to carry news items of celestial importance. However, Twitter is very good at telling me about signs and portents. Many are unusual, which makes them newsworthy. It is occasionally difficult to sort the natural disasters from the unnatural ones, but I catalog them all and look for patterns."

"What do Twitter and portents have to do with western ideals of beauty and the general good looks of angels?" Ceri was positive she did not want to follow Barachiel down the rabbit hole of "unnatural disasters."

"Right! That's what I was going to tell you. On Twitter, there is much discussion about what is attractive and what is not. It is interesting how many forms are considered attractive. Many of my siblings have taken no real corporeal form and appear as they are expected to where they visit. Very few decided on bodies like this one, and we all look quite different, although the bodies we chose fit an idealized form from wherever we were when we chose them." Barachiel tipped back his chair and balanced on the back legs, then leaned to one side, bringing the chair onto a single leg.

Ceri watched in fascination. Barachiel was one of the most fidgety people she'd ever met, but somehow his inability to be still was interesting and not distracting. Not distracting in a bad way, she corrected.

He lost his balance and windmilled his arms wildly until the chair thumped down onto all four legs again. The comical surprise of it all made Ceri laugh.

"I'm not used to balancing without my wings, but Andras says I may not use them in mortal gathering places." He shifted the chair a little, then repeated his earlier actions until he was once more balanced on one chair leg. "I understand that this has something to do with my inner ears, but I'm not sure why. Do you know?"

Ceri furrowed her brows. "I don't. You know as much as I do about inner ears and balance, possibly even more if you've been thinking about it. I don't usually."

The legs on Barachiel's chair hit the ground with a long thump. Ceri startled, even though she'd seen it coming.

"Are you okay now?" he asked.

Ceri bit back the panic at the thought of him walking away and leaving her alone with her thoughts and fears. "I don't know."

"I'm not leaving you here until Andras returns. Have no fears about that. I merely mean, are your breathing and heartbeat happening at an acceptable rhythm and rate to have a serious conversation?"

She took a deep breath and pushed the panic away. She was okay, breathing steady, regular pulse, not-too-tight shoulders. "Yes, although I don't want to."

"Humans do not care for serious or uncomfortable conversations, I have observed. That surprises me, as most celestial beings find those to be the only conversations worth engaging in. Your habit of engaging in trivial details is distracting." The frown he directed at her was disapproving, and she bit back a giggle.

"You're on Twitter," she pointed out. "Do you have an account? Do you tweet?"

He crossed his arms and replied stiffly, "I don't see how that's any of your business."

"Oh my god, you do!" She clapped her hand over her mouth. "I'm sorry!"

"For what?"

"For taking the name of your lord in vain." Ceri hadn't spent a lot of time worrying about the ten commandments, and was a little sketchy on a few of them, but she knew that was the big one for some people. She thought the later ones were probably more important, but not everyone had the same moral code.

"Do you worship the Most High?" Barachiel asked.

"No. I'm not an atheist—hard to be one after the events of the last few months. I mean, once you've gotten drunk with a Greek god or been kidnapped by an Etruscan goddess, not to mention the influx of deities in December, it's hard to be an unbeliever. But I do not follow any prescribed religion or spiritual practice."

"Then you did not take the name of my lord in vain. Not that most people interpret that correctly anyway. If you're interested, I can lead you in a discussion about the true meaning of many of the biblical passages that are misinterpreted by unintelligent leaders and too-trusting followers, but not today." He tipped back on his chair again. "I wish this was one of those chairs that spins in circles.

I'm very fond of those. They disrupt my inner ear functions and cause me to lose my balance in a most delightful way."

Conversations with Barachiel were less a linear progression and more like trying to untangle a bunch of necklaces that'd been sitting in a jewelry box for a couple weeks unsupervised.

"Portents? Real talk?" she prompted. Then another thought struck her. "Give me your phone."

"My phone? Why?" Barachiel's chair thumped down again, and he looked...worried.

"I'm going to put my number in it, so we can text. I'll give you Andy's, too."

He appeared to mull it over, then dug it out of the pocket of his jeans and handed it to Ceri. "Please do not send nudes, but me-mes are okay."

Ceri choked and coughed. "I promise to send you zero nudes. And meme is a single syllable."

"Oh. Okay. You're the first person I've said that out loud to. Although I instinctively speak your language—all languages at once, in fact—there are a few pronunciation rules I've yet to understand." He took the phone back and looked expectantly at it.

"What are you— Oh." Ceri pulled her phone out of her jacket pocket and opened her messages. She had the message she'd sent herself from his phone, so she added him to her contact list, then sent him a .gif of Jesus jumping on a pogo stick.

His phone played the opening bars to the Imperial Death March from Star Wars. He grinned in delight, opened his messages, and frowned for a second, then laughed. "That is very funny. Thank you, seer." He tucked his phone away, folded his hands on the table, and looked at her.

No, that wasn't right. He wasn't looking at her. He was looking *into* her. It was uncomfortable without being totally unpleasant. She had the slightly hysterical thought that, after this deep dive into her where he was peeling away the layers of her mind and soul to look deeper and deeper, a couple nudes would be less exposure.

"You are barely hanging on," he murmured as he backed out, putting everything back where he'd found it.

It was remarkably like being peeled like an onion then returned to its original state, flaky, papery skin, and all.

"I'm fine," she retorted, then rolled her eyes at herself. She was clearly not fine, or they wouldn't be here.

"You are doing quite well for a mortal. Most would've succumbed to the madness within a few days, instead of nearly half a year. Congratulations." He nodded at her in what almost looked like respect.

"Most humans wouldn't have accidentally done that deep dive into him," Ceri pointed out.

"You mistake me. I meant most humans with your ability, not the more mundane and uninteresting ones. You are remarkably strong of mind, even for one of your kind." He reached into his... Ceri wasn't sure where he was reaching. His hand wavered in and out of existence, like she was looking at it through dark, rippling water.

He pulled his hand out and in it was Andy's feather.

Relief flooded over her, and she took it. The last of the horror that had survived Barachiel's presence disappeared when she slipped it inside her shirt and pressed it against her skin. "Thank you."

"You are welcome. I spoke with your old one, and he explained his theory about the feather. It is interesting, and perhaps not one I would've thought of, although I *am* infinitely intelligent, and I am pleased to see it works. You should value the old one more. He is more than most of you but hides it well. The other old one, the scary woman, she is the same. She wears a face meant to distract from her true self, but it is wavering now. I am hopeful I will be here to see her when it falls away." Barachiel stood and leaned against a wall, then sat again and tapped his fingers on the tabletop.

Ceri put away the information about Morgana, as well as the tidbit about even an angel finding her scary, to think about later when the fate of the town wasn't on her shoulders.

Barachiel leaned forward, and every trace of playfulness fell off his face. He truly looked like the kind of angel who needed to yell "fear not," now. "You know what's happening, at least a little. But I need you to understand the entire picture and not merely your part in it. This will be difficult to hear, but it is necessary before we can take the next steps. Do you understand why?"

Ceri was almost certain she didn't, but she nodded anyway.

"Your mind will not survive what's about to happen; it will not be restored. Are you ready?"

Paska and Russell slid in next to Ceri, each carrying a pitcher of beer. Paska had one glass, and Russell two. He slid one to Ceri, filled their glasses, and took a drink.

Ceri drank without registering the taste of the beer, although she really should think about it since she'd likely never think about anything again.

"How long?" she demanded.

"How long what?" Barachiel asked.

"Until you destroy my mind to save the town?" She took another long drink and set the nearly empty glass on the table.

Russell refilled it, then leaned back and regarded the angel silently.

Paska glanced at Ceri. "We are here as your advocates in place of the demon who is being kept busy by another of these winged visitors. A Black man who looks like he's never smiled and wouldn't know a joke if it hit him in the face."

"Ah, Uriel has arrived," Barachiel said in satisfaction. "That is good. As for how long," he pulled out his phone and glanced at the screen before tucking it away again. "Approximately twelve hours, and even that is cutting it too close. Fortunately, there are few preparations to make. The only requirement is to have the old one—" he waved at Paska "—as well as the one who shines like a prism, Andras, and Uriel and me. And you, of course. We couldn't do this without you."

"Where is Drew?" Ceri asked, trying to wrap her mind around what Barachiel had just told her. Her mind that would only exist for twelve more hours.

"On his way," Paska replied tersely. "He stopped by Mirror Images to do a sweep in there for anything that might not belong. I don't suspect he'll find anything. You haven't been at your shop for several weeks, but it is better to be safe. There is still one missing, and I don't like missing things."

She'd almost forgotten the reason she and Andy had left his home and come here in the first place. The earthquake and the "you're going to die in twelve hours" news drove out almost everything else.

She sucked in a breath, pressed the feather under her shirt into her body, and said, "You're just in time. Barachiel was just telling me that my mind cannot be restored, but presumably, it's necessary to do whatever it is they're going to do and destroy me if I don't want to kill everyone in the town."

"I didn't say you'd be destroyed. Only that your mind would not be restored to the state in which it was before you looked too deep and saw too much. There is no way to return you to your previous level. Your gift of seeing is too strong, and now that you've seen eternity, every time you look unguarded into anyone who has touched heaven or hell or any of the planes between, Earth excepted, you will be drawn in. And when your guard is down, it won't even take a deliberate look. You cannot be a seer when you've already seen everything, or you'll find yourself back in this same place in a decade, or a year—maybe less, if you continue to be unguarded around Andras." Barachiel paused and looked at her expectantly, but she didn't know what to say.

"I don't understand," she confessed.

"He's saying that healing your mind and the rift you've created in Oracle Bay is incompatible with keeping the sight. If you live through this, you will no longer be a seer," Uriel said from the doorway. He was a small, unassuming Black man with a shiny, bald head, dark brown eyes, and skin so dark and smooth that it looked like the softest silk.

The angel obviously has a great skincare routine, Ceri thought with another near-hysterical giggle.

"There is no need to imply she may not live through this," Barachiel said. "It will only make her more nervous and incite panic at a crucial moment that could make our jobs harder and her life status more precarious. It is better if she believes she will survive, regardless of facts."

"You know we can still hear you," Russell said. "You are not reaching your 'don't incite panic' objectives right now. Can't you guys, I don't know, talk to each other in your heads or something?"

Barachiel and Uriel turned their attentions to Russell and tipped their heads in the same direction and at the exact same angle. It was eerie, and another bubble of hysterical laughter escaped from Ceri's lips.

Barachiel's shoulders relaxed, and he turned towards Ceri. "We were merely making a distasteful joke. If everything goes as planned, your life is not in any danger. But Uriel was correct that you will not be a seer *when* you live through this event."

"I thought angels couldn't lie," Ceri said.

"Whatever gave you that impression?" Uriel scoffed. "It's only demons who tell the truth. It's how they snare you in temptation."

Another nugget of information to be tucked away and drawn out later to examine.

"Get on with it," Paska said. "If you're waiting on Drew, he just walked through the door. We've only a few hours to go; set it up so we can knock it out. I'd like to get a nap in before the big event. I want to be on my toes, and I haven't slept in a couple weeks, so it's long overdue."

Ceri was going to need a new mental storage space for all the questions that were coming up. She gasped. "Will my memories be gone? Everything? Will it be amnesia after, or will I start over with a child's mind?"

The look Barachiel gave her could only be described as patronizing befuddlement. "You read too much into what I'm saying, when I only speak truth. Unlike some other angels," he didn't look at Uriel, but his words were pointed, "I don't lie. If we take Uriel's skepticism about your chances of survival as truth, my statement that you won't be a seer when you live through it is still true. You won't be anything if you don't. Now, let's move on."

Drew walked in, looked at the two angels, and curled his lip before sitting in the empty chair next to Paska.

"Tomorrow morning, six of us will need to gather in an open space that no one will mind losing, as it will become unusable for a few centuries after. The necromancer should be there as well to hold the spirits who haunt Ceri at bay. Convincing them that getting too close to the yawning maw that will open into hell will likely result in them being drawn in should be enough. Of course, any who would like to cross over are free to do so, but it is my experience that most would not choose to willingly go into hell." Barachiel took a breath and exchanged a glance with Uriel, who took over the thread of the narration.

Uriel stared directly at her, and the intensity of his gaze made her squirm. He didn't have the good-natured cheer of the other angel. "It is our job to restore balance to this earth, and we are here, not because we care about this town and its inhabitants, but because you cannot be permitted to destroy the balance. What you did was foolish in the extreme. It brought danger and instability to this world. If the rift is allowed to open in the physical world when your mind becomes too small to hold it, passage between the hell you can't stop dreaming about and the town you're deeply rooted to will open, making it possible for all manner of hell's denizens to venture forth. I hope you can see why that's not the ideal way to preserve the balance between heaven and hell."

"Of course," Ceri said. She could. Absolutely. But she felt defensive at the suggestion that she'd been foolish, although perhaps she had been. She'd known Andy wasn't what he'd pretended to be, and she dove into his mind to search for the answers about the Etruscan goddesses without caution, the way she would've if she'd scried a mundane human.

Uriel continued with barely a pause. "You will stand with us. The others need to be further back if they don't want to be incinerated. The Fallen One may stand closer; he is unlikely to be consumed by hellfire, although the unfiltered purifying light of heaven may be too much. The prism will stand in the spot we designate." He looked at Drew.

"Am I the prism?" Drew asked, looking around the table.

"Yes," Uriel confirmed. "Have you not already seen this? This is who you are, not only for these purposes, but always. You take light and scatter it, separating the purity and singleness of it."

"Okay." Drew's expression was almost as unreadable as Uriel's, but Ceri saw sadness in his eyes.

She knew him well enough to know the knowledge that he separated light, interrupting its "purity," would cause him to resurrect the guilt he felt too often and for no good reason. "Prisms make beautiful rainbows," she said, reaching across the table to grab his hand.

"Rainbows are impure," Uriel growled.

"Okay," Ceri said. So far, Uriel was not endearing himself to her —or to anyone. "Then what?"

Barachiel looked at the other angel, and before Ceri could blink, he had a sword in his hand and was holding it at Uriel's neck. "You no longer serve Her, which makes you expendable in my eyes. You may not be familiar with humans and their standards for kindness, but you do not get to bring your wrath to this place. Causing deliberate pain to these people is unnecessary to achieve your aims." Barachiel stepped back, and the sword disappeared. He sat, and the mask he'd dropped reappeared along with a slightly crooked smile. "You need to chill your rolls right now."

"It's either 'chill' or 'slow your roll,'" Russell muttered.

"Right. Uriel, chill, or I will ask you to leave." Barachiel turned his gaze back to the oracles around the table as Uriel took a seat next to him, pulling the chair as far away as he could while staying in the alcove.

"The old one will stand near the prism. He will know when the time is right for the prism to act. He is connected to the earth more than any of you and will know when the rift is close enough to be affected but not so close to risk opening and sucking us in before it is too late. Then Uriel and I will pull the knowledge of how you opened the rift out of your mind and use our combined powers and Her light to destroy the wound in your head, which should restore balance, prevent the mouth of hell from opening, and save the day!" He beamed at them.

Ceri caught the word he'd added to stick to his truth. "Should restore balance?"

"Nothing is ever certain, is it? I cannot make promises, but I am confident we will succeed." Barachiel squared his shoulders and exuded waves of confidence.

"You have skipped a great many details," Paska chided in a gravelly voice.

"It is difficult to know all the details until the event itself," the angel replied. "What more would you know now?"

Drew counted on his fingers. "What does 'acting' mean for me, what's Andy going to be doing, will the rest of us be in danger, and what will Ceri need after it's all over?"

"You will know what to do when it happens," Barachiel promised. "As for the rest, there is always a modicum of danger when heaven and hell come into conflict."

"Collateral damage is inevitable and no cause for concern," Uriel muttered from his place in the corner. "It is not important."

"It is when we might be the collateral," Drew said. "And the other questions?"

"Andy knows his role, and it is of no concern to you. As for the seer, as she was called by her nan before her parents named her a witch and tried to eliminate her in the name of the god they didn't understand, I will take care of her and return her to you when she is ready." Barachiel smiled gently, and buffeting waves of confidence washed over the table, adding a layer of comfort even more powerful than it had been earlier.

Every last shred of doubt, every question Ceri had, was washed away in the knowledge that Barachiel would take care of everything, would take care of her. She didn't need to worry.

"You waste your powers on them," she heard Uriel mutter. "They are mere mortals, and they must do as we say, whether they like or understand it."

"It is better for them to go forward with confidence. It makes them less likely to second guess things at the wrong moment and create difficulties we have to adjust for at a crucial time. And my power is infinite, so it cannot be wasted. You forget yourself, Uriel. Do not tempt my anger again." Throughout his chastisement of Uriel, his smile never wavered.

Ceri heard what they were saying, heard why Barachiel was soothing them, but she didn't care. If he was confident, it made sense he wanted them to feel the same. Her breathing slowed until she was floating in a calm, meditative state.

Barachiel dimmed the intensity of his smile, and the fog of calm lifted, leaving behind peace and acceptance. He stood, patted his pockets, and pulled out his phone, handing it to Paska. "Please insert your contact information into my phone and then send a message to yourself so that we can text. I would like the prism to do the same." He looked at Russell. "You may, too, if you like. But you may not send nudes. Any of you."

The others looked just as taken aback as Ceri had been by the suggestion they might send the angel nudes, but they entered their numbers anyway.

"You may have altered our emotions now, but there will come a time when you'll need to answer for that," Paska said. He had a flask in his hand and was giving the angel a measured stare.

"That may be true, but it will not be today, nor will it be tomorrow." Barachiel put the phone back in his pocket, pulled it out a moment later to check it, then put it away with a look of comical disappointment. "If the old one must rest, the rest of you likely need to as well. Once Uriel leaves this alcove, Andras will be here in seconds, and he will be displeased that he was compelled to stay away by a lesser angel than he once was. So unless you wish to be here to listen to his complaints about being left out of such an important discussion, I suggest you walk away now."

Russell and Paska left the alcove, followed a couple minutes later by Uriel.

"I will leave you now to look for an appropriate place to meet in the morning. I will text you the location when I have found it. Be there at first light." He strode out of the alcove, dodged around Andy, and disappeared out the door.

"What the hell is going on here?" Andy asked, with only the faintest hint of a snarl in his voice.

"I'll catch you up, but can we find a place to sleep?" Ceri asked.

"I'll take you home," Drew said. "Well, I'll take you to Bill's. Andy, you can come too, I guess. And we'll fill you in on the way there."

twenty-three

Ceri paced in the center of the large field south of town where the peninsula was widest, and she could see neither ocean nor bay. There were a lot of cranberry bogs nearby, but this field was unused. She didn't know who it belonged to and whether Barachiel had gotten permission, but she put that worry out of her mind.

Andy wasn't pacing. He was standing stock still about thirty feet away, radiating sulphur. His eyes followed her, but he didn't speak.

Ceri was okay with that. Any efforts to reassure her might be lies, and she didn't need a dose of realistic expectations right now. He'd confirmed he knew his part in it, but wouldn't talk about it, which made Ceri even more nervous than she'd been already.

Drew was waiting in the car. He said it was because it was too cold and damp outside, and he didn't want to subject himself to either before it was necessary.

Ceri had her suspicions that he was staying away from her so his nerves wouldn't spill over onto her.

The sound of another engine approaching drew her thoughts

away from the two men she was here with. Any distraction was welcome at this point.

Russell parked behind Drew's car. He and Paska joined Ceri a few moments later.

Paska looked worn, and the lines of exhaustion were out of place on his typically youngish-looking face.

Russell's eyes were unfocused. He looked around. "They're all here, and they're buzzing, although I can't tell if it's with excitement or concern. I'll talk to them and draw them away; they likely won't leave altogether. They are attached to you and will fade out too much to be comfortable for them if you're out of sight. I'll stay with them to make sure they don't forget why they're not surrounding you, hoping to catch your attention." He opened his arms, said something Ceri didn't catch, and backed away and up the road.

She didn't feel any different, although she'd rather anticipated she would.

Paska walked up next to her and pulled her into a rough embrace. "You've got this, Ceridwen."

Ceri was so taken aback by the uncharacteristic display of affection that she was slow to return the hug. "Thank you, Paska. And thank you for finding answers and for being here."

"You're the most interesting thing that's happening this month, so of course I'm here. But I will have a word with that angel about how to properly send a location. 'Find the dying land in the middle of it all' was not terribly useful." Paska stepped back and tipped his head at Andy, who was still unmoving.

"At least he learned how to do a group text. And he did clarify when Drew asked." Ceri shrugged, looking around for the angels who were, in her opinion, late. The sun was up and the ground was steaming as the early morning rays hit the damp ground.

"He did, and the advice that we'd find the dead land in the middle of the red-stained water led us here once we realized he was talking about cranberries. And gave us some coordinates. I guess if things might light on fire, might as well do it on nonarable land surrounded by bogs." Paska took a drink from his ubiquitous flask and untied the leather pouch that held his runestones. He squatted, brushed the area in front of him clear of the small sticks and leaves that covered the ground, and scattered the bones.

Ceri looked past him at Andy. She walked around Paska and into Andy's waiting arms.

"I need you to know something before this starts," he said, not quite meeting her gaze.

"Tell me after." She put her hands on his shoulders and stood on her tiptoe to brush her lips against his.

He pushed her back a little but didn't let go. "It has to be now. I need you to know before everything gets started and I cede the careful control I've developed in the last few decades to someone else. To angels."

Ceri dropped her arms to her sides. "Okay. Tell me now so I can kiss you before everything starts. I need this since we didn't get very far last night."

Andy rubbed one hand over his forehead. He caught her gaze and held it long enough that Ceri was getting nervous. "I love you."

He said it so quietly and so matter-of-factly, that she didn't immediately grasp what he was saying. "What?"

"I love you." His voice was stronger this time.

Butterflies erupted in her stomach, and she felt a little light-headed. Perhaps declarations of love disrupted one's inner ears.

"It's okay if you don't feel the same way. I know you would prefer to keep things casual between us, but I didn't want to go forward this morning without telling you." His gaze dropped to their feet.

Ceri knew what she was supposed to say. She was even almost sure she felt the same. But she couldn't get the words out. She'd not told a single person she loved them in anything but friendship in over three hundred years, and breaking that barrier now felt impossible. She opened her mouth, but before she could offer an equivocating reply, he crushed her lips in a kiss.

It was hard and passionate. He was pouring every ounce of his fear and anger and lust into her, and she returned the same. She was about ready to push him to the ground and finish what they'd started last night, audience be damned, but pulled back instead. It was not the time nor the place.

"If you are finished with…that…we will start. I don't want to be here all day." Uriel's voice was dripping with contempt.

Ceri whipped around. She hadn't heard them arrive, but the angels were standing in the middle of the field with their wings trailing behind them.

Paska stood, scooped the bones back into his leather bag, cinched it, and hung it from his belt. "It is a good time to start, and the bones are favorable today." He walked back towards the car, turned around to look at the angels, then took five steps to the left and three to the back. "This is the place."

Ceri reached up and kissed Andy again, gently this time. She might not have been able to tell him how she felt, how she might be feeling, but she tried to let him know with her lips. Her chest tightened and her throat grew thick with unshed tears. "See you in a few," she whispered against his lips.

He didn't answer, just brushed her lips with his again, then let go. His silvery wings spread out behind him. "I love you," he said. "Don't forget."

"I won't," Ceri promised before taking her place with the angels.

She looked around. Russell was almost out of sight up the road, and Drew had joined Paska.

Andy had taken his place between the angels and the oracles, although closer to the latter.

"I'm ready," she said to Barachiel.

"You're not, but it doesn't matter," Uriel said. "Because it's time."

· · · · ★ ★ ★ ★ · · · ·

Ceri gasped under the weight of the angels' hands on her head. Her mind burst open—if she'd thought it too wide before, she'd been sadly mistaken. She saw the birth of the universe, the birth of galaxies, of solar systems, planets, moons, life, and gods. It streamed into her too fast, and she tried to move away, to hide, to run away and never look back.

"Cease your movements, child," Barachiel said to her. "No harm will come to you."

Ceri stopped trying to escape physically, but she couldn't help trying to shut down her mind, to stop seeing everything. Blacking out would be a mercy.

"If you relax your mind, relax yourself, this will be easier on you," the angel's voice echoed in her mind. Or was he speaking aloud? She couldn't tell.

She saw every blade of grass that ever was or would be, every grain of sand, every star, every birth and death. And each new thing that came into existence split into infinite numbers of possibilities. Every path that could be taken was mapped out before her and behind her and all around her.

Tears slid down her face. The rush was slowing now. She could see past the deaths of stars to something dark at the end of the tunnel. There were more deaths now than births. More endings and few beginnings. The darkness grew, and she shut her eyes against it. It didn't work, didn't block out the vision.

Something new appeared in front of the darkness. A tree— ancient and gnarled. It exuded impossible age, and Ceri knew the tree was the oldest thing in the universe. It'd been born, fully formed, when the universe erupted out of the nothingness she didn't want to contemplate, and now it would follow the universe back into the nothing.

Ceri trembled. The tears streaking down her face intensified. It was too old, too beautiful to die.

The tree finally reached her, and there was nothing else to see.

It split open. Inside was fire and screams. The hell that she'd experienced for the last few months stood in front of her.

"Now!" she heard Paska yell through the haze of tears and pain and sorrow and eternity.

Her skin heated, and white light surrounded her.

At first, nothing happened. The flames rose higher, burned hotter. The tree blackened, leaves turning to ash and branches curling from the heat.

Then someone stepped into the space in front of the tree. The light from the angels beside her had splintered into a million colors and wrapped Andy in rainbows.

He stepped into the burning hollow in the center of the tree and raised his arms.

"No!" she screamed. She tried to run to him but couldn't. It was too far away and too close. There was no way to get there, no way to save him.

His light doused the fire, and the tree snapped closed around him and slowly moved away. The darkness of the nothingness receded until there wasn't even a pinprick.

And then her mind unspooled. Everything that had rushed in, rushed out again with increasing speed, stripping her bare.

She heaved, fell to her knees, and vomited, but it didn't stop the tide from going out. It spun around her. She was caught in the center of an infinite vortex, the calm in the eye of the storm of the universe.

And then it was over. There was nothing left.

White light exploded in the now-empty space that was her mind and broke into a million pinpricks.

She screamed.

And darkness claimed her.

twenty-four

Ceri opened her eyes slowly. For a moment, she thought she was suspended in her mind in a field of endless white, but as her vision cleared, hazy blobs resolved into walls and floors and soft, overstuffed furniture. Color began saturating her vision.

The furniture turned beige, then tan, and resolved into a rich brown. The walls were blue, and the floor, a golden oak color, was covered in deep, red rugs.

"You may sit, if you'd like." Barachiel's voice echoed in the room.

"Where am I? Am I dead?" she asked. Her voice was dry and raspy, and she wished fervently for a glass of water.

"You're not dead. I was confident you wouldn't die if you'll remember. And we're in your mind still—you must regard this as a safe place, because this is where you fled to at the end." Barachiel materialized in front of her, and behind him a fireplace took shape.

Ceri stood up, wavered on her feet, and walked to the nearest chair. She curled up in it and pulled the blanket that had appeared on the arm over her body. There was a glass of water on the low table beside her, and she drained it. "Why are you here?"

Barachiel sat across from her. "I needed to be here to guide you through the next part. I told your friends that I would take care of you when it was over, and so here I am." He shifted on the chair. "This is a very comfortable chair. I like your secret mind room. Much cozier than most people's."

Ceri didn't know what to say, so she waited. She didn't feel different, didn't feel like she'd lost the sight, but until she gazed in a mirror and concentrated, would she know?

"You no longer have the ability to scry into the future," Barachiel said.

"You told me it would be that way." A pang hit her chest at the loss of something that'd been a part of her since she was old enough to gaze into a basin of water and wonder what the future held. "Will I age now?"

"I do not know how time will affect you going forward; there are many possibilities." He crossed one leg over the other.

"Did we do it? Is Oracle Bay safe? My friends?" There was something else she needed to ask, something that was at the edge of her mind. "Andy? What happened to Andy?"

"Andras sacrificed himself to quench the hellfire at the end of the universe. He took the light She sent us, the light refracted by your prism friend so it wouldn't burn away his soul, and walked into the tree that holds everything." Barachiel's eyes softened. "He did more than any angel would've willingly done."

Tears ran down her face. "He knew what he had to do before we started." It wasn't a question. It was why he'd told her he loved her, told her to remember. He knew.

"He did. Uriel informed him, and he did it anyway. Without him, without Drew, you would've been lost. Uriel and I could've prevented the rift from opening, but the results wouldn't have been the same. He was in favor of dropping you into a black hole to stop it. It was the easier, more expedient choice. But this was better."

"Not for Andy," she whispered.

"Maybe not. Only time will tell. But now, we have much to do before you wake. Close your eyes and look inward."

Ceri quailed at the thought. "I'd really rather not do any introspection right now."

"It is necessary. Do it." His voice didn't waver in its command.

She did as she was told. The field of stars confronted her again, the pinpricks she'd seen before her mind shut down. "It's so beautiful. What is it?" she breathed.

"This is everything." Once again, Barachiel's voice echoed around her. "We could not send that much through your mind and seal the rift while leaving you your sight.

Ceri huffed a little impatiently. "I know. You told me. Repeatedly."

"Look at one of the stars—look as closely as you can."

Ceri grimaced but did it anyway. She picked a light point and stared. "This is stupid. What am I supposed to see other than a dot of light?"

"Concentrate. You need to want to see the star. You want to know everything about it." His voice was calm and rhythmic. He'd be great at reading meditations for her favorite app.

She stared at the dot of light and concentrated on wanting to know, so she could learn whatever lesson Barachiel wanted to teach her about being mundane and go home.

The dot of light expanded, and she shrieked and tried to take a step back. Since she was inside her mind's mind—can you get a headache thinking about brain inception?—she couldn't step back. The dot rushed towards her, then encompassed her. Her jaw dropped. She was looking into a galaxy. She recognized the characteristic spiral arms dark with stars.

"What is that? Why do I have a galaxy in my brain?" Wasn't galaxy brain some kind of slang? It likely wasn't supposed to be a literal description.

"You can let go of it. Once you stop concentrating on it, it'll go back to being nothing more than a tiny star in your mind." His voice was no longer echoing. "When you've let it go and everything looks as it did when you got here, open your eyes. You'll be back with me in your comfortable room."

Ceri let it go and watched it zip away. She looked at another dot and was tempted to see if it was the same. But only a little. It would be better to step back and find out what Barachiel had to say about what'd happened to her. She opened her eyes. She was back in the comfortable room. Another glass of water waited for her. She downed it and waited for the explanation.

"You've already seen too much to have it all torn away. Taking away your sight would've crushed you, eventually. You'd still have the memories of everything you'd seen—but they'd be dim and distant, like those of January 13, 1832." He smiled at her expectantly.

"What happened on January 13, 1832?" She was more tired than she would've thought possible, considering she was unconscious.

"I don't know, and neither do you, which is the point. You might be able to pinpoint something if you thought about it long enough. You'd find an event you remembered and count backwards from there, retracing your steps to get to January 13, 1832, only to find it wasn't worth remembering. But if your sight was gone and nothing stepped in to replace it, the memories wouldn't know where to go, so they'd stay and take up space. They wouldn't dim and fade into the background. You'd go mad. Slower than you were this time, and with less cosmically devastating consequences, but some part of you would be aware of what was going on, would watch as your mind dissolved, as your behavior got more and more erratic, and you began to believe you were caught in your memories, talking about what you were remembering. It wouldn't be a pleasant way to die." Barachiel sighed and clasped his hands over one knee. "So instead of shrinking your mind, I expanded it. You don't have the mental capacity of an angel or other divine being—you are still mortal—but you have everything you did before. Only now you have room for it all. And soon you'll have the knowledge to access what you need and keep the rest locked away."

"But my sight?" Ceri asked.

"It's gone in the way you're used to, but you'll be able to use the same mediums to find what you want to know. You won't be accessing the future the same way, but the results will be the same. As long as you learn how to only find what you need and don't lose yourself in your mind. That won't drive you mad in the same way, but if you stay too long, you'll wander in there forever. Your body will become catatonic, and eventually you will wither and die. I have seen it happen to one of my brothers, although I believe he did it on purpose. Eternity had become too much for him." His expression was sorrowful and deadly serious, and a chill ran down Ceri's spine.

"How do I keep myself from looking?" Her heart was beating hard in her throat, and she took a deep breath to calm herself.

"I'm going to show you how to shut the door to the stars in your mind. It will be there, and your subconscious can pull the information you need to keep plying your trade. Small insights may still occur, although rarely, and they will flash in your mind. You will never again be subject to seeing things you didn't intend to look for when you walk by a mirror or look in a pool of water. It will take deliberate effort to see." Barachiel leaned back and grinned. His carefree persona was falling back into place.

They must be almost done then. "Okay. Tell me how."

"I can't tell you. There are no words. But it's easy. Watch."

With his last words, the lights blinked out, and they were back in the starry darkness.

"It's simple." He reached up, grabbed something, and yanked it down. The stars turned from bright pinpricks of light to dim, barely visible blurs. He snapped his fingers, and the cover retracted. "Your turn."

Ceri reached up and grabbed hold of the hard material that met her hand. She tugged down, but it didn't budge. "It won't move," she complained through teeth gritted with effort.

"Don't think too hard about it," he advised. "Imagine it as a window covering. The ones that you pull down, then have to tug just right to make it go up. But sometimes, they don't go back up because you pulled it too far out, and then you have a stupid window covering that just hangs there."

"Should I not pull it too far down?" Ceri asked. She reached for the bottom of the imaginary blind and pulled gently. It moved, and she slowly drew it down between this part of her mind and the other, newer, bigger part.

"It's not a real shade," Barachiel said. "Why would you think you could pull it too far down?"

Ceri shook her head. His transformation was nearly complete. She kept pulling until the shade was at her feet. Then she let go gingerly and stood. It stayed in place, and her mind felt…freer. "What will happen to me now?"

"I don't know. You will be able to make your future—within reason, of course. Stay out of the secret rooms. If you feel you need to look around the shade, text me. Do not come here alone. And do not tell anyone you don't trust with your life about the access you have to the secrets of the universe. Now open your eyes. It's time to wake up."

"Wait!" she said, reaching towards him.

Barachiel shrunk back. "Do not touch me."

"Sorry. I just… Where is Andy? Is there a body? Something to hold?" The tears she'd been keeping back flowed, and a hiccupping sob tore through her.

"His body is there," Barachiel said, tilting his head to look at her. "Why wouldn't it be?"

"Well, if he died walking into a giant end of the universe tree, I wasn't sure if there'd be anything left." Her shoulders heaved as she took a deep, wracking breath in an effort to get herself under control.

"Andras is not dead. Why would you think that?" The angel snapped his fingers, and her eyes flew open.

Ceri wasn't in the cozy room in front of the fire. She blinked, trying to figure out where she was. She was half sitting, half laying down on something that was harder than her imaginary chair but not uncomfortable. There were silvery translucent shapes hovering in the corners of the ceiling, but she wasn't ready to deal with ghosts yet, so she pushed them out of her mind.

"You're awake," Andy said. His arms tightened around her.

She'd woken cradled in his arms and sitting in his office at the Pour House. "Why are we here?" she asked. Her voice was raspy. Apparently, all the imaginary water and talking didn't translate.

Andy tipped her upright and helped her adjust her position so she was sitting on his lap. He handed her a glass of water and stared at her while she drank it. "Barachiel said you'd be okay, and that you'd wake soon, but I didn't believe him until I saw your eyes open."

Ceri finished her water. "How long have I been out?"

"Not long—maybe an hour or two. It's just ten in the morning now." He took her empty glass and set it on his desk.

"Ten? But we didn't even get started until almost eight, and if I was only unconscious for two hours, that means the whole thing took... How long?" Ceri's mind was swirling with the sudden intake of too much information, but before it could overwhelm her, it dissolved past the curtain, and she was left light again.

"About five minutes before I did my part." He shrugged, then winced.

"Are you okay? What's wrong?" Ceri slid off his lap and turned to look at him. The bare skin of his chest and shoulders was blackened and peeling. "What is this?"

"Burns. It was hot in that tree." A crooked grin appeared on his face. "Not as hot as some other places I've been in."

"Pervert." She smiled back.

"A little, but you like it." He stood and stretched. Large flakes of paper-thin blackened skin drifted to the floor. "In another hour, I'll look as good as new, but the healing process is very uncomfortable."

"That's all it takes to heal burns this badly?" Ceri reached out and hovered her fingers above an angry looking burn on the inside of his left bicep.

"That's all." He grabbed a shirt from the file cabinet that he used for his spare clothes and put it on. "Are you hungry? Despite my directive to stay closed today, Brandy has the place open for weekday brunch. Paska, Drew, and Russell are downstairs waiting for you, and I believe the rest of the charlatans are on their way to make sure you're okay."

Ceri's stomach growled, and she wrapped her arms around her middle.

"That answers that question. Let's get you downstairs and get you fed." He held out his hand, and she took it.

"Before we go, there's something I need to tell you." Her voice quavered with nerves. "Two somethings, actually."

Andy sat down again and pulled her onto his lap. "Tell me."

"I'm still a seer. Kind of. The angels did something to my mind so everything could fit without driving me crazy. I have the whole of... everything in there. I don't want to tell many people. Not yet, at least. It's new and weird, and it's so tempting to jump in there and look around. I have my own Wikipedia, my own Google, and I want so badly to dive in." Ceri stopped talking and hoped Andy would say something.

"Did Barachiel show you how to protect yourself?" he asked with no inflection or emotion.

She nodded. "He did. And he said I'd still be able to pull the truth of the future out if I want to, but to stay on this side of the magic imaginary curtain in my brain."

"Okay. That's good—my mind is like that a little, too, so if you ever want to talk about it, you can ask me. I don't know how I feel about him doing that without telling you, though. It's too much for one person." His arms tightened around her waist, then dropped to his sides. "What's the second thing?"

Ceri stood up and took several steps away from him, then turned around. This was a lot harder than telling him about her new, giant brain. She opened her mouth and closed it several times before she could get started.

"Ceri, you're making me nervous." His voice was tight, and when she looked at him, she saw the tension in his jaw and around his eyes.

She bit her lip, exhaled forcefully, then blurted, "I love you, too."

He was off the chair and in front of her in the blink of an eye. "Do you mean it?"

She smiled up at him. Saying it felt better—a weight was gone now. "I do. I love you, Andras Sterling."

"I love you, too, Ceridwen Kenny." He kissed her, and it was magnificent.

Her knees buckled, and he pulled her back into his lap on the chair.

Her stomach growled again, and she laughed against his mouth. "Food, then make-out session?"

Andy stood and let her slide down the length of his body. "That's a good idea. I wouldn't want you to pass out from lack of sustenance during the hours of plans I've made for us."

"Hours? That sounds ambitious." She linked her fingers through his and tugged him out the door and down the stairs.

"That's just for starters."

His low laugh made her shiver in anticipation.

She pushed open the door to the bar. The spirits who'd been following her rushed at her, pushing her backwards into Andy. "Stop it," she muttered. "We'll talk in a minute."

They swirled around her in agitation and made no move to retreat. She resolved to ignore them, and stepped through the doorway, coming face-to-back with Felicity and her niece, Joanna.

The too-cheery server was wearing a sundress that left bare her shoulders, arms, and most of her back.

"Oh hey, Felicity. Are my friends here?" Her eyes caught on the vibrant ink covering Felicity's body. Besides the tattoo of poppies growing around the skull and the one of raven carrying a bouquet of purple orchids, there were pink and blue tulips with their stems twined around what looked suspiciously like a femur, a bright purple iris twining around a rib cage, red roses sprouting from a fresh grave, and a daisy chain that'd been cut in half by a rusty, serrated knife.

Felicity turned around and tucked her hands behind her back.

Ceri looked from the poppy in the skull she'd already seen to Felicity's face.

"Surprise." A grimace twisted the woman's face, and no trace of cheer remained. She took half a step back, cocked an arm, and plunged a knife into Ceri's chest.

twenty-five

Ceri stared down at the knife sticking out of her body. "Ow." She must be in shock—there was no way a stab wound in her chest warranted only an "ow."

The stench of sulphur filled the room from behind Ceri.

"I will kill you for that," Andy said.

Ceri reached out a hand towards him. "Wait. Please. Can you just grab her without killing her?"

He growled but did as she asked, grabbing Joanna with his other hand as she slowly backed away, a look of horror on her face.

Felicity gaped at her and didn't struggle against Andy's restraint. "How are you still standing? What are you?"

Ceri took a deep breath—Felicity had missed the lungs and everything else vital. The knife was preventing any blood from leaking out, too, so she didn't need to worry about bleeding to death. "I think you're out of practice," Ceri said. "You missed everything important." She winced. It'd been a long time since she'd been stabbed, and it didn't feel any better now than it had then. She'd have to be slow and careful until she could get this out. But for now, she could stand it long enough to get the answers she wanted.

Brandy walked into view. "Felicity, you're late. You were supposed to be on the floor twenty minutes ago. This is the last warning I'll give you. Next time—" she rounded the corner and skidded to a halt, her hand flying up to cover her mouth. "Oh my god. I'll call an ambulance."

"Wait a minute, Brandy," Ceri said. "I'm okay for the minute. I need to get to the alcove. How many people are out there that need to be distracted?"

Brandy took a deep breath and looked at Andy. When he nodded, she threw her hands up in the air. "Fine. I'll wait. There are three tables, all towards the window instead of your alcove. I'll send Zeke over to distract them with the free mimosa special we're having today as of right now. If you stay on the left side of Andy and..." Her face turned red as she stared with a vitriol that surprised Ceri. "I cannot think of a word strong enough to describe her right now. I will text my bff. He's Scottish and knows all the best insults. But stay to their left, and no one will notice you."

"Thank you," Ceri said carefully. It didn't hurt exactly, not if she didn't think about it too much, but it wasn't comfortable, either.

"You owe me. Both of you. Maybe you'll finally tell me what's going on with your weird group of fortune telling friends and stop pretending the monsters of the world aren't real." Brandy looked at the women Andy was holding onto. "Wait a moment, please." She disappeared into the employee break room behind them and reemerged with two pairs of handcuffs. She cuffed Joanna, then Felicity.

Ceri looked at Brandy, who was wearing a slightly sheepish grin to go with her hard, angry eyes. Ceri made an encouraging noise, since Andy seemed incapable of speaking right now, and she didn't want to speak too much.

Brandy glared at her. "Do not die in my bar." She turned around and stalked into the bar.

A moment later, Brandy leaned around the corner and jerked an outstretched thumb towards the main room. Ceri shuffled to the left of Andy and trailed behind him to the alcove. Andy paused to let Ceri walk in first, then shoved Felicity and Joanna in behind her before standing in the doorway to block her escape.

"Excuse me?" The soft question came from behind Andy. Ceri leaned forward, gasping in pain, and peered around the imposing form of her... Her everything.

"What's going on?" Joanna asked, eyes wild and panic fluttering in her throat.

"That's an excellent question," Drew asked. He looked like he was on the verge of panic as well.

"It's fine, I'm fine," Ceri said. She pushed the pain back. She wanted to shove it behind her fancy mind curtain but couldn't concentrate enough to figure out how. This hurt a lot. She didn't remember it hurting this much last time.

"Um, sweetie, you have a giant knife sticking out of your chest," Misty said helpfully.

"I'm aware," she said. The dryness of her tone rivaled Morgana at her best. *Not bad,* Ceri thought to herself. Morgana was definitely the right person to emulate here. "Felicity stabbed me."

"But why?" Sandy asked, nose wrinkling in confusion. "It's not like you're out-of-control cheery and need to be taken down several notches."

"Paska, check out her ink." Ceri tilted her head towards the woman trapped between a table full of oracles and Andy.

Paska looked her over, but there was no surprise on his face. "Crass."

Felicity glared at the man. "You're calling me crass? You drink whiskey from a pint glass."

He grinned at her, but there was nothing friendly in his expression. "At least I don't tattoo myself with memories of the people I murdered." He patted the leather pouch on the table in front of him. "I make runes from their bones and carry them in a pouch made of their skin. Like a civilized person."

Ceri curled her lip. She'd known she didn't want to know anything more about the pouch he carried everywhere.

"Why are you here?" Ceri asked. "I don't even care what you are and how you've lived so long. I want to know how you found me and why."

Felicity laughed. It was short and hard and full of contempt. "Do you think this is a movie, and I'll confess my dastardly plot that I would've gotten away with except for the meddling town weirdos?"

Jezebel leaned forward and covered her mouth with her hand, gasping dramatically. "You guys, she thinks we're weirdos. That really hurts; it's like she's stabbed me, too."

"Hurts to my core," Morgana agreed. The look on her face should've been enough to have Felicity wetting herself in terror, but the waitress cum serial killer—or was it the other way around?—just looked down her nose at Morgana.

"Not to kill the atmosphere—I love a good back-and-forth insult festival as much as the next person—but is there a reason you're here instead of on the way to a hospital?" Russell asked. His voice was steady, but his eyes were darting wildly between the knife in Ceri's chest, the handcuffed Felicity Andy was still holding onto, and the space above Ceri's head where her ghost army was apparently lingering.

"Yes." Ceri nodded. "Can I sit down, though? There's a giant knife sticking out of my chest, and it is uncomfortable." Drew stood and helped Ceri to his chair.

"Sorry," he muttered. "Little shock, here. I thought I was all out for the day, but Oracle Bay continues to surprise me."

Ceri looked around. All seven of her ghostly hangers on were in the alcove with them. "Russell? Can you talk to them without opening yourself up the way you did last time? I think I can now, but I don't know how and don't want to mess anything up."

"All seven at once? Or do you want them to choose a spokesperson as before?" Russell was the only one who didn't look like he was in shock.

Even though the others were playing it cool, dry, and sarcastic, Ceri saw their faces. Everyone was a few shades paler than usual, and Sandy, Misty, and Jezebel all had their phones on the table.

"All at once if you can. I want to offer them a deal, but before we do, I have another question." She kept her gaze fixed on Russell. If she turned around and looked at Andy, not only would it hurt like hell, she'd lose her nerve.

"Shoot," he said, leaning back against the wall.

"What would happen if the ghosts all jumped into a person?" She crossed her fingers in her lap and hoped the idea teasing at the edge of her awareness was knowledge and not wishful thinking.

"What ghosts? What are you talking about?" Felicity asked, and for the first time since the stabbing, she didn't sound icy and collected. It was nice to have a break from the exclamation points, though. She'd been standing very still in front and to the left of Andy, although her eyes darted between the oracles in front of her and the door behind her.

"Don't speak," Paska said. "You do not have the right to ask questions now."

Russell was quiet for so long, Ceri had to resist the urge to scream at him to hurry. She might be playing it cool—chilling her rolls, if she was going to channel Barachiel—but getting stabbed hurt a lot, and she was nearly at the end of her pain tolerance for the day.

"I'm not sure. It's technically not possible, of course. A spirit has a difficult time possessing a body that's not open to them, and when they do take over a person, they do not share well. Seven spirits flowing into a body that's resisting them is unprecedented as far as I know." He tapped his chin with the fingers of his right hand and regarded the air above her head. "However, it is possible that seven spirits—a significant number in several cultures—in one unwilling body might destroy that body, and if not the body, the mind."

"I don't understand," Joanna whispered. She slid down the wall and drew her knees into her chest.

Ceri spared a brief second to try to feel sorry for the girl, then turned back to Russell. "When you say impossible, why is that?"

"Nearly impossible," he corrected. "They are already attached to you, and they are strong enough to have survived a hundred years without being moving on. It's a difficult call to resist. My guess is Felicity isn't eager to play host to the ghosts of the people she murdered, either."

"What are you talking about?" Felicity demanded. "Just have me arrested so I can get away from all of you."

"But if there was a pathway opened?" Ceri asked.

"It'd have to be pretty powerful," Russell said.

No one else was speaking, and for that, Ceri was grateful. She was almost at her breaking point. Had reached it the day before. And she just needed this done so she could go the hospital and have the stupid knife pulled out of her body before she passed out. Again. "She's here. The knife that's in my chest is the same one she used to murder at least thirty-five people. The jewelry she stole from them and the piece she took from me are in Paska's creepy leather pouch. My blood, her knife, and the trophies of her victims... Will that be enough?"

Russell nodded slowly, and an anticipatory smile curved his lips. "It should be."

"I have the serrated blade, too, if it helps," Paska offered. He reached into the inside pocket of the trench coat hanging over the back of his chair and pulled the horrible, blood-stained knife out, setting it on the table. He poured the bag of jewelry out next to it.

Ceri felt the hum of the ghosts around her pick up as they spotted their jewelry. "What about the spirits? What will happen to them?"

Russell didn't look away from the spirits. "They'll be released if she dies and will have a choice to move on from this plane or stay. They will not, however, have a choice about releasing you."

"And if she doesn't die?" Ceri asked. She didn't look at Misty or Sandy. They were the youngest here, and she didn't want to see what they thought about her conspiring to murder the woman who'd stabbed her.

"They'll be trapped inside her." Russell's answer was simple, and he glanced at her once before turning his attention back to the spirits.

Drew leaned forward and stared at Felicity. When he spoke, his voice vibrated in anger and fear. "If the ghosts don't kill you, I will. And it will be much, much slower."

"Can you get them out?" she asked, knowing Drew was not bluffing. The ghosts would be freed either way, but watching Drew torture and kill a woman might be too big a shock to the younger oracles' senses. Might as well let them believe it was an empty threat for now.

"I don't know. I can try, but there's no guarantee." Russell leaned back again and rested his head on the wall behind him, looking up at the ceiling.

Ceri nodded. "Okay. Offer them this: they can take their revenge by crossing through the conduit you're going to open for them, through me, through their jewelry and their murder weapon. Once inside Felicity, they are welcome to do as they please. And should she die, we would strongly encourage them to move on. And if Felicity doesn't die, we will get them out, or will try at least."

Russell nodded. "This will take a couple minutes. Talk amongst yourselves."

Ceri felt Andy's hand rest on her shoulder. "You okay?"

She wasn't, and she knew he knew. But there was no other answer to give. "Fine, but I'll be happy when it's over."

"Me too. Once again, my plans have been foiled by this... I'm going to need the number of Brandy's Scottish friend. He would be a useful man to have on speed dial. I need more curses."

Ceri saw Russell's head jerk towards them momentarily at the mention of Brandy's Scottish friend. She grinned inwardly. Maybe she knew what ranked number one for Russell on Brady's greatest decisions.

"Just a little longer," she murmured, not sure if she was bolstering herself or reassuring him.

"Do you want to know the why and how?" Misty asked. "Why she's here trying to terrorize you and how she's lived this long?"

Ceri bit her lip. She could find out. It was as simple as pulling up the shade just a little, and it'd save anyone else from trying to delve into the cesspit of Felicity's mind.

"I can find out," she said. "I'll need a mirror or something."

"Don't be ridiculous," Misty said, rolling up her sleeves. "You've had a big enough day already. No need to do more." She peeled off one glove, stood, and placed her hand on Felicity's cheek before the other woman could flinch away.

"She's completely mad," Misty said. "Her mind has been fractured for decades, although it wasn't when she committed the string of murders in LA in the 20s. She's been looking for you almost as long. She's obsessed with you—and even though she kept killing, and in the same pattern as before, she doesn't get the pleasure she did once because she's constantly looking over her shoulder for you. You ruined her life."

"I don't think you should feel too badly about that," Jezebel said, looking pointedly at the knife.

"How'd she find me?" Ceri asked.

"She knew what you were when she met you in LA. You questioned her about the death of the woman she worked for—the woman who hired you to save her. She's been visiting psychics ever since. When she heard about Oracle Bay, the town with more psychics per capita than anywhere in the world, she was certain she'd found you. Her only end game was to find you, terrorize you past your breaking point, and then kill you like she'd killed the others. Once you were dead, she would've killed six more to complete this cycle so she could move on to the next town." Misty took a deep breath and withdrew her hand from Felicity's cheek.

Drew asked, "What is she? She doesn't feel like us... But now that her disgustingly cheerful mask is gone, she feels wrong."

Misty wrinkled her nose in disgust. "She's... I guess she's a witch. She's found a way to stay young through sacrifice to one of the darker gods. I don't know him, but he likes blood, she enjoys killing, so they have a deal." She shuddered. "She's filthy inside. Touching her was like licking a sewer."

Felicity was vibrating with rage. "Let me go, or you will feel the wrath of my god. He won't stand by while I'm harmed."

Ceri laughed, then winced as the knife vibrated against her breastbone. "I've met a few gods, and I can say most are remarkably uninterested in their followers most of the time. I'm sure your god is no different."

"They're ready," Russell said. "They have agreed. I will need to create the pathway now. Brace yourself. This will be unpleasant."

Ceri watched in fascination as blue light formed above the pile of jewelry and the serrated blade on the table, arced to her, swirled around the knife—into her chest and back out again, then stretched to Felicity. It was beautiful. She took a deep breath as the first spirit stepped gingerly onto the bridge. She was whisked into the stream, zipping around the jewelry, in and out of Ceri's chest like an icicle lightning bolt, and into Felicity.

Felicity's hair rose like she had her hand on a Spencer's static electricity ball, but before Ceri could enjoy that, another icy form dipped in and out of her chest. The other five followed in rapid succession, and by the seventh one, Ceri was gasping and sweaty. Perhaps this had been a mistake. She closed her eyes and tried to breathe through the pain haze.

"Oh my god," Sandy whispered. "What's happening to her?"

Ceri opened her eyes and followed Sandy's gaze to Felicity just in time to watch the woman disintegrate. For the briefest moment, Felicity's shape held, formed perfectly in ash and dust. Then it burst outwards. Seven spirits erupted from the center of the dust that rained down on the table.

Ceri coughed as the dust entered her lungs. The pain that had become a dull ache in the last few moments intensified, and she knew she wouldn't last much longer.

"Gross," Russell muttered. "I have murderer in my mouth." He looked up at the spirits hovering near the ceiling.

Ceri couldn't understand them, but the aura they gave off was satisfied.

"Are you ready?" Russell asked. He must have gotten an affirmative answer, because he sketched a rectangle in the air, and it opened. The ghosts streamed through, one by one. The last one stopped in front of Ceri and brushed her cheek with an icy hand before following the rest. The door snapped closed, and Russell closed his eyes and leaned back. "No one else attract any ghosts for the next couple months, okay? I don't want to do that again for a while."

"I'll do my best," Jezebel said. Her eyes were wild, but her voice was steady. "Are we done here? Are we good? Other than being stabbed, Ceri looks okay, right?"

Ceri smiled—or she tried anyway. She was positive it was more of a grimace. "I'm good. Thanks for checking on me. I'll see y'all later."

She looked around at the people who'd cared enough to show up to make sure she was okay. They sucked a lot when they didn't believe her, but most of them had redeemed themselves already. Jury was still out on Morgana.

"Where's Joanna?" Drew asked. "Isn't that what you called her? The woman who was here with Felicity?"

She was gone.

"How'd she get past you?" Drew asked Andy. "Not accusing you of anything, just commenting on her sneakiness."

"I let her leave," he said. "She was terrified out of her mind and about to wet her pants. I can find her later if need be. Besides, she's still cuffed, so she probably won't get too far. But for now, I think Ceri needs a little medical attention. If you don't mind...?"

Drew helped Ceri to her feet. "I'll check in on you later. Misty and

I are going to head over to your house, give it a deep clean, and get it ready for you to come home."

"Thank you," Ceri said. She swayed on her feet. "We need to go now. I am not going to make it much longer."

Andy scooped her into his arms. His wings flared around him, and he looked up at the ceiling.

"Please don't break another ceiling," Brandy said from the doorway. "There's an ambulance three minutes out. I'm sure your way is faster, but my way has actual medical professionals and no broken beams."

Andy straightened his legs from the half-crouch he'd been in, and Ceri watched his wings fold and disappear. Brandy didn't look shocked. Not even mildly surprised.

"Fine," he said. "But only because of the EMTs. I don't care about the roof."

"I know." Brandy patted his arm. "That's why you have me."

Ceri let her head slump back against Andy's chest as he carried her through the bar under the blanket Brandy had brought. "When this is over and I'm back home, wanna go to karaoke with me and watch the carnage?" she asked.

"I will not sing," he replied, but she knew he was wavering. Just a little.

She smiled up at him. It was like looking through a soft filter. Her vision was faltering as the pain intensified. "I kinda love you."

"I love you too. Now hush and let someone else take care of you for a change."

Ceri closed her eyes. She barely noticed when she was transferred to the gurney and was unconscious before they were out of the parking lot.

"WE HAVE TO STOP THIS," ANDY SAID WHEN SHE OPENED HER EYES. "I HAVE had my fill of waiting for you to rouse from unconsciousness."

Ceri smiled. "I didn't mean to get stabbed."

"That may be true, but if you could take care to avoid all further stabbings, I would appreciate it." He was holding her hand, and his thumb stroked the soft skin of her palm.

"I'll do my best, but no promises. After all, we live in Oracle Bay." Her eyes drooped a little, and she opened them wide in retaliation. "When can we go home?"

"Tomorrow," he said. "You were lucky, according to the doctors. The knife somehow missed everything vital."

"We'll have to figure out where we're going to live," she said sleepily. "I've gotten used to having you around, so we should probably just keep doing that."

He squeezed her hand. "I will move into your house. It's bigger, has a better view, and it's yours. Also, it doesn't have scorch marks on the ceiling of the guest room."

She laughed softly. "That sounds wonderful. I'm going to sleep now, Andy."

"I love you, Ceridwen," he said as she drifted off.

"I love you, too." She smiled at him, then let sleep take her under, secure in the knowledge that he'd be there when she woke up. She wouldn't have to go to sleep alone.

Ceri looked down at the silver mirrored tray centered on the low vanity Andy'd brought with him when he'd moved in with her. What she saw made her gasp, and her hand flew to her mouth.

Andy was by her side in an instant. "What is it? Are you okay?" His wings flared out behind him, and he pulled her into his body.

"I'm fine…" Her voice trailed off while she tried to make sense of what she'd seen. "You and Barachiel are going to be making a trip soon. There is something weird happening on the other side of the state. Really weird."

"Weirder than apocalypses and gods and fortune telling?" His grip on her relaxed, but his wings stayed out.

She turned and punched him lightly on the arm. "It's not fortune telling. It's prognostication."

"So not chicanery, then?" He grinned at her and kissed her when she wrinkled her nose at him. "I'm sorry. Please continue telling me about the weird place Barachiel and I get to visit."

"It's all demons, monsters, magic, and children too powerful to not attract the notice of something darker." Ceri furrowed her brow as she tried to untangle the threads of what she'd seen into a narrative that made sense.

"Want me to get the annoying angel? He's downstairs. I can hear him rummaging around in your cabinets, which is weird because he refuses to eat or drink anything since I got him drunk on whiskey last year."

"He's probably trying to throw us off the scent of his eavesdropping." Ceri grinned at him and ran a single finger along the outside edge of the silver wing closest to her.

Andy growled low in his throat, and the noise weakened her knees and set her pulse pounding in her throat.

"I think the angel can wait. We have a few things to..." he raked his gaze up and down her body "...discuss."

"If you want to talk to me, wouldn't it be easier to just do it now then send me away, rather than talking about me, causing me to eavesdrop on your carnal activities? Unless that's the point, and you're exhibitors." Barachiel's voice echoed through the room, even though he was on the floor below and their door was closed.

"I hate it when you do that," Ceri replied. "Your 'FEAR NOT' angel echo gives me the creeps. But since you're already eavesdropping, I guess we can talk now, and have our carnal exhibition later."

"The term is 'exhibitionist,' not exhibitor," Andy muttered as he tucked his wings away. "And as much as I don't mind an audience, it'd never be you, angel."

"That's a relief. I have absolutely no desire to be a part of anyone's carnal activities, either as a spectator or a participant. It's just...icky." The obvious distaste in his voice made Ceri grin.

Then she registered what Andy'd just said. "Did you just say you liked an audience?"

He shrugged and winked. "I know a place if you're ever interested in walking down that path."

She tapped her index finger against her lips, trying—unsuccessfully—to keep the mischievous smile off her face. "I wonder if it's the same place I'm thinking of."

"You are a wicked, wicked woman, and I am the luckiest man in the world to have you in my life." He pulled her close and ran his hands down her sides and around her back, pulling her close.

Her eyes drifted closed. She lifted her face towards him, anticipating the kiss she knew was coming. "I think I might be the lucky one." Ceri tightened her arms around his neck as his mouth met hers, and she opened to his questing tongue.

"I am still here, and I am listening to everything!" Barachiel yelled.

Ceri took a reluctant step back. "To be continued?"

"Let's get rid of your unwelcome house guest, then I'll endeavor to show you how much I love you."

"Deal." She walked down the stairs, her mind turning back to the vision. There were three women. No...four? But the fourth was different. Other. Ceri shook her head. Ugh. None of it made any sense. Four women. Three children. Or was it three women and two children? Or no children? The images had flickered among several possibilities, and it was hard to get a bead on what was real now.

"Okay, lay it on us," Andy said, grabbing a couple beers out of the fridge and handing one to Ceri.

"It's confusing, and all I really know for sure is that you two will be called to go there. You'll be there on a job, maybe. But pay attention to what you see; there's more going on than what you'll be there for." She blew a wisp of hair out of her face in a huff of frustration. "I'm sorry I don't have more. The vision was cloudy—like I was looking in through a grimy window."

"When? Will I have time to pack?" Barachiel asked. He looked politely interested.

"What do you have to pack?" Ceri asked. He was entertaining but completely exhausting. She knew he wasn't as much of an airhead as he pretended to be—she'd gotten a peek at what was underneath his mask—but he made it difficult to remember there was more below the surface.

Barachiel shrugged. "I might need a bathing costume. Or my dancing shoes."

Ceri grimaced and tried to erase the image of Barachiel in a "bathing costume" from her mind.

"Do you know where on the other side of the state?" Andy asked, drawing her attention away from the awful picture that had formed in her head of the beautiful angel wearing an old-fashioned bathing costume, flowered swim cap, and Irish dancing clogs.

She took a deep breath and looked at her own personal fallen angel. "Have you ever heard of a town called Eden Valley?"

* * * * * ★ ★ ★ ★ * * * ·

READY FOR MORE? KEEP READING FOR A SNEAK PEEK AT TEMPEST IN A Teapot, Psychics of Oracle Bay book #6, the first in a 2-book Morgana arc!

want more amy cissell?

And why wouldn't you?

Love it, hate it, somewhere in between? Please leave a review for **Hell and High Water** at Goodreads, Bookbub, or your favorite online retailer.

Links to all retails sites are at:
https://books2read.com/HellAndHighWater

Reviews are always appreciated & allow me to keep writing what you love!

Sign up for Cissell's Epistles at https://amycissell.com for new release updates, exclusive content, and a bevy of book recommendations! (You'll also get to choose a free book as a thank you for hanging out!)

Come hang out in my Facebook Reader Group - the Amyzonians can always use another shenaniganator. (It's a word. Promise.)

https://www.facebook.com/groups/amycissellauthor/

Join my patreon - https://www.patreon.com/ACissellWrites - for early access to books, free copies of my digital books, free paperbacks, and access to my entire back catalog!

· · · ★ ★ ★ ★ ★ ★ · ·

tempest in a teapot

Morgana crossed her ankles, smoothed down the slim pencil skirt she was wearing, and steadfastly avoided her reflection in the window of Gate D6 in the Portland International Airport. There was no way in hell she wanted to spend any more time than was necessary looking at the stupid brown bob, pearl necklace, and salmon-colored sweater set she'd been hiding in for the last year.

"It's necessary," she muttered to herself with clenched teeth. She couldn't risk blowing her cover now, no matter how far away she was from Vancouver and the string of murders that had stopped a month ago as abruptly as they'd started. The killer had struck three times in Seattle, but with none of the precision and rigidity they'd shown in Vancouver. And now they'd dropped off the map again.

Morgana was tired of working for the Silver Eye—had been for a couple decades—but this would be her last job. She'd spent too much time hiding who she was over the centuries, and a year of dressing like a PTA president at their behest, regardless of the reasons, was too much. She'd saved five witches in the last year, one from a rogue warlock, two from vampires, and the last two from mundane cis men who used a different kind of power to subjugate the innocent. But she hadn't saved anyone from the blood witch who'd gone on a rampage in the Pacific Northwest in the last couple months. As soon as either she or another of their operatives found the blood witch, Morgana would cut ties with the organization that'd been set up centuries ago to protect witches and other magic users.

Her stomach clenched, and she forced a breath out through her nose and tried to concentrate on the fierce joy she took from putting abusive men in their places and not her overwhelming nervousness. Her hands twisted in her lap until her knuckles turned white, and she had to force herself to relax her fingers before they cramped.

"Afraid of flying?" a man asked, dropping into the seat next to her.

Morgana stiffened. She hated talking to strangers, and when she wasn't dressed up like a PTA president, strangers never talked to her. "No."

"It's a pretty common fear." His voice was deep and husky, everything Morgana liked in a voice.

The seats creaked a bit as he shifted his weight. Morgana glanced over to her left to see long, blue-jean-clad legs finished with black Dr. Martens stretched out next to her. The man's presence and invasion of her personal space might irritate her, but that would not stop her from admiring the strength evident in his thighs.

"I'm not afraid of flying," Morgana said, although this time a lot less forcefully. She looked back down at her hands. She wanted to see this man's face even less than her own at this point. If he was as attractive as his voice and legs hinted, she'd risk blowing her cover. And if he wasn't, Morgana would be disappointed, and she'd had enough of that lately.

"My name's Donovan Davies," he continued in his slow, easy voice, completely oblivious to—or perhaps ignoring—her dismissive tone. "Are you heading out or heading home?"

"A little of both," Morgana admitted. And before she could stop herself, she tilted her head up and towards him. Oh my goddess, he was even more beautiful than he'd sounded. Long, black hair with streaks of grey spilled over his shoulders, and light, honey-brown eyes glowed against his russet skin.

The man chuckled, and Morgana realized she'd been staring. She felt a flush start at the base of her neck and held it back with a force of will she'd been honing for centuries.

"Are you going to tell me your name?" Donovan asked.

"No." Morgana pulled her phone out of the ridiculous handbag she carried to match her prim librarian persona and tapped the e-reader app. She wished she had a physical book with her. Those were a better deterrent.

"Have it your way." He didn't get up to leave.

Morgana glared at her phone, then back to Donovan to give him a piece of her mind. His eyes were closed, and the lines on his face that marked him in his mid-fifties had smoothed out. There was an energy emanating from him, and it raised goosebumps on Morgana's skin. She recognized it, of course.

Power. The kind that drew people to Oracle Bay. But his was somehow different, and Morgana couldn't put a finger on it. A smirk quirked up the corner of her mouth when she considered all the things she could put a finger on.

She shut down that line of thought immediately. Now was not the time to appreciate attractive magical men. Although she—and the Eye—believed it more likely that the blood witch was a woman based on the type of magic used, she couldn't discount anyone. This man had power, but he didn't feel like a warlock, nor did he feel like a person who'd bound themself to the goddess. At least, not quite. There was something earthy about him, though.

"Like what you see?" Donovan asked without opening his eyes.

Morgana gritted her teeth. She should've known better than to assume someone with that much raw power emanating off them would be unaware of scrutiny no matter how tightly their eyes were closed.

"No." She left it at that and turned back to her book after a quick glance around the gate area. There were a few empty seats for the flight that was due to leave in less than an hour, but all of those were next to other people as well, and she would not give him the satisfaction of moving seats.

"Hmmm... Are you always such a liar?"

She gasped at the audacity of his question and forgot her resolution not to look him in the eye again. She met his gaze, ready to kill him with a look. She'd done it before, although it'd been a long time since men were so intimidated by her reputation that she could induce heart failure with a glance.

The dancing amusement in his light brown eyes did nothing to quell her anger; in fact, it ratcheted it up a few notches. "How dare you?" she growled under her breath. "You don't know me, and you accuse me of dishonesty?"

His gaze unfocused, and for a second, it felt like he was looking through her instead of at her. "From where I'm looking, the entire package, from your sensible coral pumps to your bland brown bob, is nothing but a lie wrapped in beige. You can't tell me this is who you really are. The fire in your voice doesn't match the country club couture, sweetheart."

Morgana's jaw dropped. Calling her dishonest was one thing—he was a stranger, and she'd forget that handsome face soon enough—but calling her sweetheart? Anger rose in her chest with a force she'd not experienced in more years than she could count.

It was all she could do to hold the power back. There were a lot of reasons not to lose her temper in an airport. The most pressing one right now was the need to arrive at her destination before sunset to begin the Beltane festival with the coven she'd founded six hundred years ago. She seldom traveled back for the holidays, but they'd requested her presence to ascertain the innocence or guilt of a junior member of the grove in a crime serious enough to summon her for but not so serious—she assumed—that they needed her in anything more than her capacity as a witch rather than an agent of the Silver Eye.

Turning this impertinent disrespectful man into a toad, or better yet, a cockroach that would make Kafka jealous, would likely disrupt her journey and result in a lot of unwanted attention and uncomfortable questions.

She clamped her mouth shut so hard her teeth clacked together, the shock reverberating through her head. She turned back to her book and swiped through to the next page.

A low chuckle beside her had her grinding her teeth. Morgana checked the time. Boarding wasn't due to start for another thirty minutes, and there was a bar just a couple gates down. She stood, grabbed her cheerful pink and black polka-dotted carryon, and stalked towards the bar. She seldom drank when traveling in case there was an emergency landing and no one else could fly the plane —that man had been right when he'd guessed she was afraid of flying—but today would have to be the exception to the rule.

She sat on a stool at the bar, and as soon as the bartender appeared, Morgana ordered without looking at the menu she held out. "I'll take a shot of your best Irish whiskey and a glass of your house red."

The bartender, a nice-looking white woman in her mid-twenties with a blond undercut and a plethora of facial piercings, titled her head at Morgana. "Whiskey and...wine? Most people do beer."

"I don't like beer very much, and if I'm going to drink in an airport, I'm going to enjoy myself," Morgana said.

"Okay, ma'am! They're your drinks. Do you want to make them doubles?" The woman smiled cheerfully as she pulled a large wine glass and a small tumbler out from under the stainless-steel bar.

"Both of them?" Morgana asked, glossing over the "ma'am" in her mind. "I didn't know you could make wine a double."

"Sure, it's just a double pour for only fifty percent more. It's cheaper than buying two glasses." The woman paused, waiting for Morgana's answer.

"I will have a double of the wine, but only a single shot of whiskey," Morgana decided.

"You got it!" A couple minutes later, the bartender placed a wine glass, delightfully full, next to a couple fingers of Redbreast 25.

Morgana tipped the whiskey back and drank it one swallow, grimaced slightly at the burn, then took a sip of the water the bartender had discretely placed next to her elbow. Then, she turned her attention to the wine. Twenty minutes to drink the equivalent of two very generous glasses of wine wasn't a lot, but she was up for the challenge.

She was halfway through her glass, and her shoulders had relaxed enough to be below ear-level, when her phone pinged with an incoming text. She glanced down at it and wrinkled her nose.

A notification of a group text greeted her, and since she was part of only one group text, it was the group of psychics she'd aligned herself with in Oracle Bay. It was an unusual community. They were all quite different and, in another place and time, wouldn't have become the tight-knit group they were. But a small town has ways of bringing people together, especially a town like Oracle Bay, with the highest per capita number of genuine psychics in the United States.

The town was full of tarot readers, astrologers, palm readers, and scryers. They even had a prophet, a fallen angel, and a necromancer. And whatever she and Paska were—witches are what the modern age called them, but neither of them were modern, and they were much, much more than "witches."

She opened the text, unsurprised to see it was from Misty. Mystic Greene was one of the youngest in the group, but she was the only one who'd grown up in Oracle Bay, and that gave her access to a deeper well of power than most of the others. She was also the owner of most of Main Street, the president of the Chamber of Commerce, head of the informal city council, and chair of the fall bazaar, Halloween party committee, and the Yule Ball.

In other words, she was in charge of a lot of things, and she very much liked to add to the list.

Morgana sighed, took another drink of wine to brace herself against whatever committee Misty was forming and recruiting her fellow psychics onto, and opened her text messages.

Misty: *I can't believe Morgana left town without saying goodbye!*

Drew: *I can. She's wily like that and has been doing it every week for months. She definitely has a double life that doesn't include us. Probably a secret husband and some secret babies. And a few skeletons in her closet.*

Paska: *We all have skeletons in our closets.*

Ceri: *Not all of our skeletons are literal, Paska.*

Paska: *I don't keep skeletons in my closet.*

Ceri: *No, you keep them in a leather pouch made of human skin that you wear on your belt.*

Paska: *And in my garage.*

Jezebel: *Is there a point this text is coming to, or am I cool just muting y'all and scrolling through the inanity later?*

Drew: *Wow. Morgana's been gone less than a day, and already, Jez is gunning hard to be her replacement. Too soon, Jez, too soon.*

Morgana rolled her eyes and thumb typed. *I didn't say goodbye because I will only be gone a few days. I told the old man and the fallen angel I was leaving. It did not seem necessary to announce my departure as though I was nothing more than a dirty bus leaving the station. However, since you all seem so concerned with my absence, you may expect me to return a week from tomorrow. Now, I hear my flight being called. I am going to turn off my phone. Please restrain yourselves on this message thread.*

She closed the text app and went back to her wine. She ignored the first seven text notifications, then sighed and opened it up with the eighth.

Ceri: *I can't believe you told Andy & he didn't tell me.*

Andy: *The witch told me this morning, and I haven't seen you since.*

Sandy: *Airport? Where are you going? Why didn't you ask someone for a ride? Are you at PDX or SeaTac?*

Russell: *Are you sure I need to be included in this group chat? If I sic ghosts after every one of you, will you delete my number?*

Andy: *If I have to be on the list, so do you. I'm not even an oracle.*

Drew: *Sandy had good questions, Morgana. Where are you going and why didn't you ask for a ride?*

Paska: *Why do you think she'll volunteer her business over text when she didn't tell any of you in person? It's like you don't know who you're talking about.*

Jezebel: *Why would we, though? It's hard enough getting to know regular people.*

Morgana shoved her phone in her purse, finished her wine, and dropped three twenties on the bar. She made a quick detour into one of the ubiquitous stores selling books and magazines, before walking to her gate.

First class seating was being called when she got back, so she pulled out her boarding pass and strode forward to join the queue.

She stowed her bag with the help of a flight attendant, ordered a glass of sparkling wine, accepted the hot towel, pillow, and blanket, then settled into her seat with the three paperback thrillers she'd purchased.

Movement next to her pulled her attention away from the book so she could accept the wine. Instead of the flight attendant she expected, her wine was being passed to her by the man sitting down next to her. None other than Donovan Davies.

"We're seat mates," he grinned. "Isn't this fortuitous?"

TEMPEST IN A TEAPOT IS THE FIRST HALF OF MORGANA'S ADVENTURE! ONE-click your copy now!

PSYCHICS OF
ORACLE BAY
BOOK 6
Tempest
in a
Teapot
USA TODAY BESTSELLING AUTHOR
AMY CISSELL

raising a demon

MIDLIFE MAGIC IN EDEN VALLEY #1

Raising a Demon is the first book in Midlife Magic in Eden Valley, a magical new paranormal women's fiction series. Eden Valley & Oracle Bay are in the same universe, and there are some crossover characters and cameos!

Being a single mother has its challenges, but Evie never imagined that "the talk" would involve Ouija boards and pentagrams.

Evelyn Addams is forty-three and fabulous. She has a great kid, fantastic friends, and doesn't need a man to complete her. But when she catches ten-year-old Lily summoning a demon to ask for birthday wishes—and the demon who turns up is Evie's summer fling from eleven years ago—her comfortable life is shattered.

Reuniting with an old flame is tricky enough but finding out he grows horns and a tail makes a romantic reconnection downright complicated. And when Lily is kidnapped by her newfound grandfather, the last shred of her old life is destroyed, and everything goes to hell.

Will Evie and her friends rescue Lily from hell before the lights go out and the lost souls come out to play? And can she ignore past and Luc's family complications to take a second chance on love and learn how to raise a demon's daughter? Get your copy of Raising a Demon today!

http://www.books2read.com/raisingademon

acknowledgments

Thank you so much to my amazing developmental editor, Suzanne Lahna! Your feedback, advice, and magical validation were invaluable.

And without my favorite wine-drinking witchy friend, Shéa Macleod, my magic narrative would be infinitely less magical.

My kiddo - Liana - is my most ardent supporter and best encourager, even though I will not let her read my books.

And last, but not least, my partner in business, crime, and marriage, Chris... Thanks for keeping my commas honest and getting me wine when I'm too stressed to open my own bottles.

amy cissell – i spell trouble

Amy can be found on most social media channels @acissellwrites. Come visit her website at amycissell.com for blogs & books! (autographed copies, if you want!)

Amy Cissell is a USA Today Bestselling Author of urban fantasy and paranormal romance novels. She lives in Portland, OR with her husband, her haunted house-obsessed daughter, their three cats, and the murder of crows she's conspiring to turn into her vengeful army.

When she's not working or writing, she's sleeping because that's all she has time to do! There are few things Amy loves more than a well-timed pun, a good book, a glass of wine, and time at the Oregon Coast.

Although she reads anything and everything, her first love is fantasy. Eleven-year-old Amy discovered fantasy when she 'borrowed' her father's copy of The Hobbit and an enduring love affair (mostly with dragons) was born.

also by amy cissell

Paranormal Romance

Psychics of Oracle Bay

Not in the Cards (October 2018)

First Hand Knowledge (November 2018)

Wing and a Prayer (January 2019)

Belle of the Ball (December 2019)

Hell and High Water (June 2022)

Tempest in a Teapot (April 2023)

Elements of Surprise (April 2023)

Dead Giveaway (2024)

Bad to the Bones

Shoot for the Stars

Fun and Prophet

Box Sets (ebook only)

Seeing is Believing in Oracle Bay (Books 1-4)

Paranormal Women's Fiction

Midlife Magic in Eden Valley

(complete series)

Raising a Demon (June 2021)

Devil and the Deep, Blue Lake (September 2021)

Valley of Angels (November 2021)

Guardian of Eden (February 2022)

Eden Valley World Novellas

Match Made in Hell (June 2021)

Hell's Bells (December 2021)

Fall From Grace (January 2022)

Devil May Care (February 2022)

Box Sets

Welcome to Eden Valley (Novellas 1-4)

Vamps in the Vineyard

Here to Slay (September 2022)

Vamps in the Vineyard Novellas

(newsletter subscribers only)

Stakes and Stems (September 2023)

Slay Bells Ring (January 2023)

Contemporary/Urban Fantasy

An Eleanor Morgan Fantasy Adventure

(complete series)

The Cardinal Gate (February 2017)

The Waning Moon (June 2017)

The Ruby Blade (October 2017)

The Broken World (March 2018)

The Lost Child (June 2019)

The Iron River (May 2020)

The Dark Throne (February 2021)

Box Sets (ebook only)

Eleanor Morgan Books 1-4

Eleanor Morgan Books 5-7

Ghosts of Valhalla

As Yet Untitled (late 2023)

www.ingramcontent.com/pod-product-compliance
Lightning Source LLC
Chambersburg PA
CBHW060913210726
48293CB00006B/2078